Megan

Megan

CAROLE LLEWELLYN

LARGE PRINT
Oxford

Copyright © Carole Llewellyn, 2008

First published in Great Britain 2008
by
Robert Hale Limited

Published in Large Print 2009 by ISIS Publishing Ltd.,
7 Centremead, Osney Mead, Oxford OX2 0ES
by arrangement with
Robert Hale Limited

British Library Cataloguing in Publication Data
Llewellyn, Carole.
    Megan
    1. Women domestics - - England - - Bristol
    - - Fiction.
    2. Bristol (England) - - Social life and customs
    - - Fiction.
    3. Great Britain - - History - - George V,
    1910–1936 - - Fiction.
    4. Large type books.
    I. Title
    823.9'2–dc22

ISBN 978–0–7531–8398–4 (hb)
ISBN 978–0–7531–8399–1 (pb)

Printed and bound in Great Britain by
T. J. International Ltd., Padstow, Cornwall

In memory of my mother, Edith Mary Iles.
For Barrie, Robert, Clare, Amy and Sophie,
with love.

Acknowledgements

Thanks to Brixham Writers' Group for their help and support, especially Kate Furnivall for being so generous with her time, advice and encouragement. Also warm thanks to my dear friend Keith Emery for his patience and technical help in setting up my computer.

CHAPTER
ONE

1919

Megan Williams stepped down from the big brute of a steam train. She did not allow herself to think of what lay ahead. Not yet.

The dimly lit station had an eerie feel to it, with steam billowing out from under the train's engine and rising up to meet the yellow glow of the platform's flickering gas lamps. Through the haze Megan could just make out the outline of dark figures rushing to and fro, all going about their business as if there were but a minute to live. No one seemed to notice the lone figure stepping from the train, and into a strange new world.

Bristol's Temple Meads station was as big as a rugby field, yet totally covered by a high glass-domed roof. The platform was packed. Men, women and children — some dressed up to the nines, others looking shabby and poor — were intermingling, yet miles apart. Megan stood still, trying desperately to shake off the feeling of utter loneliness. Then she remembered her promise to her mother to look presentable at all times. She laid her small suitcase on the ground to allow her to replace the few unruly curls that had escaped from under her hat and to adjust the buttons of her coat. As she raised her coat collar against the chill in the air she caught a waft of her mother's rosewater cologne.

"'Twill be no sixteen-year-old daughter of mine that turns up in Bristol with no warm overcoat," her mother had argued in her Bristolian accent, not lost even after living twenty years in Wales. She had been adamant about it and insisted on cutting down her own Sunday-best coat to fit Megan's tiny frame.

Megan took a deep breath before retrieving her suitcase, reminding herself that this was an exciting new world and she must be strong, her family in Nantgarw, a small mining village in South Wales would expect nothing less. As she slowly made her way along the platform she spotted a sign, which confirmed she was indeed on PLATFORM 14. Now all she had to do was find the bench near the exit and wait. These had been Lizzie's instructions when she had written to confirm Megan's appointment. Eventually, after walking the length of the platform, she found the bench in question. As she settled herself down, her nerves were taut, her mouth was dry. How different it would have been if she had been a lone traveller in the valleys. By now someone would have wanted to know who she was, where she was going and more to the point, was she in need of help. The English were obviously more reserved.

Her eyes were drawn to a woman on the other side of the platform, holding tight a tiny baby draped in a ragged shawl. The young lad at her side looked in a sorry state, his thin arms and legs showing through holes in his clothes, his hand held out begging from passers-by. A lump came to Megan's throat. Thank God her family were safe in the valley — but for how long?

"Have you seen anything of the guard?"

Megan visibly jumped as the young man sat with a hard thud next to her on the bench.

"Well, have you? What's the matter, cat got your tongue?"

"No, I mean yes, the guard passed me no more than a few minutes ago," Megan answered.

"Good, that means he'll not be back this way for another half-hour or so. You see, I'm about to sneak on to the train, don't believe in wasting good money on a ticket," he said, in a rather matter of fact way. Almost as if it were a regular event.

Megan stared in disbelief. He looked to be a few years older than she was. He had a stocky build with thick black hair shining with brilliantine — obviously applied to groom it away from his tanned face. He was quite well dressed if somewhat flashy, and her overall impression was that he took pride in his appearance.

"Going by your accent, I'd say you just got off the train from Cardiff."

Megan nodded.

"You got a name?" he asked.

She didn't answer. Her mother had warned her about talking to strangers.

"Please yourself. I'm off to Swindon races. Mind you, I could do with a bit of luck. A little kiss from a pretty girl like you would do it."

"You must be mad!" She made to move away.

"Don't worry yourself. I'll not stay where I'm not welcome. It's time I was off anyway." As he stood up to leave he leaned over and, taking her completely by surprise, he gave her a quick peck on the cheek.

"How dare you?" In shock, Megan raised her hand believing anyone that brazen deserved a slap, but he simply swerved, thus avoiding her blow. Then flashing a wicked smile he quickly turned and left.

As she watched him dart across the platform towards an incoming train she still couldn't believe his outright cheek. At the same time, she guessed she would always remember her very first kiss, although she thought it might be wise to keep this little encounter to herself. It wouldn't do to give others the wrong impression.

The station clock read twelve thirty and her doubts returned. What if no one came to meet her? What if Lizzie had made it all up? What if there was no position? Her mother had barely managed to scrape together the cost of a one-way ticket, so if no one came how would she get back home? Megan dismissed such thoughts. Of course someone would come for her, and of course there was a position. Not even Lizzie would play such a cruel trick. Anyway, hadn't she been the one who suggested Megan apply for the position of kitchen maid at Redcliffe House in the first place?

"Hello, you must be Megan Williams?"

Megan looked up at the tall good-looking young man standing in front of her. She was about to answer, when he continued, "I'm Sidney Partridge. I've been sent

4

from Redcliffe House to collect you. I hope you haven't had too long a wait?"

"No, not at all," she lied, so pleased someone had at last come for her. "And thank you for your trouble, Mr Partridge."

"The name's Sidney. The staff up at the big house don't stand on ceremony, so I shall call you Megan, if that's all right?" Again, he didn't wait to be answered, but gave her a big friendly smile. "I must say you don't half look like Lizzie."

Megan had the urge to tell this stranger that although as cousins they might look alike — both slim and of small build and both with masses of dark brown curly hair — the similarity definitely ended there. But stopped herself. She had to try harder to think better of Lizzie . . . if only for her Aunt Margaret's sake.

"Be — Is that all your luggage?" he asked, pointing to her old suitcase.

She noticed how he instantly corrected his Bristolian dialect.

"Yes, but I can manage it thank you."

"Well, if you're sure, follow me," he said, striding off.

Megan followed. Sidney Partridge was a good six inches taller than she was, with shining blond hair and fair skin, so unusual to Megan as all the men in her family were very dark. Soon they were out on to the street. After the darkness of the railway station it took a while for her eyes to become accustomed to the bright daylight. This morning, as she prepared to leave Wales, dark clouds gave promise of rain. The weather, like her mood, had definitely changed for the better. It had turned into a beautiful spring day, with bright sunlight shining through wispy white clouds, although as often expected in early spring, there was still a slight chill in the air.

Everything around her seemed larger than life. The front of the railway station was even more impressive than the inside. She shaded her eyes with her hand as she looked up at the high ornate facade of the station entrance, with its large stone pillars and elaborate carvings. She had never seen anything so grand.

"Your transport awaits, ma'am," Sidney said, bending over in an exaggerated bow. "Samson, meet Megan."

Turning around, Megan stopped dead in her tracks. In front of her stood the biggest horse she had ever seen — twice as big as the rag-and-bone man's who was a regular down her street. Samson was hitched to a long wooden wagon. High above the driving seat a white display board advertised CASTLE BREWERY in bold black letters. Instinctively she took a step backward, she had never been this close to a horse before.

Seeing her reaction, Sidney attempted to reassure her. "It'll be all right, he don't bite, honest. Come around this side and I'll give you a leg up. I really must get a move on, I don't want to be late back to the depot."

Megan hesitated. "I-I thought you worked at Redcliffe House."

"I'm sorry, I should have explained. My ma is Mrs Partridge, the cook up at the big house. She asked me to come and collect you. You see I have to go past Redcliffe House to visit one of our taverns. I'm working alone today picking up the empties. Mind you, it's a help that Samson here knows his way around."

Satisfied with his answer but not too sure about the mode of transport, she slowly walked around to where Sidney stood. Taking her arm, he gently helped her up. Then pulling himself into the seat next to her he took hold of the horse's reins, giving them a gentle tug.

"Walk on, Samson, and you be on your best behaviour. We have a young lady on board, so no leaving dirty parcels in the street, do you hear?"

Megan tried to muffle a laugh, but when Sidney laughed out loud she did also.

"Mind you, most days I shovel it into buckets. The gardener up at the big house swears by it to grow the rhubarb, so think on if you're ever offered a slice of Cook's rhubarb tart." They both laughed again.

For a while they travelled in silence, as Sidney steered Samson expertly out of the station and on to a long cobbled street, stretching as far as her eyes could see, narrowed by the large high buildings which lined either side. There were so many other vehicles on the road. Automobiles, omnibuses, bicycles, horse-drawn carriages and ahead of them an electric tramcar. She had never seen one before, although she knew from her relatives that Cardiff and Swansea had them.

"Whoa, boy." Sidney pulled the horse's reins, steering him away from both the oncoming tram and a big black automobile — just like the one Tommy Bevan, the undertaker, drove back home.

She watched spellbound as Sidney manoeuvred Samson in and out of the traffic and at one point made a clucking noise with his tongue. This seemed to encourage Samson to pull them faster up a small gradient and over a large wooden bridge. The sound of Samson's hoofs echoed around them, as she caught her first glimpse of the harbour.

"This is Bristol Bridge," Sidney informed her. "Those ships in the bay are tea clippers, all being unloaded before setting off again. Look, up there's a sign that should make you feel at home." He pointed to a small iron sign on the side of a building saying Welsh Back.

"It's a street that leads down to the harbour. I'll take you there one day, if you like? When we've got more time, that is."

Megan felt her colour rise. "I'd like that," she said quietly. Then quickly changing the subject, "Do you deliver the beer with Samson every day?" she asked.

"No, not every day. Three days a week I'm apprenticed to the cooper. He's the man who makes all them wooden barrels that hold the beer. You see, at eighteen I have ambitions."

Leaving the bridge they entered a maze of even busier streets.

Megan had never seen so many people coming and going. There were fine shops and street hawkers everywhere, and men carrying billboards with the latest news. FIRST ATLANTIC FLIGHT RACE! she read, and the idea of such an adventure made her dark eyes shine. Once across a wide square, her attention was attracted by the bright red lights of the Hippodrome Theatre advertising a variety show. How she wished her family could see this colourful sight. Then, as if reading her thoughts, Sidney asked about her family. She told him of her mother, father, three brothers and two sisters left at home in Wales.

"I could never imagine having such a big family," Sidney responded, "with me being an only child and all. You see my dad died when I was only five years old. That's when ma and me went to live with Gran."

"How sad," was all Megan could say at first but it did not seem enough somehow, so she added, "My father's not very well; he's been finding it a struggle to get to work, which is why I needed to find a position. The timing of Lizzie's letter couldn't have been better. I aim to work hard and get on as well as she has."

A frown appeared on Sidney's face. "Don't you be too eager to follow in the footsteps of that madam! I'm sorry . . . it's none of my business," he added, obviously embarrassed by his outburst.

Megan didn't understand. Surely, no one could dispute that Lizzie had done well. Hadn't she started as a scullery maid only three years ago? And look at her today — a parlour maid no less!

Sidney quickly changed the subject and insisted on naming every large grey-stoned building they passed, St Augustine Church, the Royal Hotel, Bristol Cathedral, the City Library. Megan doubted she would remember them all. Although puzzled by his reference to Lizzie, she put it to the back of her mind. There was so much to take in.

"Are we nearly there?" she enquired. For although she was enjoying her tour of the city, she was impatient to arrive at the house where she would not only work but live.

"Not far now, we just follow the signs for Clifton Suspension Bridge."

Skillfully, he turned Samson in and out of the narrow streets then on to Clifton Road and finally into a side street, and up to a parade of superior dwelling houses.

"Here we are then, Victoria Square," Sidney said, slowing the horse down to a stop outside a large white terraced house. "This be — Is your employers' town house. There's also a country house in Devon. I've been told it's grand by all accounts, though I've not seen it myself."

Megan looked skyward. She had never seen such a tall narrow house. There were so many windows, some had black painted wrought iron balconies overlooking a central floral garden.

Sidney moved Samson slowly along the front of the house, past the ornate iron railings, before finally bringing him to a halt once more. Then jumping down on to the pavement he offered her a helping hand. She hesitated.

He seemed to sense her mood. "There's no need to be afraid. I'll come into the house with you, you'll not be alone."

"I'm not afraid," she lied.

He didn't argue. While keeping hold of her hand he slowly brought her through a side gate.

"Only the toffs use the main entrance. This is the way in for the likes of us."

The steps led under the street. It was very dark, cold and damp. They stood in a small yard in front of a large wooden door. Sidney raised his hand towards the door's metal latch. For a brief moment Megan's heart raced . . . she felt the urge to run away to return home, to her family, to safety. Almost instinctively, she reached out to pull Sidney's hand from the latch — but it was too late! She could only watch as he pushed open the door.

CHAPTER
TWO

The heavy door opened into a huge kitchen. The whole place was a hub of activity as workers busied themselves round a large wooden table, which dominated the long high-ceilinged room. One was chopping vegetables, another rolling out pastry and yet another placing blue-and-white crockery on to a silver tray. There was a lot of lively chatter and banging of pots and pans. It was little wonder no one heard them enter.

To the left of the table a rather large girl, with bright red hair, balanced precariously on top of a ladder, her arm stretched out, straining to reach one of the many copper-bottomed cooking pans adorning the huge wall.

"You be careful, Sally Tomkin, don't you go falling off that ladder. If you were to land on poor Agnes, you'd surely flatten her," an older woman called out from beside a big black cooking range which dominated the opposite wall.

"Yes, Cook," the girl on the ladder answered in an unusually loud gruff voice.

This caused everyone to laugh, but the laughter stopped abruptly when at last they noticed Sidney and Megan standing in the doorway. From an anteroom off the kitchen someone whistled a tune, breaking the awkward silence. But not for long, for this also ceased when an imp-faced young man came to investigate the sudden quietness of his fellow workers.

Sidney spoke first.

"Hello, Ma, this is Megan Williams. She's the new help."

This seemed to satisfy everyone's curiosity and they continued about their work.

"Sit her by the fire, lad, she looks half froze to death. Sally, get down from that ladder and get this young 'un a cup of tea."

"Yes, Cook," the girl said as she began to descend.

This again brought giggles from around the room as one of the other girls mimicked Sally's gruff voice repeating, "Yes, Cook,"

"Enough of that, get on with your work!" Cook shouted in a voice you knew would be obeyed. But her tone soon changed, becoming gentle as she spoke to Sidney. "Would you like a cup of tea, Son?"

Mrs Partridge was a rather plump woman in her early forties. Her pretty face had a high colour, flushed no doubt from regularly standing over a hot cooking range. Her plaited brown hair, with just a speckle of grey, she wore neatly tied at the top of her head. As she walked across the room towards the fireplace she wiped her hands on the white apron, which failed to cover her well rounded figure. Although her appearance differed greatly, her Bristolian accent reminded Megan of her own mam, so much so that she was tempted to go over and give her a big hug. But no, it wouldn't do to make a spectacle of herself.

"No thanks, Ma, I'll pass on the cuppa. I'd better get myself back to the depot," Sidney said, and then taking Megan's hand he walked her to the chair beside the fireplace. She gripped his hand, not wanting him to leave, not wanting to be alone. He smiled down at her. "Don't worry, you'll be fine. You can tell me how you get on when I return later for supper," he whispered.

Megan nodded, forcing a smile.

As the door slammed behind him, the girl called Sally handed a cup of tea and a piece of fruit cake to Mrs Partridge who in turn placed it on the small table beside Megan's chair.

"That should keep you going till supper. We'll all get to know each other then." Cook glanced around, making sure her words were understood by all. "So we'll have no idle chatter now, understand?" Then returning her gaze to Megan, "Mrs Jarvis, the housekeeper, will be in to see you directly. Try to remember her bark's much worse than her bite."

Megan nodded.

"That be all right, child. I understand. You just sit quiet for a while and gather your thoughts. Anyways, I've got work to do." Cook patted Megan's hand before making her way back to the cooking range.

Megan sat clutching her suitcase, reluctant to let go of her little piece of home. Cook's kindness had only made her feel even more homesick.

It seemed ages before she heard . . .

"Hello, Megan."

Looking up, a wave of hope swept over her as she saw Lizzie and a tall, thin, middle-aged lady standing before her. Of course, she thought, I'm not alone. I've got my cousin. From now on we shall forget our differences and become friends. After all, we are family. And blood is thicker than water.

Megan couldn't help noticing how smart and in control Lizzie looked, wearing a black calf-length dress and crisply starched white hat and apron. Megan gave her a friendly smile but it was not returned.

"Megan, this is Mrs Jarvis, the housekeeper. Don't just sit there, where are your manners? Stand up and say good afternoon to Mrs Jarvis and for goodness' sake let go of that scruffy suitcase."

Although confused by her cousin's obvious unfriendliness, Megan sensed that she should follow her instructions. It wouldn't do to cross swords, at least not on her first day. Slowly she placed her suitcase on the floor and stood up.

"Good afternoon, Mrs Jarvis," she said, pleased that her voice sounded confident. She wasn't about to show Lizzie, or anyone else for that matter, how unsure she really felt.

Mrs Jarvis was dressed in a long plain black dress. She was slim and neat, with pointed features which made her lined face look rather stern.

"Good afternoon to you, Miss Williams. In a while Lizzie will show you to your quarters. Once there you will unpack your . . . mm . . . luggage . . ." The housekeeper hesitated, looking down at Megan's battered suitcase before continuing, "As soon as you're settled come to my office. I trust you'll not keep me waiting long?" Then, without another word, she turned and left the room.

During the time the housekeeper had been in the room, everyone had busied themselves. But as the kitchen door closed behind her, all work came to a stand still, and once again Megan became the centre of attention.

"Follow me," Lizzie said, leading the way across the kitchen.

Megan picked up her suitcase and followed on.

"See you later, child," Cook whispered, as Megan passed by.

Then one of the older girls shouted out, "Don't you go paying heed to Lizzie Williams. We all know how that snooty cow got her job!"

"Hush, all of you, and get on with your work," Megan heard Cook command as she followed Lizzie out of the kitchen and up a steep flight of stairs.

If Lizzie had heard the girl's ungracious comments, she gave no such indication.

"From now on, Megan, you will have to learn to stand on your own two feet. Don't think that you'll have an easy time of it, just because you're my cousin."

Megan was about to protest that she didn't for one moment expect any such thing, but Lizzie hadn't finished what sounded to Megan like a well-prepared speech.

"From time to time as parlour maid, I might have to be hard on you. But it'll be for your own good — you'll do well to remember this."

They reached the top of the stairs and the familiar scent of lavender polish wafted over her. They were standing in a long hallway, well lit by the daylight shining through two tall windows at the far end. The light reflected on the highly polished wooden floor only partly covered by a plush red carpet runner — obviously chosen for its perfect match with the red and gold flocked paper which adorned the high walls.

"All upper-house staff have furnished rooms on this floor. The housekeeper's office, where you must go as soon as you have unpacked, is the room nearest that large door there." Lizzie motioned to the door at the end of the hall marked Private.

"Never enter that door unless under instruction of work, do you understand?"

Megan nodded. She didn't really, but something told her she soon would.

"Also on this floor are the rooms of Mr Hutchins, the butler-cum-chauffeur, and Sybil Davies, milady's maid, which is by far the nicest of all the staff quarters. Sybil Davies will soon be leaving the house to take up another appointment and I have been promised her position . . ." For a few moments Lizzie's thoughts seemed to be elsewhere, then as if realizing she had spoken out of turn, she grabbed Megan's wrist, squeezing it hard. "You forget I told you that, no one is to know . . . it's a secret, our little secret . . . do you hear? I don't want you clecking like you did when you saw Billy and me behind the colliery sheds. I haven't forgotten how you couldn't wait to run and tell my dad.

If it hadn't been for your meddling I wouldn't have had the strap or been sent away," she said fiercely.

Megan tried to pull her arm away but Lizzie's grip was far too tight. "Lizzie, I told you before it wasn't me who clecked. It was Mervyn the coal. He saw you when he was loading his sacks," she protested.

"I didn't believe you then and I don't believe you now! Still, in a way you did me a favour. I wouldn't go back to Wales for all the tea in China. I'm getting on here, and I don't want you putting a spanner in the works." Lizzie squeezed her grip harder on Megan's arm. There was no mistaking the hostility in her eyes. "Say you promise not to say a word about my intended promotion. Say it!"

"OK, I promise. Now Lizzie, let go ... you're hurting me!"

Lizzie released her grip. She seemed satisfied as she opened the hallway door leading to yet another flight of stairs and began to ascend as if nothing untoward had happened.

Megan's wrist was still stinging as she followed on behind. She felt disappointed. Aunt Margaret, Lizzie's mam, had led her to believe that Lizzie had been told the truth about Mervyn the coal, but it was obvious she still blamed Megan. So why had she helped her get the job? And why was she being so secretive about her intended promotion? One thing was clear. If Megan had hoped to look on Lizzie as a friend, she had been greatly mistaken. It was obvious her cousin intended to make life as difficult as possible for her — she was indeed on her own.

"These stairs lead to the rest of the staff quarters. All rooms are allocated in order of seniority," Lizzie said, as they entered another long hallway. This one, covered in brown anaglypta wallpaper, was very dark, the only light coming from a small fanlight high in the ceiling. "My room is at the top of the stairs, close to the water closet yet far enough away from all you kitchen workers. There's a water closet on every floor and you'll be allowed one bath a week. Always use the closet on your own floor and be sure to leave it clean — or you'll answer to me!" Lizzie snapped, not even bothering to turn around.

They walked along the bare floor boards until she stopped outside a narrow door. Unlocking it, she turned to face Megan.

"This is your room. If I were you I would unpack quickly then get myself down to Mrs Jarvis's office. She doesn't much like being kept waiting." She brushed past Megan, without so much as a "good luck" or a "so long", leaving her to enter the room alone.

To call it a room was somewhat of an exaggeration. It was no more than a cupboard with just enough space for a small iron framed bed. Above the bed a makeshift shelf held a white candle and a small black book. Megan walked over to investigate, instantly recognizing the Holy Bible.

Lifting her suitcase, she placed it on top of the dark-green quilted eiderdown covering the bed. It was as well she didn't have many clothes, for there was no wardrobe, only a few coat hangers placed on a thin rail

19

behind the door. There was barely enough room for Megan to turn around.

"It's a good job I'm thin or I would have to walk backwards to get out," Megan thought. But as small as it was, for the first time in her life she had a room to herself.

Megan decided she would unpack her few belongings later, "Just take off your hat and coat, girl, and get yourself down to the house-keeper's office."

Leaving the room, she turned the lock of her bedroom door. Placing the key in her dress pocket she was surprised how this small act filled her with quiet satisfaction.

Lizzie Williams stood back to view the oval mahogany table. It looked perfect. The time taken preparing the table before each meal was time well spent. There would be no complaints when she was on duty. Before setting the table she had examined every piece of cutlery, crockery and glassware, and sometimes wondered if the kitchen staff deliberately sent up dirty cutlery in the hope of getting her into trouble. They were all jealous of her because she had bettered herself. Just wait until they found out that she, Lizzie Williams from Nantgarw, was soon to be the newly appointed milady's maid. "Then they'll have to show me the respect such a position deserves!"

Lizzie knew only too well the cause of their jealousy. Master Harold had favoured her above the rest of them. He liked his women young, petite and willing — she had been all three. He had been very generous to her, not only by speaking to Mrs Jarvis and recommending her for promotion but in helping her financially. She couldn't see anything wrong in accepting his money. After all, everyone liked to buy nice things, didn't they? In time Megan would thank her. Mind you, she'd have to change from being such a prude.

As Lizzie made her way to the housekeeper's office she felt pleased with how well her plans were falling into place. Megan had eagerly accepted the position offered, and with her looking so much like a younger version of Lizzie, it wouldn't be long before Master Harold turned his attentions toward her naïve cousin. Then she would be free to enjoy her new position and set her cap at someone her own age. Someone with ambition and good prospects. She had no intention of spending her life in service.

Megan tapped on the office door.

"Enter," Mrs Jarvis's stern voice called from inside the room.

Opening the door, Megan knew this was her chance to do well — she was certain she would not fail. With growing confidence, she entered the room.

"Come closer, child, where I can see you," the housekeeper beckoned from behind a large oak desk.

Megan crossed the room and stood directly in front of her. The housekeeper's ice-blue eyes were fixed on Megan. It seemed an age before she spoke.

"I run this house like the captain of an ocean liner." Mrs Jarvis stood up and began pacing the floor. "If you think of this house as being surrounded by the high sea it might help you to resist any outside distractions, for these ultimately lead to day-dreaming and in turn will surely reflect on your work. Your new position as kitchen maid is subject to a month's trial period. I expect no less than your best effort regarding your work. It will do you well to remember how lucky you were to obtain this position and that it's your cousin Lizzie you have to thank for this. I trust you will not let her down?"

Megan sensed she was not expected to give an answer; the housekeeper was merely relaying the facts, and it was obvious to Megan that Mrs Jarvis thought highly of Lizzie. In silence she watched the housekeeper bend over a small table in the corner of the room, then picking up a strategically placed water jug, administered to a large trailing plant, before continuing.

"Most of your duties fall below-stairs. For all these you answer to Cook. However, some of your duties will take you above-stairs, for these you answer to the parlour maid. If I receive any complaints from either Mrs Partridge or Lizzie regarding your conduct, it could result in my terminating your employment and sending you home. Do you understand?"

"Yes, Mrs Jarvis," Megan answered, hoping her voice didn't reveal the sudden dread she felt at the thought of being sent home in disgrace . . . surely, this could not happen? Her earlier feeling of confidence had certainly been short lived.

"Remember, Megan, you're on a month's trial. There'll be no second chance."

They were interrupted by a knock on the door.

"Come in." The housekeeper walked back to her seat, "Ah, Lizzie. Take young Megan and find her a uniform. She'll need to report to Mrs Partridge directly. I trust you will make sure she has everything she needs for her new position?" Her voice sounded a lot softer.

"Yes, Mrs Jarvis." Lizzie looked towards her cousin. "Follow me, Megan, let's go and get you sorted out." Even Lizzie's voice sounded friendlier, but Megan sensed it was only an act, put on for the housekeeper's benefit.

As they left the office the housekeeper had a few final words. "Megan, I don't want to see you in this office again until the end of your trial period, is that clear?"

"Yes, ma'am."

Once out in the hall, Lizzie closed the office door behind them. "You heard her, cousin dear, so you'd better keep on my right side or I'll have you back in her office before you know it."

"You'll have no cause for complaint about either me or my work," Megan's voice was strong. From now on she would have to find a way to stand up to her cousin, while at the same time making sure she did her job well.

"I'm glad to hear it," was all Lizzie said, as she motioned for Megan to follow her.

Megan pondered on Lizzie's motives. Why had she recommended her for the job? Her cousin had not exactly welcomed her with open arms. On the contrary, she'd made it perfectly clear that her dislike for Megan had not changed.

"Come on, for goodness' sake stop dawdling!" Lizzie urged impatiently.

Megan quickly caught up with her.

Lizzie stood in the middle of the long hallway, holding open a large cupboard filled with shelf upon shelf of clean linen, all in neat piles — white on the top two shelves, then pale blue, next black and brown until finally on the bottom shelf, grey. It was from this shelf Lizzie took a long dark-grey tunic and two aprons — one light, the other dark-grey — both with matching cotton caps.

"You will keep your uniform clean and tidy at all times. The light-grey apron you wear for kitchen duties and the dark you keep for cleaning the fireplaces above-stairs, is that clear?"

Megan nodded, observing again how much her cousin enjoyed giving her orders.

"Your duties above-stairs will mainly be cleaning out and laying the fires, this you will do after all the Fothergill family have gone to their beds. Most nights this should be around midnight." Lizzie seemed to find this statement amusing but the joke was lost to Megan and her cousin chose not to enlighten her.

"Tonight and only tonight I will show you what's expected of you, after that you'll be on your own."

Somewhere in the distance a clock began to chime. Megan counted . . . one . . . two . . . three . . . four.

"I have to go, I've the dinner to serve. You get yourself into your uniform and report downstairs to

24

Cook. I shall call for you around eleven o'clock tonight."

The clock chimed . . . five. Lizzie turned and hurried towards the door marked Private. As she opened the door Megan caught sight of a tall grandfather clock which was loudly chiming for the sixth and final time. For a little while Megan didn't move, she needed to gather her thoughts. There was so much to take in, would she ever fit in? Slowly she turned and made her way up the stairs to her room.

Once in her room she unpacked her few belongings. First, the going away present from Mamgu Williams — a mirror, hairbrush and comb, all with matching mother-of-pearl handles — they were the prettiest things Megan had ever owned. Very carefully she placed them on the shelf next to the Bible. Next the gingham toilet bag, lovingly made by her dear sister Olive from an oddment of material, holding safe her soap, flannel and pumice stone. Megan hung it around the bedpost at the bottom of the bed. Then taking out her flannelette night-dress she placed it under the ticking-covered pillow. Her underwear would have to stay in the suitcase; it would serve as a drawer in the absence of one in the room. Closing the suitcase she attempted to push it under the bed but something was stopping it. Reaching under, she moved a white porcelain chamber pot to one side. This enabled her suitcase to slide under with ease.

Megan changed into her uniform, carefully hanging her best chapel dress on the rail behind the door. She wondered when she would get to wear it again. The housekeeper hadn't mentioned if she would be entitled to any time off or, more importantly, what her wages would be. Megan had thought to ask but decided to wait a while, to see how the land lay.

"Come on in, young 'un, and sit yourself next Sally," Mrs Partridge beckoned to Megan as she entered the kitchen.

"Can I help you, Mrs Partridge?" Megan offered shyly, struck by the warmth of the greeting after the coldness of Lizzie.

"No, sit down, child, and eat." Cook patted the wooden bench. "It has been a long day for you and it's not over yet, for you're to meet Lizzie later. She's to give instruction about your work above-stairs. Tomorrow will be time enough for you to acquaint yourself with the job down here. Move over, Sally, and let young Megan sit in." The cook gave a few tuts of annoyance as she spoke to the same girl with bright red hair who had earlier been balancing on the ladder.

The table around which everyone sat was laden with food and almost unrecognizable from the hive of industry it had previously been. As Sally slid along the bench seat she gave Megan a friendly smile — something Megan was grateful for, even though the girl's teeth were as black as soot. This could have been easily avoided with regular brushing with bicarbonate of soda. Megan had been lucky her mam had instructed her in this practice. Her resulting white teeth were proof enough of its efficiency.

26

Cook busied herself at the cooking range, while everyone else stared at Megan in silence.

"Now don't you worry about this lot all staring, 'tis only because you're new. I'll tell you their names directly, not that you'll remember them all in one go, mind, but with working alongside them every day you soon will."

Megan did as she was instructed and took the seat on the bench next to Sally.

"That be right, you sit yourself down." Cook's voice was warm and friendly as she made her way towards the table carrying a huge teapot. "While the tea's brewing, I might as well get on with some introductions. Well, as you probably heard me say, that big lump right next to you is Sally. She doesn't say much — thank God, for her voice be as deep and as loud as a fog horn."

Everyone around the table laughed. Sally seemed to take it all in good humour, because she was still smiling when cook continued, "Next to Sally be Agnes. She be leaving Saturday and 'tis her job you be filling. Silly girl's gone and got herself in the family way, so she's being sent home to Somerset. Mistress Fothergill insists on paying her train fare even though she's been let down badly. Just shows you how kind the mistress be, that's what I say."

Megan glanced at the young girl in question. She was a frail little thing with light blonde hair. Her head was bowed down hiding her face; her shoulders jerked as she gave a little sob.

"Enough of that, Agnes, what's done is done. It is something that happens all too regular to you young 'uns. Think you'd have more sense be now!" Cook looked toward Megan. "Ignore her, she'll stop her sniffling shortly. S'pose it comes with her condition," she said raising her eyes before continuing the introductions.

As Cook had rightly said, Megan struggled to remember everyone's name straight off — next to Agnes sat a young man whose name she couldn't remember, but she knew his job was washing the pots and pans. Then there was an empty seat — this she was informed was for Lizzie.

"If and when 'her ladyship' cares to join us," the lad said in a sarcastic tone which was not lost to Megan.

"Watch your tongue, Percy Smith! Kindly remember Lizzie is Megan's cousin and if Lizzie sometimes chooses to eat alone, then 'tis naught to do with any of us." Cook glared at the lad. Megan sensed she spoke more in defence of Megan than in support of Lizzie.

Next to where Lizzie was to sit were two much older girls, one called Sadie, the other Alice.

"This seat next to me is for Sidney." The cook's eyes shone with pride when she spoke her son's name. "Sidney tries to eat with us most evenings. It be his reward for doing favours for the household, like taking the time to pick you up from the station. Heart of gold, my Sidney has." She looked towards the back door as if anticipating his arrival, and at that precise moment the door opened.

28

"Hello, folks, are you all waiting for me?" Sidney asked, flashing a wicked grin at them all. "Well, I'm here now and I be starving." He gave his mother a gentle kiss on the cheek as he took his seat opposite Megan.

"Hello, Megan." He spoke to her with the ease of an old friend, which pleased Megan. "I can see you've settled in. I must say you look grand in your uniform. Must feel strange though, eh?" He flashed her a smile.

She felt her colour rising. "Yes, it does a bit," Megan answered her new-found friend, hoping no one had noticed her blushes. She was not used to compliments regarding her appearance.

"I know you're all eager to find out more about Megan here, so later I shall allow you to ask her one question each, but first we must eat." Cook had spoken.

On Cook's instructions they began passing around the plates of food. Slices of home-cured boiled bacon, potatoes, baby carrots, hot beetroot and a lot more. Megan was surprised at the amount she ate because earlier she had not felt in the least bit hungry. When they had all finished eating, Cook stood up and, carrying a large teapot, walked to the fireplace. "All right, you nosy lot, while I wet the tea you may ask Megan your questions — no badgering her, mind," she said, as she lifted a huge black kettle of boiling water off the open fire.

One by one they each asked a question.

"How old are you?"

"Where have you come from?"

"What's it like living in Wales?"

"Did you travel all the way by train?"

"Have you got any family, besides Madam Lizzie?"

The only one who declined a question was Sidney, but then he already knew most of the answers. Megan's honest replies seemed to satisfy everyone's natural curiosity.

"There, Megan love, it's as well to get all the questions over first as last, that's what I says. Now is there anything you would like to ask us?" Mrs Partridge asked, as she sliced a large fruit cake into portions and passed them around the table.

Megan hesitated but a friendly smile from Sidney gave her the confidence to speak.

"Well, I-I would like to know more about the people who live above-stairs? Who exactly are my employers?"

Cook smiled to herself as she poured out cups of the hot brown tea. "It is only natural for you to be inquisitive," she said, then taking a deep breath, "Well, first there be your main employer, Mistress Gertrude Fothergill. She be such a nice lady and never no trouble. Very sad though, she lost poor Mr Joshua Fothergill not six months ago. Shame it be, him such a good husband and business man. Well respected he was all over the country . . ." Cook gave a deep sigh.

Megan sensed her genuine compassion, remembering how Sidney had told her about the death of his own father, so his mother understood only too well what it felt to lose a beloved husband.

Cook shook her head and gave another deep sigh before continuing, "The mistress has two sons. Master Robert, he be a military man — an officer, and. like his

30

dad, a true gentleman. He was in France during the war. The sights he must have seen have sadly taken their toll on him, for he be a shell of the man he once was. Anyways, then there's Master Harold. Since his father's sad demise he has taken over the running of the family's tobacco business. Now, he be a different kettle of fish. How two brothers can be so different mystifies me. He's certainly no gentleman, and you'll do well to give him a wide berth, child. There I've probably said too much. But I do try to warn all my girls to stay clear of him. Some take heed, others choose to ignore it."

Megan couldn't help notice the knowing looks that passed around the table.

"Lizzie likes him," Percy sniggered.

"We all know why she likes him," Alice — or was it Sadie? — said. Megan was having trouble remembering which was which.

"Hold your tongues, all of you. Lizzie must rely on her own conscience and I'll not have her spoken about behind her back, is that clear?" Cook was on her feet. "Come on, hurry and finish your tea and get this table cleared away."

The mood had changed. Megan wished she understood more, but sensed there would be no further answers tonight.

"You best take yourself to your room, child. You've had a long day travelling. No doubt you could do with a few hours' rest before starting your duties later tonight." Cook smiled "What time are you meeting Lizzie?"

"Eleven o'clock, Cook."

"She'll show you the ropes. She knows the job inside out and I have to say 'twas one she did exceptionally well. Although be prepared. Your cousin can be a hard taskmaster."

"Thank you, Cook. If my mam was here she'd tell you that I'm no stranger to hard work."

"I'm sure she would. Now go on, off you go."

Once back in her room Megan undressed down to her petticoat, lay on the bed and wished she were back home helping her mother prepare the evening meal. Now she would even have welcomed the noisy and often irritating banter of her five younger siblings. Cook had been right, it had been a long day. Megan fought the sudden urge to close her eyes and give way to sleep. She couldn't risk oversleeping. Instead she cast her mind back over the events of the day.

She remembered how especially clean and tidy her own family house had looked this morning and guessed that her mother had made a special effort, wanting her eldest daughter to remember it at its best. But in truth Megan needed no such reminder. Of course, it was always nice to see the house looking spick and span, but what she would remember most was the closeness and love of her family.

She thought of her dad who had felt it necessary to dress in his Sunday best to send her on her way — such a proud man. She swallowed hard, and decided to let her mind cling for comfort to that last moment when she had walked with her brother across Carn Mountain.

They had set out just before dawn, Jess eager to accompany her, if only for the first section of her six-mile journey to Llan Station. For a while they'd walked in silence, afraid to speak, not wanting to spoil their final precious time together; only their footsteps on frost-covered grass broke the sombre silence. After about a mile the familiar sound of the colliery hooter echoed around the valley, calling the miners to work and heralding the start of a new day. Above Nant Colliery, where the mountain path forked, they stopped. It was time to say goodbye.

Jess turned to her. "Megs, it's not too late. There's still time for you to change your mind. You don't have to leave."

Megan's temples throbbed and her throat burned as she fought to hold back the tears.

"You know I can't turn back now, Jess. I have to go. It's all arranged. Lizzie's expecting me."

"Why did *she* have to interfere? We would have managed somehow."

"You know that's not true. Do you think I'd be leaving if there were any other way?"

"Well, I think that cousin of ours is up to no good. Hell bent on getting back at you."

Megan had to admit that the same thought had crossed her own mind but she'd decided to give Lizzie the benefit of the doubt.

Megan reached out, gently touching her brother's shoulder. "Please Jess, let's not argue. And as for Lizzie, I think it's time to let bygones be bygones. I'd much rather you wished me well."

"Oh Megs, you must know I wish you well." His voice had become tender. "*Duw*, there's biting the wind is this morning, it's even making my eyes water."

Megan knew better, but let it pass. She would never embarrass her brother. Of all her siblings, Jess had always been the one she felt closest to. Closest in age and also in understanding.

"Don't you worry about me, Jess, *bach*. I'll be fine. You just concentrate on looking after Mam and the others. I know she's worried about Dad — he looks so frail. And that cough of his doesn't seem to be getting any better."

Jess, at seventeen only a year older than herself, stood proud and tall. And rightly so, for she knew he worked as hard as any man.

"You know you can rely on me, Sis." He looked down towards the colliery. "I'd better go. If I'm late for work they'll dock my wages."

She put her arms around him and gently kissed his cheek. "Go on, off to work with you, Jess Williams. I've a train to catch."

"God keep you, Sister."

She watched as he took the path down the valley where the morning mist hovered like a shroud, watched as he ran the last few yards to the colliery gates. Just before entering he turned and gave a last wave. Then he went out of sight.

Megan opened her eyes to darkness. For a while she lay puzzled. The bed felt strange to her, where was she? Then it came to her: *of course, I'm in Bristol. I must have dozed off. I'd better shake myself. Any time now Lizzie will be calling for me!* As she jumped out of bed she fumbled for the matches above the bed and lit the candle. The room was cold. She hastily dressed, then wrapping her mother's coat around her shoulders, sat on the bed to wait for her cousin. In the distance Megan heard a clock chime. She counted. It was eleven o'clock. Her bedroom door opened.

"Come on, let's go," Lizzie commanded.

Megan let her coat fall on to the bed and left the room. She followed Lizzie down the back stairs, through the door on the ground floor marked Private and into the main entrance hall with its black-and-white-chequered, marble tiled floor. Megan stood in awe at such opulence. The winding staircase, covered in a plush red carpet runner, seemed to reach right up to the high ceiling with its elaborate centerpiece — a large chandelier that shimmered as draughts caught the many candles that lit it. But the candles seemed different to those Megan knew. These were covered with glass baubles.

"Come on, we haven't got all night. I'd like to go to my bed sometime soon," Lizzie grumbled.

As Lizzie escorted her first into the dining room and then the parlour, Megan was amazed by the splendour of the ornaments and furnishings.

"Each night when you clean out and lay the fires, you will touch nothing, do you hear? There is an inventory made of all valuables every week. So don't think you could remove even the smallest item without it being noticed."

35

"But —" Megan was about to challenge Lizzie for suggesting she, Megan Williams, would steal anything. She was stopped by Lizzie's hand over her mouth.

"There's to be no argument. I'm here to tell you what's expected of you, and you'd do well to be quiet and just listen, for I don't intend to repeat myself. Now, each night when all above-stairs have retired, you will first clean out and lay the fire in the dining room and then do the same in the parlour. You never light them, this duty falls to me as parlour maid."

Although Megan stayed silent, she had been tempted to ask Lizzie if she'd ever tried to teach her granny how to suck eggs? For hadn't she — Megan Williams — been laying and lighting coal fires since she was old enough to lift a bucket?

"Well then, what are you waiting for? The sooner you start, the sooner you finish. It shouldn't take you more than an hour. Most nights you should be in bed by midnight."

Megan was sure Lizzie was laughing at her.

"What's so funny?"

"Nothing, *dear cousin*. Well, nothing that concerns you, anyway."

Megan, too tired for riddles, let it pass.

CHAPTER
THREE

It was late in the day when Jess returned home. His body and clothes were black with coal dust after a long hard day down the pit, so he looked forward to a long soak in a hot bath.

Following in his father's footsteps, Jess had joined the colliery at just thirteen years of age. His job as a collier's assistant meant he had to work a ten-hour shift each day underground. It saddened him to think what fate had in store for him. He had seen what a lifetime of working down the pit had done to his dad, once so strong and healthy, reduced to an old man before his time, constantly coughing and wheezing and fighting for every breath, symptoms common among the many men who worked amid the dusty and damp conditions of the coal mine. Jess thanked God that women and girls were no longer allowed to do such work, as had been the case in Mamgu's day.

Mamgu, his paternal grandmother, lived not a stone's throw away, at the bottom end of King Edward Street. A sprightly woman, despite her years sorting the slag, looking after her husband and bringing up three children, she still managed not to look her sixty-eight years. Jess's father was the eldest of her children. Next

37

to him had been Ivor — Lizzie's dad — but sadly he had passed away last year. It had hurt his wife Margaret that Lizzie wasn't able to come home for the funeral — the truth was she hadn't wanted to, she had never forgiven her dad for taking a strap to her. Mamgu's youngest child, Maude, had married well and lived in Cardiff. Her husband, Jack, worked in the shipping office, near the docks. Jack had often hinted to Jess that if he ever wanted a job . . . but Jess knew it could only ever be a pipe dream. He couldn't move away from the valley. His family needed him here.

Opening the back door into the kitchen, he was surprised to find thirteen-year-old Olive sitting by the fireside crying her heart out.

"Whatever's wrong, *cariad?*" Jess spoke softly, as he crossed the room to her, making sure to avoid the empty tin bath which dominated the centre of the room.

"I'm sorry, Jess. B-but your bath's not ready . . . and it's all my fault," she cried.

"Shhhh. Don't you go upsetting yourself. Now isn't there plenty of time for me to have a bath?" Jess tried to comfort her.

"But . . . Megan . . . always . . . had . . . your . . . bath . . . ready," Olive sobbed.

"Where's Mam?" he asked, putting his arm around her shoulder.

"She's . . . upstairs . . . with . . . Dad," she cried.

The poor lamb, Jess thought, she looks as if she's got the weight of the world on her shoulders.

"*Duw*, I was only thinking as I walked home from work, how nice it would be to have a cup of tea and a Welsh-cake before my bath today. So you see there's no rush, honest. Now, while I lift the bucket of water on to the fire, you go make a nice pot of tea, righto?"

"Jess, are you sure, you really don't mind?" She looked up at him with her big brown eyes.

Jess gave a smile. His little white lie had at least stopped her crying.

"Of course I'm sure, but only if I get two Welsh-cakes, mind you."

With ease, he lifted the large bucket of cold water and placed it alongside the two kettles already filled and heating on the black-leaded hob above the fireplace. Olive stood up and placed a tender kiss on his cheek; she didn't seem to care about his dirty face.

"Thank you, Jess, you're a *browd* in a million. I'm so lucky to have a brother like you."

"Get away with you," he said, acting as if embarrassed.

Olive gave a little giggle. Jess watched as she reached for the brown china teapot on the dresser. She looked such a frail little thing and he knew the job of looking after the family was becoming too much for her.

Since Megan had left, their dad's illness had taken a turn for the worse and he was now confined to his bed. This meant their mam had to spend more time looking after him, which in turn put even more work on to poor Olive. Jess looked out of the kitchen window, across the backyard and into the garden where young Phyllis was playing happily with baby Evan. At only eight years of age Phyllis handled the energetic toddler well. Although this was something to be grateful for, it still left Olive to cope alone with the everyday running of the house. Under protest, Bryn attended the local school every weekday, so could only help with household chores at night or on the weekend.

"What do I want with schoolin' anyway? As soon as I'm thirteen I shall follow you down the pit. So what do I want with reading and writing?" Bryn had argued.

Jess tried to explain how important it was. He had learned to read and write and thought it a privilege to be offered schooling. He vowed that whatever their objections, he would make sure his brothers attended school. It wasn't so important for the girls. He paused at this thought . . . Megan had been different, he reasoned, remembering how she had pestered him to teach her. And how they'd read for hours by candlelight from a book of short stories he'd managed to pick up for a penny from the rag-and-bone man.

Megan had been quick to learn. When Minister Jenkins asked her to read the Sunday school lesson, Jess had felt such pride. He gave a deep sigh . . . his Megan had been gone for nearly three weeks and still there had been no reply to his letter.

"There you are, Jess *bach*, a nice cup of tea and two Welsh-cakes. Now you sit yourself down by the fire," she said, carefully placing them on the table.

Jess did as she bid.

"There's spoiling me you are. With treatment like this, I might take a late bath every day."

His sister's face beamed, pleased with this small praise, especially as it came from Jess.

Jess was not joking. It wouldn't hurt him to change his routine. By doing so, he could save Olive the job of lifting the heavy bucket on and off the fire — which to her must have been a backbreaking task — and do it himself. He didn't know how she'd managed it for so long, and felt guilty that until today he hadn't noticed how ill she looked. Her skin had become pale and seemed to highlight the contrasting dark rings under her big brown eyes, eyes which had somehow lost their brightness.

"Lift those big feet of yours if you don't want them covered in damp sand," Olive said with mock severity, while at the same time flashing him a lovely warm smile.

Jess quickly obeyed her. It was good to see her in better spirits. As he lifted his feet, she scattered the damp sand over the stone floor. Inevitably, when he undressed for his bath a residue of coal dust would fall from his working clothes and instead of falling on to the stone floor it would stick to the damp sand, making it easier to sweep up later.

As Jess ate his Welsh-cakes he stared into the fireplace, wondering what was to become of them all when the inevitable happened. There was no mistaking the signs of progressive lung disease — he'd seen it so many times with other mine workers — and knew it was only a matter of time before his dad's lungs gave up completely. Then they would have to leave their tied house and God knows where they would go. With him not old enough to be taken on as a full-time collier, he was not entitled to a colliery house.

"I think your water is ready now, *browd*. So you get yourself undressed and I'll fill your bath." As she made to walk toward the fireplace Jess put his hand out to stop her.

"No you don't! From now on I fill my own bath."

Jess was sure he hadn't imagined her sigh of relief as she turned away. Then placing a bar of carbolic soap into the tin bath, she made for the back door.

"I'll just go and get the washing in off the line and check on the *babas*."

Around this time Olive usually made herself scarce, allowing Jess some privacy to have his bath. After a long soak in the hot water, he scrubbed himself down with carbolic soap, in an attempt to rid himself of not only the dirt but also the cockroaches and fleas which seemed to thrive underground. Stepping out of the bath he dried himself with the towel which Olive had left warming on the wooden clothes horse in front of the fire.

Once dressed in his grey serge trousers and charcoal collarless shirt, he carried the tin bath outside and emptied it down the drain, then hung it and his dirty working clothes in the wash-house next to the privy in the back yard. As it was Friday he wouldn't need them again until Monday morning. He decided that in the morning he would help Olive wash and dry them in readiness for another week's work.

Returning to the kitchen he sat himself in his father's big armchair by the fire and savoured the feeling of being free of dirt and grime. Maybe he'd have forty winks before going upstairs to see his dad. He was just dozing off when he heard his mother's footsteps slowly descending the stairs. As she reached the bottom, her face was white, drained of all colour.

"Mam, what's wrong? Is it Dad?" Jess jumped from the chair and rushed over to her.

"Your dad's gone from us forever, Son." Mary Williams put her hands together and fell to her knees in prayer. "God! Bless my husband's poor soul. But what's to become of us?"

Jess put his arms around her, lifting her up, "Oh Mam, I'm so sorry. He was a good man and —" He fought back the sudden tears. "Come on, Mam, don't you worry. We'll be fine, honest." As he led her to the armchair he struggled to make his voice sound convincing. "I'll make you a nice cup of tea before I go and fetch Mrs Griffith."

For as long as Jess could remember, Mrs Griffith had been laying people out, but she was getting old and he wondered who would take on the unenviable task when she was no longer around.

"Just give me a few minutes and I will see to your dad, Son. You go and get Doctor Rees and Mr Bevan, the undertaker." Her voice was calm, almost too calm.

"Please, Mam, let me call and get Mrs Griffith?"

"No, Jess! Your dad made me promise not to let 'that woman' near him. For years he secretly feared her; it was as if he believed that just being close to her, somehow brought him closer to death. Many's the time he would cross the road to avoid meeting her face to face, so I'll not be letting her near him now."

Jess knew there would be no arguing with his mother.

"Where be Olive?" she asked.

"She's getting the washing in down the garden. The little ones are playing down there as well."

"On your way out, tell her to take the children to your Aunt Margaret's. She's to tell her what's happened and ask her to keep the children away until the undertaker has been and gone."

"Right, Mam," he said, handing her a cup of tea. "Will you be all right on your own? I'll be as quick as I can."

"I be fine lad. I had nothing to fear from your dad when he was alive, so I'm sure . . ." She didn't need to finish her sentence, he understood what she meant.

As Jess made his way down the garden path, he could clearly hear his mother's sobs. He should have known she would not cry in front of him. She was far too proud. Even in poverty there was no doubting the love his parents had felt for one another. Jess himself grieved for the loss of his dad, but there were no tears. His father was at peace at last. No more pain, no more fighting for breath, no more suffering the humiliation of having to rely on his wife and family for everything. Jess was determined to remember his father as one of the strongest, proudest and most respected men he knew. A good man, much loved and admired by everyone who ever knew him.

44

As he walked down the garden path, Jess had to duck his head under the washing line which Olive had lowered to remove the clothes. His sister stood with her back to him at the far end of the line, and appeared to be having some difficulty removing the last few items of clothing as they swung fiercely to and fro, catching the high wind as it swept down the valley. The battle won, she bent over, carefully folding each item before placing it into the raffia laundry basket strategically placed at the side of the path.

Young Phyllis and Evan busied themselves, retrieving the spent clothes pegs and depositing them into the wooden box attached to the side of the laundry basket. As Jess drew closer the familiar fresh smell of newly washed and starched laundry wafted over him, and for some strange reason this momentarily gave him a feeling of well-being. Hearing his footsteps, Olive turned to face him. Their eyes met. The look he gave her said it all.

"Dad?" she asked.

He just nodded. She turned, covering her face with her pinafore in an attempt to hide her tears from the little ones.

"How would you two like Olive to take you to Auntie Margaret's for tea?" Jess asked, trying to sound light-hearted. He knew when his mother felt the time was right she would tell them about their dad, in her own way. He felt relieved that that particular job hadn't fallen to him. Either way, a few hours of blissful ignorance wouldn't hurt them.

"Are you coming too, Jess?" Phyllis asked.

"No, *cariad*. I shall see you when Olive brings you home later."

"What's wrong with Olive? Why is she covering her face with her pinny? Does she want to play hide and seek? I like playing hide and seek . . ."

"No, Phyllis. No hide and seek, not today. I think Olive must have something in her eye. Listen, if you take Evan and wait by the gate, I'll see if I can help her remove it."

Satisfied with his explanation, they turned and headed towards the high gate which opened on to a dirt lane.

Jess moved closer to Olive. "Are you all right, Sis?"

Dropping the apron from her face, she flung her arms around his neck. "Oh Jess . . . poor dad . . . I didn't even get to say goodbye. I should have gone up to see him this afternoon, instead of sitting by the fire feeling sorry for myself. I didn't even get to tell him how much I loved him," she cried.

As he held her close, he felt her warm tears trickle down the side of his neck.

"Don't you go fretting yourself. I'm sure Dad knew how much we all loved him. He's at peace now. From now on it's Mam who's going to need all our support. Us older ones must be strong for her."

He hoped that appealing to her sense of family duty would halt the flow of tears. It worked. Almost instantly she stopped crying and pulled herself away from him. Then, taking a small handkerchief from her apron pocket, she blew her nose. It was more a gesture than a necessity, a way of telling him she had composed herself.

"Of course, I'm being selfish again . . . poor Mam. Shall I go to her?"

"No, not right now. I think she wants to be alone with' — he was about to say Dad, but aware of the images it might bring to her mind, instead he said — 'alone with her memories. You look after the little ones. Take them to Aunt Margaret's, explain what's happened and how Mam wants the children away from the house. I'll let you know when it's time to come back home. Come on, I'll walk part of the way with you," he said, putting an arm around her. His thoughts went to Megan — without doubt Dad's favourite. She would have to be told and soon. He knew how hurt she would feel at not being able to be with her family at a time like this.

It was nearly midnight when Megan wrapped her grey serge tunic under her knees and knelt down in front of the dining room fireplace. The rest of the household staff had already gone to their beds, but she could plainly hear the raised voices coming from the parlour and knew she was in for yet another late night.

"What gives you the right to interfere in my affairs anyway?" a gruff voice shouted. Megan instantly recognized the voice of Harold Fothergill.

"I consider it my duty to protect Mother's interest," Master Robert's softer voice answered. Although Megan had not met either man yet, over the week she had learned to distinguish their voices. She felt she shouldn't be listening, but the closeness of the two rooms made it unavoidable.

"Duty! Don't give me that. You're afraid Mother will leave everything to me, I can see right through you." Harold's voice was getting louder.

"The way you're behaving with your excessive gambling and drinking she'll have nothing left to live on, never mind leave," Master Robert replied.

"You've always been jealous that it was me Mother chose to take the helm of the business. All you could do was go off and play at soldiering." Harold gave a loud laugh.

"It's no good talking to you when you've been drinking, I don't know why I bother. I'm just glad Father didn't live to see what you have become. I'll bid you goodnight."

Megan heard the parlour door open and close, then heavy footsteps crossed the hall and slowly climbed the stairway. Master Robert, at least, had retired for the night. The unmistakable sound of clinking glasses told her Master Harold was pouring himself another drink, so she might as well take her time brushing the black-lead into the grate. In the three weeks since she started her new job, not once had she gone to her bed before two o'clock in the morning . . . except for her very first night when Lizzie had shown her around.

That first night Megan had gone to her bed just after midnight. Lizzie failed to mention this was due to the changed arrangements of their employers. In particular that of both Master Fothergills. Harold, who was away visiting friends in London, and Robert, away in Gloucester where he had been admitted to the military hospital. The mistress, being without company, had decided to retire early and catch up on some reading. Sadly, Lizzie led Megan to believe that this was the norm.

The very next day Master Harold returned home and the situation changed. Megan soon found out how he liked to stay up until way after midnight every night. Master Robert although away most of the week, began spending his weekends at home as part of his rehabilitation treatment, but he was no trouble and usually retired early, not long after his mother. Mrs Partridge had murmured in hushed tones something about "shellshock".

Getting up off her knees, Megan admired her efforts, more than satisfied with the well laid fire and the highly polished grate, although she was sure Lizzie would manage to find fault with it. Every day she made a point of criticizing Megan's work, sometimes making her lay a fire several times over — there just seemed no pleasing her.

The clock in the hall chimed, telling her it was one o'clock. Megan now understood why Lizzie had found it so amusing when she'd told her "most nights you should be finished around midnight".

Megan listened at the wall. Everything was quiet. At long last Master Harold had gone to bed. Lifting her coal bucket, she made her way to the next room. Slowly she opened the parlour door. As usual the room was in complete darkness, but over the weeks she'd quickly learned that by leaving the door open, light from the hall chandelier would shine in, making it a lot easier to complete her duties. The parlour fireplace was small. It had ornate tiles replacing the black lead surrounds of the large dining room fire-basket. *This'll not take me long*, she thought. Megan's last job every night was to stoke the fire in the kitchen, assuring Cook of warm ovens to prepare the breakfasts. With a bit of luck she might be in bed before two o'clock, giving her at least a few hours' sleep before having to rise again at five o'clock to begin another day.

As she crossed the room to the fireplace she heard the door slam behind her, plunging the room into darkness. Instantly she knew she was no longer alone. She felt panic. She heard footsteps walking towards her, someone with laboured breathing. She wanted to run but somehow her legs wouldn't move. An odour of stale whisky filled the air. Almost immediately, a man seized her, a big and heavy man, holding her so tight she could hardly breathe and pushing his lower body roughly against hers. She felt fear like she had never before experienced. Who was he? She wanted to move away, but couldn't. She wanted to scream out, but couldn't. It was as if it were happening to someone else.

"Come to me, you young sweet thing. I've missed you so much, you little minx," the man whispered in her ear as his wet mouth lavished kisses all down the side of her neck. He reeked of whisky.

As if shocked out of a trance, Megan began to struggle free, her clenched fists hitting out at him, but to no avail. He was far too strong.

His large arms were now holding hers behind her back.

"Come on. You know you love it." He pulled her down on to the floor, falling heavily on top of her, the weight of his body pinning her down.

Suddenly she knew her attacker, his deep well-spoken voice unmistakable. It was Master Harold.

"Sir! You're hurting me. Let me go!" she screamed, instantly silenced when his mouth and tongue found her. She felt sick, she could hardly breathe, but still she fought in vain to wriggle free.

He ignored her plea and forced a clammy hand down the front of her tunic, roughly fondling her breast. Again she screamed out.

He give a sinister chuckle. "I do love it when you play hard to get, but no point overdoing it, eh?"

She felt his wet lips slide across her cheek and down her neck, his prickly, unshaven face scraping her skin. His mouth finding her earlobe, first sucking then biting, hurting her.

Summoning all her strength, she attacked harder, fists flying, legs writhing. "Leave me alone, you-you brute," she cried out fiercely.

This time he covered her mouth with his hand. "Enough of that, I say. We don't want to wake the rest of the house, now do we? I know why you're angry with me — Harold has been away from his little Lizzie far too long, but I'm back now, just feel how my body wants you." She felt revulsion as he thrust himself even harder against her.

Megan tried to scream out that she was not Lizzie, but his hand still covered her mouth, silencing her. She flinched as his teeth bit into the side of her neck. In vain she fought to free herself but he was far too heavy and strong. She could not budge him. It was abundantly clear what he intended to do to her. And that she was powerless to stop him. As he lifted her dress and roughly pulled at her under-drawers, her whole body stiffened with fear, she screamed in her head, "Please God! . . . No!"

Suddenly his heavy body was lifted off her.

"You animal! Leave the poor girl alone." It was Master Robert, his voice angry, almost unrecognizable. "I'm ashamed to call you my brother."

"Why don't you mind your own bloody business! You can't order me around. I'm not one of your regimental lackeys," Harold shouted.

"No, but I can stop you inflicting your unwanted attentions on this helpless young girl."

Megan could just make out the outline of the two brothers as they sized up to one another in the darkness, then she heard Master Harold slump into a chair. And only a moment later, Master Robert was gently taking her hand, helping her to her feet,

"Are you all right? Please, don't be afraid. Leave everything and get yourself off to your room. You'll not be bothered again tonight."

Hastily, she straightened her skirt, her hands shaking. As she rushed past Master Robert, she only managed to

52

whisper, "Thank you," eager to escape to the safety of her own room.

She ran all the way up the two flights of stairs, afraid to turn around in case *he* had somehow managed to follow her. Out of breath, she unlocked her door and entered quickly. For a while she stood leaning against the door listening for the sound of his footsteps, while trying to control her breathing. Eventually, satisfied she had not been followed, she threw herself on to the bed and finally gave way to tears. But she did not forget to give thanks to God and Master Robert for saving her from evil.

Robert Fothergill marched out of the living room leaving Harold slouched in the chair. The drink had finally taken full effect. He wished he could believe that the drink had sparked off his brother's attack on a young member of the household staff, but he knew better. Harold was a drunkard, a bully and a gambler.

Robert couldn't stop shaking. He hadn't felt such anger since . . . he stopped himself . . . he didn't want the images of the carnage he'd seen returning to his already troubled mind. Night after night, he'd been haunted by nightmares so vivid he could clearly hear the screams of young soldiers as they lay dying in the mud. Some were as young as fifteen, having lied about their age in their eagerness to enlist. They were not prepared for war. Most had only joined for the regular wage, three meals a day and a uniform. He felt angry at such a waste of life, and guilty that he had survived. It didn't help when everyone told him how lucky he was to have been months in the trenches without being maimed or scarred. It was true, there were no visible scars — they were all in his head. He felt somehow responsible. After all, wasn't he the one, who, knowing how futile it all was, ordered men to go over the hill? Day after day hundreds of men, who obeyed without question, died. And still the directive from his superiors insisted on pushing forward . . . why?

Tonight at least his insomnia had been a godsend. He dreaded to think what Harold might have done to that young girl, if he hadn't decided to seek out one of his old law books from the bookcase in the parlour. He hoped from now on she would be extra vigilant. He wouldn't put it past Harold to try again.

It was a long hard night, and the next morning Robert awoke in a cold sweat. Would the bloody nightmares ever go away? There was a tap on the door. Hutchins entered carrying his breakfast tray.

"It's almost six-thirty, sir. You asked me to call you, but I can see there is no need, you are already awake."

Robert watched as Hutchins set the tray on the small bedside table. He liked Hutchins. He was a gentle, caring sort of chap who, while often inquiring as to Robert's general health, never once commented on his cold sweats or questioned the disarray of the bedclothes.

"Begging your pardon, sir, but would you like me to run your bath before I go and fetch the car?"

"Thank you, Hutchins, that would be fine. My train is due to leave at eight. Let's hope I shan't have to make the trip for much longer."

Robert knew that the doctors at the military hospital were more than pleased with his progress. Each day he was getting physically, if not mentally, stronger, and, at least by day, he found it easier to cope with what the doctors called his "post-war trauma". The hospital and its staff had done as much as they could for him. His discharge date was almost in sight, and from then on it would be up to him to cope alone as best he could. Robert had felt somewhat better since, after a lot of cruel soul-searching, he'd come to the conclusion that his future no longer lay with the military. He'd decided the time had come to set the wheels in motion to resign his commission. He intended to return to studying law and hoped one day to be called to the Bar, as had been the case before a mistaken sense of duty had prompted him to take up a commission to fight for king and country.

Harold's earlier drunken accusation that he was "only playing at soldiering", truly hit home, for it was not without truth. Robert certainly had never been prepared for actual war. Oh yes! He had passed with flying colours, the training, the exams, the theory, but it had all seemed a game, almost as if he were merely acting out a role — so far removed from the real thing.

The day of his passing-out parade he, like his parents, had felt great pride. After all, he was the first commissioned Fothergill male. He had visibly preened himself as he marched by in his made-to-measure, red and blue uniform of the Highland and Somerset's. Acting the part of an officer so well, he even started to believe in it himself.

Then, before he had time to adjust to his new-found position, a rude awakening. Only three days later he was being sent off to Ypres in France, to take command of a unit on the front line, and he soon became aware of the reality of war in all its glory.

"Will there be anything else, sir?" Hutchins had returned from running the bath, and was anxiously looking at the clock on the wall.

"No. You go. I shall ready myself and be down before seven-thirty."

Later that morning, Lizzie, going about her duties above-stairs, met Master Harold in the hallway. Normally he would have walked straight past her, never acknowledging her, always careful not to give the slightest hint of their *understanding*. His mother would never forgive such impropriety, especially when it involved someone in her employ. Lizzie bobbed a polite curtsy, expecting his usual token nod. Instead to her surprise he made a grab for her arm, drawing her close, pressing his mouth hard against her ear.

"Would you mind telling me what you thought you could achieve by last night's fiasco in the parlour? Making such a commotion that my *dear* brother thought it his God-given duty to intervene on your behalf?" His voice was low and menacing.

"But Master Harold, it couldn't have been me. I wasn't in the parlour last night," Lizzie protested.

He tightened his grip on her arm. "Well, I'm sure I didn't dream it. So don't you lie to me, girl. It's not too late for me to change Mrs Jarvis's mind about your

56

promotion, so think on. I mean to have an explanation."

"It must have been my young cousin, Megan, sir. She has recently been taken on as kitchen maid. And everyone says what a strong resemblance there is between us. Honestly, sir, I wouldn't lie to *you*." Lizzie was eager to set him straight. She couldn't allow anything to stand in the way of her new position as lady's maid.

"Mmm, Megan, you say. And exactly how old is this cousin of yours?"

"She's just sixteen, sir. If you like I could have a word with her."

"Don't bother. Why should I waste time on her, when I can have you? In fact, my sweet, I shall see *you* later tonight." Slowly, he brushed his wet mouth across her face, leaving a trail of saliva on her cheek.

"Harold, is that you in the hallway? Do come along, the staff are waiting to serve tea," Mistress Fothergill's voice called from the dining room.

"Coming, Mother," he answered, quickly releasing Lizzie's arm.

CHAPTER
FOUR

Harold entered the room. He didn't greet her. He never did. Why should he? As far as he was concerned she was his for the taking. In the flickering candlelight Lizzie watched as he hastily undressed, removing only his topcoat and breeches.

"Come here ... you little temptress, you," he whispered, as he lifted the bedclothes and slid alongside her. She felt one hand pulling at her nightgown, while the other urgently fondled her breast. His usual clumsy, pathetic attempt at foreplay.

It had been almost three years since Harold had first visited Lizzie's bed. In those early days she'd been flattered, and quite enjoyed the thought of becoming a plaything to such a well-heeled gentleman. But that had been then. Now, he made her skin crawl. Most of the time she lay back and thought of England, or was it Wales? Of late, Harold had been taking longer and longer to pleasure himself — his performance no doubt affected by the amount of alcohol he consumed. It wasn't long before she realized tonight was going to be no exception.

For what seemed like hours he grunted and groaned, trying to finish what he had been so eager to start.

58

Under her breath, Lizzie cursed her cousin. *"It's all Megan's fault! He wouldn't be bothering me now if she had given in and let him have his way."* Lizzie vowed that before the night was out, she would somehow persuade him to try again with Megan, although his threat to have a word with Mrs Jarvis had not been an idle one. She would need to box clever, at least until she officially became lady's maid. It was going to take all her cunning to bring her cousin into the conversation without alerting his suspicion. Her thoughts were interrupted when, at long last, Harold's body began to shake. She quickly responded by giving groans of ecstasy, pretending to have enjoyed it as much as he had. She had become an accomplished actress. For a while he lay on top of her, his breathing laboured, his large body heavy on her tiny frame. Eventually he slumped beside her, exhausted.

"You're a good girl, Lizzie. I can always rely on you to please me — not a bit like that cousin of yours," he said, snuggling his face into her neck.

Lizzie smiled, he'd played right into her hands. "Really, Master Harold. Fancy you not knowing when a girl's teasing you. Why, only this evening Megan told me how she wished Master Robert hadn't interrupted you last night," Lizzie lied easily.

"Well, she could have fooled me! She fought me like a wild-cat. Are you sure?" he said, slowly raising himself on to his elbow.

Aware of his sudden interest she elaborated,

"I think the misunderstanding was all my fault, sir. You see, I told Megan how you often liked being

59

teased. No doubt with her being so young and a virgin and all, she probably overplayed it."

He gave a loud belly laugh. "You little minx. I do believe you're encouraging me to transfer my attentions."

Lizzie only had to look at the self-satisfied grin on his face to tell that he more than fancied the idea, especially now he'd been given confirmation of Megan's purity. Even so, Lizzie needed to convince him that whatever happened, from now on her favours were no longer an option.

"I'm only thinking of you, sir. As milady's maid, it'll not be as easy for me —" She didn't have to spell it out. He would never risk arousing his mother's suspicion. He didn't say a word, he just lay there deep in thought. It occurred to her that he might begin doubting the wisdom of helping her to secure promotion in the first place. So she quickly added, "On the other hand, Megan will be above-stairs going about her duties *every* night."

He gave a sinister chuckle as he pressed himself against her, his body again eager for her. Lizzie was in no doubt that this time his arousal had been brought on at the mere thought of having his way with her ripe young cousin.

Megan lay on her bed. How she longed to close her eyes and give way to sleep, but her day's work was far from finished. She still had the fires to see to above-stairs. Since Master Harold's attack she'd been on her guard, especially at night, and had taken to

60

hiding in the darkness on the backstairs, sometimes for hours, until she was sure *he* had gone to his bed; most nights he was the worse for drink.

There was a tap on her door. She raised herself off the bed and reached into her pocket for the piece of fruitcake she'd been unable to eat at teatime, and not wanting to upset cook, had kept hidden. Sally was always hungry and had taken to calling on Megan around this time, hoping for an extra titbit to see her through the night. "Such a pity to waste good food," she always said. Opening the door, Megan couldn't hide her surprise.

"Lizzie, what's wrong? Has something happened at home?" She was sure it had to be bad news that made her cousin call at such an hour.

"Don't worry, Megs, there's nothing wrong at home, honest," Lizzie said, her voice unusually friendly.

Relieved, Megan remembered her manners. "Please, won't you come in? There's not much room but —"

Lizzie shook her head, "No, thanks. I can't stop. I've only called because I just happened to hear Master Harold telling his mother that he planned to stay at his club tonight. But for goodness' sake don't tell anyone that it was me who told you, I don't want to get into trouble. The mistress is already making her way to her bedroom, so I thought that you might like to make an early start on your duties above-stairs. With a bit of luck, you might get to your bed at a reasonable time for once." Lizzie smiled warmly, before adding, "I must say you're looking very tired."

"I have had very late nights recently, so I really do appreciate you letting me know the change in situation," Megan replied, somewhat taken aback by her cousin's sudden but welcome change in attitude.

"Glad to be of help. Now I must get on, the mistress will be needing help with her toilet." She touched Megan's shoulder. "Good luck," she said before rushing off down the hall.

At around ten-thirty Megan went about her duties above-stairs feeling more relaxed than usual, comforted by the thought that in under an hour she could be tucked up in her bed. She entered the dark parlour with renewed confidence, safe in the knowledge that he had left the house, and for tonight at least, she had nothing to fear. But her feeling of well-being was to be short lived. As she stepped into the room, she was hit by a strong pungent odour, putting her immediately on her guard. She knew the smell of stale whisky only too well. Sensing danger, she quickly turned to leave — but before she could make it to the door *he*, in hiding behind the door, slammed it shut.

As she backed into the blackness of the room, she put her hand over her mouth to muffle a scream, believing her only hope of escape was to stay as quiet as possible, making it difficult for him to find her.

"Where are you — you little tease, you!" Harold Fothergill coaxed, his voice sounding almost childlike and getting closer by the minute.

She took another step back, fighting to control her laboured breathing. She felt sick in her stomach, her body shaking.

"That's right, you play hard to get. What's worth having is worth waiting for, eh?" he chuckled.

She continued backing away, trying to remember the exact position of every piece of furniture in the room. If she was to escape, she needed somehow to find her way back to the door leading to the hall. Her temples throbbed, her throat burned, as sheer panic engulfed her. She knew he was getting nearer, as the fumes from his whisky breath wafted over her, making her feel even more nauseous. She cautiously edged her way around the room, arms outstretched. She needed to find her bearings. First, she bumped into the table, almost falling over the small chair close by. Then, moving on, her hand felt the cold leather of the large chair, telling her she was by the fireplace. Now that she had her bearings all she had to do was follow the wall around to the right. She stopped and listened. She couldn't hear him. He was obviously playing her at her own game. Slowly she moved away from the chair, feeling for the wall, knowing she was only a few yards from safety, but as she made a dash for the door, strong arms caught around her.

"Got you! You little minx." He squeezed her to him, instantly halting her attempt to struggle free. She was no match for him. And he knew it.

"Get away from me, you brute!" she protested.

He just laughed, totally ignoring her plea. He seemed to think it was a big joke. As he pushed her to the floor, she screamed out —

"Stop it! You're hurting me."

"Shhh, less of the screaming. I don't mind a little fight, in fact, it heightens my arousal. But let's not wake the house, eh?" he whispered. "I know you want me. Trust me, the first time is always the best."

He lay on top of her pinning her to the floor. She tried to twist away, but against his strength it was futile. Soon his whisky-smelling mouth pressed hard on hers, making it difficult for her to breathe. She felt his hands tugging at her undergarments, then warm flesh, then — pain: a pain so intense that she wanted to die. She felt her senses turn numb and when total blackness eventually came . . . she went willingly.

Megan awoke cold and alone. A rawness between her legs. Thank God, *he* had gone. He had left her lying there, breasts exposed, skirt above her waist, underdrawers around her ankles. She felt sick with revulsion. Her whole body ached. Almost in slow motion she raised herself up from the floor. As she adjusted her clothing she became aware of something in her tunic pocket and, sliding her hand in, found a crumpled five pound note. She had never held so much money, and yet she knew she would never be able to spend it or send it to her family. It belonged to *him*. Did he really believe that she could be bought? At this stage there were no tears, only shame. Yet who could she tell? No one. Except Lizzie.

It was a Sunday morning and Megan had been summoned to the housekeeper's office. She felt nervous. Why had Mrs Jarvis asked to see her? Had someone seen her burn the clothes from the other night and take a new set from the cupboard? Or maybe Lizzie — she was sure it wouldn't be Cook — had complained about her work?

Overcome with apprehension she tapped quietly on the office door, half hoping Mrs Jarvis would not hear it.

"Come in, Megan. Please, take a seat," the housekeeper said, opening the door.

Megan was taken aback. This was not the Mrs Jarvis she remembered of that first day. Although she looked the same, dressed in a plain black long gown, her face as stern as ever, her voice and manner seemed so much friendlier. Cook had always said her bark was worse than her bite. In the four weeks since Megan began her employ, she had only seen the housekeeper when she made her Monday visit to the kitchen to discuss the coming week's menus with Cook. No one dared to interrupt them, all making sure to busy themselves in silence, or suffer Cook's wrath later.

"Don't look so worried, child. There's no need to concern yourself. I just thought it was time we had a little chat." The housekeeper waited until Megan was seated before continuing, "Mrs Partridge seems most concerned about you. She tells me that of late you have become withdrawn, and not a bit like the eager, happy young girl who started with us. I must say you do look rather pale. Tell me, child. Is there anything troubling you?"

Megan bit her lip, hoping to suppress the urge to speak out. It wouldn't do to tell her about the other night. Mrs Jarvis would only think she was telling lies against Master Harold. She still couldn't believe how easily she'd been duped by Lizzie . . .

"If you're worried about your position as kitchen maid, I can set your mind at rest." The housekeeper spoke softly. "Over the past month I've heard nothing but praise for both your conduct and your work. And I'm pleased to tell you that, as from today, your trial period is at an end. Or maybe there is something else troubling you?"

Megan wanted so much to tell her the truth, but what good would that do? It would be her word against his, a fact Lizzie had been all to eager to point out when Megan told her of her ordeal.

"For goodness sake, Megan. You're not the first to have had Master Harold's attentions and you probably won't be the last. It may interest you to know that for the past two years Master Harold has favoured *me* with his advances. My advice to you is to lie back and pretend to enjoy it . . . then make him pay. Don't try to stop him, he's the master and what he wants he usually gets. You will find him most generous if you learn how to time it right. Tease him a little. He especially likes it if you ask nicely for things. But another bit of advice, if you want something special ask him before he has his way with you. It'll be too late when it's over," she sniggered.

Megan flashed Lizzie a look of revulsion. How could her cousin possibly believe that she would give herself to anyone for trinkets? She was no prude, she knew only too well what happened in the bedroom between men and women — the walls in her house were very thin and after all, her mam *had* been pregnant six times. Megan believed it was meant to be an act of love between two people, nothing like the pain and degradation she'd suffered at the hands of Harold.

"Don't look so horrified, cousin dear. Why shouldn't he pay?" Lizzie snorted.

At which point Megan gave up trying to make her cousin understand. She was alone; she would have to suffer in silence or risk being sent home.

"Well, child, is there something you're not telling me?" Mrs Jarvis asked.

"The truth is, Mrs Jarvis, I am so very homesick. You see, I've not heard from my family since I arrived." Although this was not the main reason for her unhappiness, it had caused her concern. She'd have thought that Jess, at least, would have written to her by now.

Mrs Jarvis slowly opened the top drawer of her desk.

"No doubt these will cheer you up then?" she said, holding out two brown envelopes. "I'm afraid I couldn't allow any distractions until your trial period had been completed. Now that it has, any mail for you can be collected on Sunday afternoon after three o'clock, when you will also be entitled to a few hours off. You may go from the house, as long as you be sure to return in plenty of time for tea at five-thirty."

Megan felt a warm glow envelop her. She couldn't wait to take the letters and leave, but Mrs Jarvis hadn't finished.

"Also, there is the matter of the monies due to you. I have been holding your wages of two shillings and sixpence per week in safe keeping. What would you have me do with it?"

Megan actually gave a little smile, something she had thought she would never do again. At last she could see a light at the end of the tunnel.

"Please, Mrs Jarvis, could you hold back two shillings each week to be sent home? I am sure sixpence a week will be more than enough to cover any expense I may have."

"You're very wise child. I'm sure your family will welcome it. Now take these four sixpences along with your letters, and enjoy your first afternoon off. You've earned it."

After conveying her genuine thanks, Megan left the room, and for the first time in weeks she actually felt happy. Today she could leave the house behind and forget her troubles, if only for a little while. After first changing into her best chapel dress, she intended to take a walk to Clifton Suspension Bridge. Megan had heard Mrs Partridge and the others talk of its wonderment, and how it was well worth the mile walk to see it.

"You enjoy yourself, lass. The fresh air might put some colour in your cheeks," Mrs Partridge said, as she opened the kitchen door.

"Thank you, Cook. I'll be sure to get back before five-thirty."

Megan raced up the side steps and reaching into her pocket she touched the unopened letters. Although eager to read them, she had decided to wait until she reached her destination, far away from the house, and more especially *his* presence.

As she opened the iron gate and stepped on to the pavement, her mind was elsewhere.

"What the —" she heard a man's voice.

She had collided with a tall well-dressed man, causing him to drop the pile of books he'd been carrying.

"Oh! I'm so very sorry, sir," she said bending down to pick them up.

Almost simultaneously, he knelt down beside her.

"Don't worry yourself, there's been no real damage."

Megan instantly recognized the soft voice. She stood up, hastily handing Master Robert the books, and trying hard not to make eye contact. What if he recognized her, remembered her, or even questioned her? She turned to leave, eager to be on her way.

"It's Megan, isn't it?"

It was too late.

"Yes, sir," she answered, slowly turning to face him and bobbing a curtsy.

Eventually she looked up at him. He was a lot taller than she remembered, but then it had been very dark *that night.*

"Why, only yesterday, I took the liberty of asking Cook about you. I must say she has nothing but praise for you."

"Thank you, sir."

"Is everything all right? Why were you in such a rush to get away from the house?"

She could see that his concern was genuine.

"I'm fine, sir. Honest," she lied. "You see, it's my first afternoon off, and I'm in a hurry to get to Clifton Suspension Bridge." This time, as she spoke, she looked up into his face. It was a fine face, if somewhat pale, contrasting greatly with his curly, jet-black hair, and his dark, haunted eyes.

He appeared somewhat embarrassed. No doubt he had imagined her to be, once again, in some sort of danger, "Oh! I see. Quite . . . well, don't let me keep you any longer. You go on your way . . . enjoy yourself."

"Thank you, sir," she said, adding, "for everything," as she made a small curtsy, hoping he understood that she was also thanking him for his intervention on that first fateful night.

His nod told her he had. He smiled, a friendly, uncomplicated smile, before turning to go on his way.

She did the same, and decided, despite the fact that he was a *Fothergill* male, she actually liked Master Robert. He seemed so . . . approachable. She had even been tempted to tell him about — but she stopped herself. There was no point. What could be gained from raking over old coal? It was much better to keep her shame to herself. Her mother would have been proud of her. She never did approve of people who washed their dirty linen in public.

Following Cook's easy directions, Megan walked on. As it was such a fine day, Megan hadn't bothered to wear a top coat, reasoning that if she walked briskly enough she wouldn't feel the cool wind of late spring.

Her hand reached into her pocket, making sure her letters were safe. Her four sixpences she'd hidden safely in her room. With her new-found wealth she would be able to purchase fine writing paper with matching envelopes, to send lengthy letters to her loved ones back home. Tonight, after tea, she would ask Sidney if he would kindly pick these items up from the stationer's on his next visit to town.

Megan crossed the road, leaving behind the tall, terraced houses. It wasn't long before she stood on Clifton Downs, a vast area of uneven grassy land with a wide central pathway. The pathway, well worn and bare of grass, stretched as far as the eye could see, with only a few well established trees shading strategically placed bench-seats, adding character to an already beautiful landscape. She took a deep breath. After a month of working indoors it felt good to be out in the invigorating fresh air.

She was not alone. There were many other walkers both young and old. Some walked with dogs, while others flew brightly coloured kites which soared high above into a clear blue sky. Several horse-drawn carriages, carrying elegant, well-dressed passengers, trotted by, almost close enough to touch. Megan came to the conclusion that Clifton Downs was most definitely the place to be on a Sunday afternoon. Suddenly she had the urge to run to the farthest bench, settle herself down, and read the news from home.

Megan reached the bench out of breath but invigorated. She had chosen well. The bench, positioned under a large oak tree, overlooked Clifton Suspension Bridge which spanned the great chasm of the Avon Gorge and acted like a huge canopy over the fast-moving, muddy waters of the river far below. It truly was an unbelievable sight. She could have stayed gazing at it all day had the letters not been burning a hole in her pocket. She sat down. The bench felt cold but she didn't care. Reaching into her pocket she took out the two brown envelopes. She'd waited long enough.

Mrs Jarvis had been efficient in marking each letter with the date it had arrived, enabling Megan to read them in the order intended. Hastily, she opened the first one:

Monday, 17 March 1919

Dear Megs

I hope you're well, and showing the English a thing or two. We all miss you — but don't you go worrying yourself about us. We're OK, honest. Olive is proving a great help to Mam. You taught her well! I don't suppose you'll be surprised to hear that the little ones are as noisy as ever.

Mam and Dad send their love — Dad doesn't seem to be getting any worse. He has some good days and some bad.

By the way, old Reverend Jenkins has finally hung up his Bible! Our new minister is the Reverend Elias Braithwaite. He's come up from Swansea. There's posh now, isn't it! Mam thinks he's bound to call to see us soon. 'Spect she'll be getting out the best crockery!

Please write soon. We're all dying to know all about your employers. Keep yourself well. Your loving brother,

Jess XXX

Almost straight away Megan saw through her brother's light-hearted banter. He would have guessed her feeling of homesickness, and deliberately filled his letter with nothing but good news in the hope of raising her spirits. She was grateful to him — it had worked. Before opening the second envelope, she pondered over the neat elaborate handwriting on the front. It was strange to her, and she was sure it hadn't been written by anyone in her immediate family. Intrigued as to why a stranger should write to her, she slowly opened it.

31 March 1919

Dear Miss Williams

I write to you, at the request of your family. They wish me to convey to you the sad news that on Friday the twenty-eighth of March 1919 your dear father sadly passed away peacefully in his sleep.

Although I know he suffered a long illness, his passing has come as a great shock to everyone — especially your dear mother.

I am in no doubt that your family will be in touch with you soon. Until then, be assured that my prayers are with you and all of your family at this very difficult time.

May God be with you.

I remain, your Minister,

Reverend Elias Braithwaite.

Megan stared at the letter. Her hands shaking as tears ran down her face. Her father couldn't be dead! She began sobbing uncontrollably. She cried for her dad, for her mam, and for her family — but most of all she cried for herself. Night after night she had prayed for her dad to come and take her home. With him gone . . . all was lost. It was just too much for her to bear. Again she prayed. This time, promising God that she would cope with her loneliness, Lizzie's spitefulness, missing her family and even Master Harold. "Just don't let my dad be dead," she pleaded.

"Megan, whatever's wrong?"

Looking up she saw Sidney. She wanted to answer him but couldn't speak for sobs. Instead, she simply handed him the minister's letter. After taking a few minutes to read it, he took the seat next to her.

"Go on, you have a good cry. It's best to let it all out. There be no good keeping it inside to fester." He moved closer, putting a friendly arm around her shoulders.

"Don't . . . touch . . . me!" she screamed between sobs. Then snatching her letter she ran down the grassy slope, and towards the entrance to the bridge.

"Megan, please! You've no cause to run from me. I'd never hurt you," Sidney called out, racing after her.

Megan stopped. Whatever was she doing? Sidney was her friend. How could she think he could be like that — that . . . monster!

As Sidney caught up with her, Megan turned to face him.

"Oh Sidney, I'm so sorry. I don't know what came over me."

74

"That's all right. Come on, let's go back and sit down. You don't have to say a word if you don't want to. Later, when you think you're ready, I shall walk you back to the house. When I called there earlier, Ma told me you'd been given a few hours off and where I'd most likely find you. I'm so glad I did."

"So — am — I," she sobbed.

He took her hand and gently pulled her toward the bench. By the time they reached the seat Megan had calmed down a little, her sobs less frequent.

"I — feel so bad, Sidney. I've — been so selfish. Only thinking — of my homesickness and — feeling sorry for myself. When all the while my dad . . ."

"Now, don't you go being too hard on yourself. You had no way of knowing. Finding out like this is bound to come as a shock to you. Believe me, I know. I was very young but I can still remember the day my mother had the letter telling her about my own dad."

Megan touched Sidney's arm. At least she had grown up with the love of a father. But her feeling of loss was something more. She wanted to explain . . .

"I know you think you understand, but it's not just the shock of losing my dad. It's the self-pity. It's the anger I feel at him for leaving me! You see, Sidney, in my dreams my dad came to save me, and now that he's gone . . ." She spoke quietly.

"Save you? Save you from what? Who? I don't understand."

She didn't answer, afraid that in grief she might have already said too much. Instead, raising her hanky, she blew her nose to compose herself. She stood up.

"I think we'd better make a move, I don't want to be late back. Not on my first afternoon off."

"Do you think you're up to it? I'm sure my Ma will speak up for you if you need some time off."

"No, honestly, there's no need. I'll be all right now that I've had a good cry. Anyway, I'm better off in work. Work takes my mind off all of the things that I'm powerless to change."

He looked puzzled and for a while she thought he was going to press her to explain herself. If he did, she might lose her resolve. Anyway, he was her friend, surely she could tell him . . .

"Aye, perhaps you're right. Come on, I'll walk you back to the house."

Megan sighed with relief. She had, for today at least, succeeded in keeping her awful secret.

Once back at the house, Sidney told his mother and all below-stairs about Megan's sad news. Their condolences warmed her. It helped to know how much they all cared. Later, she would have to seek out Lizzie to tell her, she was family after all.

"Sidney tells me that you be determined to carry on with your duties. Well, if that be the case, tonight at least you must have an early night. You look all done in, child."

"Thank you, I'd like that. I'm sure I'll feel better after a good night's sleep."

"Good, that be settled. Tonight, Sally can to do the fires above-stairs."

She protested, not wanting to put extra work on her friend.

76

"Really, Cook. There's no need to bother Sally. I can clean the fires in the morning . . ." It was then that the idea came to her. "Actually, I've been wondering if anyone would mind if I did my work above-stairs first thing *every* morning. Instead of having to wait until the family retire, and for the coals to cool down." Megan held her breath. If Cook agreed, it would make avoiding Harold a lot easier. For she was in no doubt that he would be back for more.

"Well, it certainly makes sense. As long as you make sure my oven's lit by five, there'll be no complaint from me."

Megan couldn't believe how easy it had been. Why hadn't she thought of it before? Then she remembered her cousin. She'd be bound to object.

"Do you think I should have a word with Lizzie?" Megan asked.

"You leave Lizzie to me. I shall say it be my idea. She'll not argue with me."

That night Megan said a prayer of thanks to her dad. Indirectly, he had saved her after all.

Two days later, Mrs Jarvis came into the kitchen and handed her a letter from home.

"I'm so sorry to hear of your sad loss, child. Is there anything I can do? Would you like to go home for a couple of days to pay your respects? I'm sure the mistress would help with your travelling expenses. Mind you, it would have to be paid back."

The thought of going home, being there for Mam, was very tempting. But after reading Jess's letter, it was completely out of the question. Now more than ever her family needed every penny she could earn, and more.

Dear Megs

Can you ever forgive me? For not writing to you myself and telling you about Dad. Mam did ask me to, but I just couldn't. I know how much you thought of him (and he of you).

It all happened so suddenly. And when the minister asked if he could do anything to help, I took the coward's way out. I'm sorry.

Please, don't feel bad about not being able to come home for the funeral. Mam understands. She's being as strong as ever, but I can tell how worried she is. It can only be a matter of time before the colliery serve us notice to quit the house. How I wish I were older. I feel so useless.

As always, your loving brother,

Jess. XXX

It was the first Sunday in August. Nearly six months since her father's death, yet Megan still hadn't come to terms with it. Life at the big house had settled into a routine. If anything, Megan worked harder, she couldn't risk being found lacking and maybe lose her position, not with the family relying on her so much. Her only respite was the few hours every Sunday.

As Megan made her way to the housekeeper's office, she hoped for a letter from home.

"I'm sorry, Megan, there's no mail for you again this week," Mrs Jarvis said apologetically, quickly adding, "I'm sure you'll have news soon."

Megan thanked her before going on her way. Funnily enough, although it had been three weeks since her last letter from Jess, she was not too concerned. Of course she wanted news from home but at the moment she knew that Jess was sulking — his pride hurt. In his last letter he'd seemed unduly upset. For some reason he believed that the Reverend Braithwaite was becoming too frequent a visitor to their house, and he had the silly notion that the minister was courting their mother!

Megan had been quick to write, telling him in no uncertain terms not to be so silly. She pointed out that surely the minister calling to the house was both kind and Christian, for without his regular gifts of food and clothes, they might not have been able to survive. She had ended the letter telling Jess he should give thanks to God and the minister for their help.

She guessed that by not writing to her, it was his way of punishing her for not taking his side, but she was sure he would write soon. It wasn't in his nature to stay angry with her for long.

It had been an exceptionally hot summer, with temperatures soaring well into the eighties. Cook had told everyone how unfashionable it was for young ladies to have tanned skin — although how this was to be avoided she didn't say. Today, like the last four Sundays, she felt the heat of the sun on her skin. She quickened her step, eager to reach the downs and *her* tree-shaded bench.

"I think you look a picture, tanned face and all," Sidney had teased.

Megan blushed. It had become the norm for Sidney to meet her at the bench, never joining her until she'd had enough time to read her letters, but in plenty of time for them to take a leisurely walk back to the house in time for tea.

Sunday teas were always special, a time when all the staff were usually in good spirits — but for some reason not today.

As they entered the kitchen they heard Sally's gruff voice.

"Milady's maid! *She's* been made milady's maid? Well, I for one don't think it's fair!" Sally had been working at the house just as long as Lizzie, but had never been promoted. For years she had had to be happy with being a kitchen maid, and she was naturally upset.

It came as no surprise when Alice, who occasionally helped Lizzie above-stairs, had been offered Lizzie's old position of parlour maid. On seeing how upset her friend was she spoke up.

"I'm sorry, Sally. If you like I'll tell Mrs Jarvis where to shove her job," Alice offered.

"I've got no problem with you, Alice, you deserve all the luck you get. But Lizzie — well it's just not bloody fair!"

"Fair or not, there be naught anyone can do about it, and swearing is not going to help neither, my girl!" Cook admonished. "Anyway, I be more interested in next Friday night and the dinner party I've to plan for.

80

These days it's not often the mistress invites guests to the house, so we'll not be letting her down, will we?"

Sally soon realized how futile her outburst had been. It would make no difference however much she objected. Everyone settled down around the tea table. Megan pretended to eat the two cakes Cook insisted putting on her plate, but when no one was looking she placed one of them into her apron pocket; she knew it would help to cheer Sally later.

At the head of the table Cook sighed, "With Lizzie queen'n it above-stairs as milady's maid, who am I going to find to help Alice on Friday?" Her eyes moved around the table.

"Please, don't ask me, Cook. Y-you know I'd just die with the embarrassment of it all," Sadie pleaded.

"Don't worry. I'll not be choosing you. You haven't ventured above-stairs in all the three years you've been here. So I doubt that you be going to start now."

"I could help out above-stairs, Cook, honest," Sally offered, her gruff voice sounding eager.

"I know you could, child. But you'd have to move swiftly around the table. And being such a big lump you'd be sure to bang every chair."

Megan felt sorry for her, but Sally seemed not to be at all upset. She even joked about it.

"Aye, the soup would probably land up in their laps if I had anything to do with it. It would be good for a laugh though, eh?"

Everyone around the table laughed except Cook, who looked tenderly at Sally, then added, "Anyways, how could I manage in the kitchen without my Sally, or

Sadie for that matter? For I be in no doubt that there be no one else I could trust to do the job as well as you two."

This seemed to satisfy Sally; there could be no mistaking the look of pride on her shiny red face. Sadie, on the other hand, simply looked relieved.

"No, there's only one thing for it — Megan — you'll have to help out. Don't look so worried, child. If Alice gives you instructions afore, I'm sure you shall pick it up in no time," she said, as she tenderly patted Megan's hand by way of reassurance. "So it be decided. Alice and Megan will serve at table next Friday night." Cook seemed pleased with herself.

Megan knew everyone regarded being chosen to serve above-stairs as some kind of honour, but she would have been pleased for Sally or anyone else for that matter to take her place. She felt no pride, only shame, knowing she would have to come face to face with *him*.

CHAPTER
FIVE

It was the night of the dinner party. Alice and Megan stood in front of Cook as she gave them a final once-over.

"Now you remember, Alice, I want the mistress to be right proud of you tonight. She deserves the best and if I have my way, she'll get it. Mind you, if you work half as well as you are turned out, I'll have no worry on that score."

"Thank you, Cook, I'll not let you down," Alice said, looking pleased with herself.

"Good girl. Now off you go and make sure everything's ready in the dining room. Preparation be nine-tenths of the law, that's what I say. Tell Mr. Hutchins that Megan will follow shortly."

"See you in a minute, Megs," Alice called out. Megan didn't answer. Alice appeared so eager to go about her duties, whereas she had been dreading this very moment all week. There was no way out. No way to avoid facing her attacker.

Cook smiled as she walked around Megan.

"Don't look so worried, child. I know it be your first time waiting on table, but I'm sure, if you follow Alice's lead, you'll do just fine. My only worry be the way that apron hangs on you. Turn around, let me see if I can tighten them ribbons."

As Cook tugged hard at her waistband, it was as much as Megan could do to keep her balance.

"Thank goodness for apron frills, that's what I say. At least they manage to fill you out a bit. We don't want folk thinking I've been neglecting to feed you, for I do believe you be even thinner now than when you first arrived."

Megan knew by the fit of her own chapel dress that she had indeed lost considerable weight. She blamed Harold for her loss of appetite. He was constantly on her mind. Not a day went by when she didn't imagine him lurking behind every door in the house, although, since Cook's intervention resulting in a new work schedule, Megan had felt a little more relaxed. As for Lizzie, she'd been obliged to go along with the new arrangement or risk crossing swords with Cook.

"It's little wonder you be off your food. Losing your father so sudden like. It must have been a terrible shock. Tell me, how are your family coping?" Cook asked.

"It's hard to tell. Jess doesn't say much in his letters. I'm sure he's keeping things from me."

Since her father's death, Megan had instructed the housekeeper to send all of her wages home. It wasn't a lot, but she knew it helped; Jess had said as much in his last letter. He had made no mention of his silly suspicion regarding the minister and their mother. He'd probably thought better of it.

84

Cook stared at her. "My Sidney be ever so worried about you. He be very fond of you, you know."

Megan felt her face flush with colour. "I feel fortunate to have him as a friend, he's always been so very kind." It was the truth. Megan didn't know how she would have coped these last months without Sidney's support.

"Friend is it? Well, if you say so. I'd say you be 'walking out'. Why else would you meet regular as clockwork every Sunday afternoon?"

Immediately embarrassed, Megan looked to the floor. She wondered if Sidney had begun to draw the same conclusion. Surely not. He had always kept his distance — which more than suited her. Master Harold had succeeded in making her fear the touch of any man. Sidney seemed to sense this, never once attempting even to hold her hand. There was no way he could believe they were "walking out". She vowed the next time they met to put him straight on this point. They were friends, and nothing more.

The bell rang from the dining room. The time had come for her to take her place above-stairs.

"Go on, child. Off you go. And good luck!"

Alice, as parlour maid, had positioned herself next to the serving hatch. Mr Hutchins, the butler, stood at the door. Megan bobbed a curtsy to him before taking her place next to Alice. He simply nodded, acknowledging her arrival. She'd only ever seen Mr Hutchins in passing for, not long after her arrival, he moved out of the house and into specially converted quarters above the garage.

Cook had made mention of it one night after dinner.

"No doubt those of us who be used to having him around the house will surely miss his presence, though I s'pose it makes sense. These days there be more need for his services as a full-time chauffeur than a butler. Mind you, it wasn't always the way. I can remember when the master were alive . . . tut . . . all those grand dinner parties' — Cook gave a long sigh — 's'pose I mustn't dwell on the past. I just wanted you to know that I expect every one of you to give Mr Hutchins the highest respect at all times." Cook had spoken.

It was common knowledge that Cook and Hutchins were great friends, and that they breakfasted alone together every morning. For some reason Hutchins chose to eat all of his other meals in the privacy of his new quarters, although, rumour had it, he and Cook often shared a late night glass of sherry.

Megan looked around the room in awe. Even with the feeling of impending doom, she could still appreciate how splendid it looked. The dining table was laid to perfection, a candelabra entwined with freshly cut flowers as its centrepiece. There were eight place settings, each displaying an array of highly polished silver cutlery, diamond-cut wine glasses and white table napkins, expertly dressed in the shape of a fan. Her eyes moved to the drinks trolley, full to the brim; the sideboard, stacked high with blue and white porcelain, all delicately decorated with a beautiful gold-leaf pattern. It was a sight to behold, and most of it Alice's doing. She certainly had excelled herself.

The door opened. Megan watched as Mr Hutchins gave a well practised bow, acknowledging the arrival of Mistress Fothergill and her guests before escorting them to the table and their assigned places. Megan couldn't get over how elegant they all looked dressed in their long gowns — one adorned with feathers, another decorated with beads, another with pearls — every one of them so beautiful. The men were smartly dressed in dark suits, brilliant white shirts and black bow ties. Megan had never before seen such a fine gathering. She wished her family, especially her mother, could be here to see it.

Then she saw him. *He* was making his way across the room to the drinks trolley. Megan's body stiffened. This man, this large, ugly man had forced her to . . . to be intimate with him. She felt sick to her stomach when he turned, heading back to the table, holding a tumbler full of whisky. She could plainly see his fleshy high-coloured face, his arrogant eyes and bulbous dark-red nose. She watched him raise the tumbler to his lips . . . she grimaced and began visibly shaking, as she remembered the night and more especially the cold wet feeling of his saliva across her face . . .

"Are you OK, Megs? You look as if you've seen a ghost. Not going to faint on us, are you?" Alice whispered.

Although Megan heard her friend's quiet voice, it sounded strange, and far . . . far away. She felt suddenly giddy, but fought to overcome it, scolding herself and repeating, "Don't you dare faint. Don't you dare faint."

She wouldn't give him the satisfaction of seeing the effect he had on her.

"Megan?" This time Alice shook her arm.

It worked. Megan quickly regained her composure. "I'm fine, honest," she whispered. "Just a bit overcome by the occasion, that's all."

"I know what you mean. I was the same when it was my first time."

With the guests all seated and, thankfully, deep in conversation, Megan was sure no one had noticed her little drama alongside the serving hatch.

Now that everyone had settled, Mr Hutchins gave a light clap of his hands, the signal for Alice and Megan to begin the first course. Alice turned, tugging twice on the rope of the serving hatch. Within seconds a large tureen of piping-hot oxtail soup arrived from the kitchen. Alice, holding a spotless white linen cloth, carefully carried it to the sideboard where Mr Hutchins waited with ladle in hand. Slowly and confidently he poured the soup into fine, pale-blue, porcelain bowls.

Megan's hands were shaking. This time with genuine nerves. What if she were to make a fool of herself? Maybe drop a plate, or break a glass? She gave herself a little shake. She knew what she had to do, Alice had gone over it so many times, she had even made Megan memorize the seating plan off by heart.

Alice nudged her. The first course was ready. Megan watched her pick up two bowls full of soup from the sideboard and begin to serve anti-clockwise around the table, starting with the mistress, then Mr Arkwright, the owner of one of the largest banks in Bristol. Megan followed her lead, serving Miss Emma Carlisle, the mistress's pretty niece, and Master Robert. As she placed the bowl in front of him he gave her an encouraging smile.

"Tell me, Robert, my man. Where do you see your future? Will you stay with your commission or do you intend to join your brother in the family business?" the banker asked.

"Neither, Mr Arkwright. Long before I joined the regiment, my aspirations lay in studying law with thoughts of maybe, one day, being called to the Bar. *This* is where I see my future."

"The law, eh? Admirable, admirable." Mr Arkwright nodded his approval.

"Had enough of playing soldier then, have you?" Harold scoffed.

Robert didn't answer, he simply eyed his brother with cold contempt.

An uncomfortable silence followed, prompting Mrs Fothergill to take the lead. "Mrs Arkwright, I do love your gown. You must give me your seamstress's card. She obviously has an eye for detail. Why, the beading on your bodice is exquisite."

"Thank you. I must say she was quite a find. I'll be more than pleased to put you in touch with her."

From then on the conversation around the table resumed, mainly small talk about the weather, the meal and forthcoming social events.

Megan was thankful that it fell on Alice to serve Master Harold and Jane Arkwright, the sallow young woman next to him, spinster daughter of the banker, which left Megan with the last two servings. She was just about to place a bowl of soup in front of the youngest gentleman at the table, Mr Arthur Walters, when he looked up and smiled at her. For a few seconds she stood motionless, soup in hands, staring at him, not believing her own eyes. A discreet touch on her arm by Mr Hutchins prompted her to set the soup down and move on to Mrs Arkwright, the banker's wife.

When she had finished, she joined Alice at the serving hatch, but she couldn't take her eyes off Mr Walters, She was sure she'd met him, yet for the life of her she couldn't remember where, or for that matter, when. There could be no denying that Mr Walters stood out, with his bold pinstripe suit. No, it had more to do with his swarthy good looks, his dark hair, heavily greased and combed away from his tanned face, and the way he sported a well-groomed, thin, black moustache.

Megan helped clear away the empty soup bowls; by then it was time to serve the second course, a poached white fish in a cream sauce. She was still puzzled as to how she could possibly know one of the mistress's dinner guests. Then it came to her, like a bolt out of the blue: he was the lad from the railway station, the one who'd kissed her. As she set the fish down in front of him, she took a closer look — yes, it was definitely him — it was definitely the lad from the station!

As she moved away from the table, Megan felt convinced that Mr Walters had not recognized her, had not even given her a second look, unlike Master

Harold, whose eyes had seemed to follow her every move, willing her to meet his gaze. This at least, she had the power to refuse.

"Mr Walters. How's business?" Arkwright asked.

"I can't complain. With thanks to Harold here."

"It's simply a case of supply and demand. I need to transport stock efficiently and you offer that service." Harold smiled. "You scratch my back and I'll scratch yours, eh?"

"Now, now, gentlemen. No talk of business at the table. Please save it for later with you port and cigars."

Mr Arkwright gave an embarrassed cough, "Quite, quite. My apologies, dear lady."

Megan wondered how Mr Walters's circumstances could have changed so drastically. How could he be at the Fothergills' dinner table? It was certainly a puzzle.

"Robert, I must say you're looking so much better, are you fully recovered?" Emma Carlisle asked. A faint flush to her cheeks indicated her interest was more than casual.

"I thank you for your concern, Cousin. The truth is, I take one day at a time, but yes, I feel that I'm well on the way to a full recovery."

"Still visiting the funny farm though, eh?"

"Harold! How could you? You'll apologize at once."

"Sorry, Mama."

Mrs Fothergill let it pass, but it was obvious to everyone, including Harold, that she'd meant him to apologize to Robert.

Robert was giving his brother a hard stare, and said quietly, "I believe you are the one who gets up to funny business, Harold, not me."

"How's finishing-school, Emma?" Mrs Arkwright quickly changed the subject.

For a fleeting moment Robert's eyes met Megan's. She was struck by the warmth in them, as if they were inviting her to laugh with him at the silliness of the conversation of those around him. Megan could not resist an answering smile, but at a frown from Mr Hutchins, she made herself turn away. She had work to do. There were another three courses to serve and she was determined to do it well.

At the end of a long evening, Lizzie entered the room, carrying the mistress's white silk shawl over her arm. She totally ignored both Alice and Megan, but Megan couldn't help noticing how, as she slowly crossed the room, Lizzie had blatantly flashed her eyes around each of the men, and in particular, at Mr Walters.

"Ladies, shall we retire to the parlour and leave the men to their cigars?" the mistress asked, rising from her chair.

As the ladies excused themselves from the table, the men stood to attention and gave a polite bow, returning to their seats only when all of the ladies had left the room.

At the same time Mr Hutchins joined Megan and Alice at the serving hatch.

"Have you two finished here?" he asked.

"Yes, Mr Hutchins. We've just sent the last of the dirty dishes down to the kitchen," Alice answered, pleased with herself.

"Good. Now you can return to the kitchen where I'm sure you'll be needed to help clear away. You both did very well here this evening. I was very pleased with your performance, and you can tell Cook that I said so."

Under his watchful eye they gave a small curtsy before leaving the room and only then did he begin offering a large box of cigars around the table.

"For a moment back there, Megs, I thought you were a goner. But you did fine, we both did." Alice chatted away as they made their way down the back stairs to the kitchen. "That Arthur Walters is a bit of all right, don't you think?"

"He's OK, I suppose," Megan answered, feeling a lot happier knowing she had survived the evening without breaking anything or giving Harold the satisfaction of seeing how distressed she was.

"OK? He's bloody gorgeous! I wouldn't mind finding his shoes under my bed, I can tell you."

They had entered the kitchen within earshot of Cook.

"Alice Parsons! I'll not have such coarse talk in my kitchen, do you hear?" Cook admonished.

Sadie and Sally laughed, "Go on Cook. Don't be a spoilsport. It's 'bout time we had a real man around the house, although I doubt he'll be looking at the likes of you, Alice."

"You don't know. Could be a real man might have an eye for a real woman."

At this even Cook had to smile, "Alright, that be enough frivolity. I'm eager to know how you got on upstairs. I can tell by how clean all the dishes be, that the meal was to their liking."

Alice set about telling her everything, making a point of relaying the message of praise for them both from Mr Hutchins.

"Well done! I be right proud of you." Cook beamed. "When I next speak to Mrs Jarvis, I shall be sure to sing your praises."

After serving the ladies their coffee, Lizzie took her position, standing behind the mistress's chair near the fireplace in the parlour. It was not long before the men, having finished their cigars, joined them. With the room alive with light-hearted conversation and everyone in such good humour it was obvious that the evening had been a great success.

As Lizzie looked on in silence she became aware of the attractive man, the one she'd earlier heard introduced as Arthur Walters, staring at her. For what seemed like an age she held his gaze, brazenly staring him out. Then, much to her surprise, he began to cross the room heading towards the fireplace, the sleeve of his jacket lightly brushing her arm as he passed by. He was standing right next to her. To her relief, the rest of the party continued chatting away, but then why shouldn't they? After all, there was nothing unusual in a man warming himself by the fire.

He edged closer to her. The musky fragrance of his cologne reached her nostrils; a distinctive smell, his smell. He was so close she could feel his warm breath on the back of her neck, making her whole being tingle with excitement as he whispered, "I may not know your name, but your eyes say it all — enticing me, drawing me, telling me we are of the same mind. Look, I need to be alone with you. And ple-e-ese make it soon!"

Her eyes darted around the room, afraid for her job yet enjoying the danger of the situation, smiling to herself when she was sure that no one had noticed him speaking to her.

"I get off on Wednesday night," Lizzie said, so quietly she wondered if he'd heard.

"I can hardly wait. I'll pick you up at seven from the end of the road," he whispered, brushing his hand across hers, before hastily retreating to the other side of the room and the company of Miss Arkwright.

Lizzie was unable to hear what he was saying, but whatever it was, Jane Arkwright hung on his every word while gazing longingly up into his eyes. Lizzie allowed herself to feel quietly confident. Mr Arthur Walters had already made his choice.

She thought she might burst with joy, he was so very handsome and obviously rich. Well, he had to be, to be a friend of Master Harold's. For a few moments she felt sudden panic. What if Harold had confided in Arthur Walters and told him about his affair with her? But she soon dismissed such thoughts, reasoning that Master

Harold wouldn't want anyone to know about his goings-on with a member of the staff.

Later that night, as Lizzie attended the mistress with her toilet, she congratulated herself on a very successful evening. It had started for her when she'd entered the dining room carrying the mistress's scarf and saw the look of envy on Megan's face. Then the way the men had noticed her, most of them flirting with their eyes, except, that was, for Master Robert but then everyone knew he was a bit funny in the head. And while she had certainly noticed Arthur Walters, he had truly surprised her by actually asking her out. Lizzie knew that none of this would have happened had she not been in the right place at the right time.

It had taken her three long years to achieve her goal to become milady's maid, three years of scheming, of buttering up Mrs Jarvis, of having to welcome Master Harold to her bed. But tonight's events told her that it had all been worth it.

Surprisingly enough, when she first set her sights on becoming a lady's maid, she harboured some doubts about her own capabilities. After all, what did she know about a lady's toilet? As it turned out, there was nothing to it really. Lizzie's daily routine consisted of serving Mrs Fothergill breakfast in bed, preparing her bath, laying out her clothes and assisting with her dress and toilet. In the afternoons, after a little light sewing, she would accompany the mistress on outings to take tea or, best of all, to the couturier for a fitting. Hardly a gruelling day. Nothing like her tedious factory work in

Wales. From six o'clock in the evening until she helped her mistress prepare for bed, her time was her own.

With so undemanding a mistress, as well as one night off a week, Lizzie had more time and energy than she knew what to do with. This should have pleased her, but instead she became even more restless, especially now that she had seen first hand how the "other half" really lived. It was the way she would have liked — no! — wanted to live. She truly believed that if you wanted something badly enough, there was always a way. And she couldn't help but wonder if Arthur Walters's timely arrival might be the answer to her prayers.

On Wednesday night at seven o'clock sharp, Arthur Walters sat in his black automobile at the end of the street.

"Wow! You look great," he said, flashing a wicked grin as he leaned over to open the passenger door.

"Thank you," she said, and slid into the passenger seat.

She knew she looked good. She'd been saving this black, fringed dress, with its short hemline, for just such an occasion. The shopkeeper had assured her the dress was the latest fashion from Paris, France. It had cost an arm and a leg, but Harold's recent generosity had made it easily affordable. If Arthur's reaction was anything to go by, the money had certainly been well spent.

"I've taken the liberty of booking us a couple of seats at the Gaiety Theatre. Is that OK?" he asked, starting the car and heading into town.

"That's fine," she said, trying to hide her excitement. She didn't want him to know that it would be her first visit to a stage show.

"What time do you have to be back?"

"Anytime," she lied, determined to spend at least one night without restrictions, even if it meant facing Mrs Jarvis's wrath.

"Good. I thought, after the theatre, we might go on to the Sefton Hotel for a bit of dancing. Do you like to dance?"

"I love it!" If he was trying to impress her it had definitely worked. She would be like putty in his hands for the rest of the night.

The evening more than lived up to her expectations. At the theatre she hadn't really known what to expect, but from the moment the Master of Ceremonies began introducing the acts she was totally captivated: from the exotic dancer to the jugglers, then the comedian, and finally the star of the show, Miss Marie Lloyd — even Lizzie had heard of her.

It was nearly ten-thirty when they left the theatre and moved on to the Sefton Hotel where they were given a table for two close to the dance floor and Arthur ordered champagne, another first for her. They flirted with each other, laughed out loud and danced. Arthur Walters moved well on the dance floor. Lizzie especially enjoyed the closeness of the slow dances, cheek to cheek. The feel of his hand softly caressing the small of her back, his lips occasionally finding her ears and sending a tingle down her spine.

"You dance like an angel, my Lizzie." He nuzzled her neck.

"I wish I could say the same for you."

"You're teasing me."

"I like to tease."

"So I see."

"Don't you? Like to tease."

"No, my sweet."

"Life's too dull without games."

"Life is exciting. And right now you're the most exciting creature in it."

Lizzie laughed. He was everything she wanted in a man and she wanted the night to last forever.

When Arthur suggested they stop off at his apartment for a nightcap, she understood full well what he expected from her. Well, he had just treated her to the most wonderful night of her life and how else was a girl supposed to show appreciation? It wasn't as if making love to him would be a hardship, she really did fancy him, and she felt confident that if she let him lie with her tonight, he would surely come back for more. And she would be a step closer to a new life away from Redcliffe House.

Lizzie sat on a long, brown, brocade sofa in the spacious sitting room of Arthur's apartment. It was typical of a man living alone, sparsely furnished with plain green window drapes and floor coverings. There were no frills, flowers or chintz. To her, the apartment lacked a woman's touch, although the fact that it was situated on Fairfield Road and the "right side of town" was definitely in its favour. Even she knew how important it was to have the correct address.

Arthur walked over to the drinks cabinet, "Gin and tonic OK?" He started pouring, not waiting for an answer.

She didn't want or need a drink. She chuckled to herself, in time he would get to know that there was no need for the preliminaries or the idle chit-chat.

"So the young girl waiting on table the other night is your cousin? Are you very close? I must say, my love, you certainly look alike. I'm betting that you share all your innermost secrets," he teased.

For some reason Lizzie felt suddenly threatened. She didn't like him asking about Megan — maybe he fancied her, too. Well, she would soon put a stop to that!

"No, we do not. In fact, we barely speak to each other. My cousin is the most self-centred person I know. If it wasn't for me she wouldn't even have a job. But is she grateful? Is she hell!"

"You surprise me." He handed her the drink, joining her on the sofa.

"Don't you be taken in by her acting all innocent-like. It's common knowledge among the staff at the big house that she's carrying on with Sidney Partridge. They meet every Sunday on Clifton Downs. And I know for a fact that he's not the only man she has assignations with either. Mark my words, Megan is heading for trouble and if I were you I'd give her a wide berth."

100

"What! You don't think that I'm interested in her, do you? Surely not."

He reached across, taking the drink from her hand, and placed it on the small table in front of them. Then, pulling her to him, he kissed her, a soft, gentle, lingering kiss. Lizzie responded, making sure he could be in no doubt that she wanted more. His kiss became harder, his mouth open, his soft, sensuous tongue searching for hers while his hand urgently fondled her breasts. She felt aroused in a way no other man had ever managed to achieve. She wanted him, needed him right now. As he rubbed his body against hers, she could feel that his need was as great as hers.

After the dinner party Cook made a point of reporting back to Mrs Jarvis. A few days later Alice and Megan were summoned to her office.

"I've been hearing good reports about you two from both Hutchins and Cook. Alice, it would appear that you have more than proved worthy of your new position as parlour maid. Well done."

Alice beamed, praise from Mrs Jarvis was a rare thing indeed.

"As for you, Megan, from now on, while still continuing to fulfil your duties as kitchen maid, I would like you to assist Alice at table whenever there is need. And for this you will receive an extra shilling a week."

Megan was overwhelmed. She didn't expect remuneration, believing it to be all part and parcel of her job. She couldn't wait to send a letter home, giving them all the good news.

It was the middle of September and after the intense heat of summer the weather had become much cooler, a sure sign that autumn was on its way. Megan settled herself on the bench, eager to read the newly arrived letter from home. She'd not heard from Jess for ages. She told herself that with money so short and her family living with the knowledge that it was only a matter of time before eviction, it was little wonder that Jess hadn't felt like writing to her.

As her fingers nervously fumbled to open the envelope, she prayed to God that this letter didn't bring with it the news that her family had been made homeless.

9th September 1919

Dear Megs

Well the worst thing has happened. Mam and the Reverend Braithwaite are to be married by special licence at Bridgend Register Office next Saturday, and we are all going to live up at the manse.

I know for a fact that our Mam is only marrying him to keep a roof over our heads. She's been worried sick since the letter came from the colliery telling her we had to move out to make room for another miner and his family.

The letter said, that if we didn't leave within fourteen days, they would be forced to send in the bailiffs! How I wish I were older and a full time collier. Then they would have to let us stay put. As it is I feel so useless. Mam asked me to write and explain things. She sends her love, along with the rest of us.

Your loving brother, Jess. XXX

Megan reread the letter. Suddenly, it was as if a dark cloud had lifted from her, making her heart feel lighter. From now on her family would be safe. Thank God, they had found a protector in the Reverend Braithwaite. She convinced herself that although the family's situation may have played a big part in her mother's decision, she must have feelings for the man or she would never have agreed to such a union.

It was almost too much to take in. A mixture of emotions overcame her. Of course she was happy for them, but part of her felt left out. Why did she always have to be satisfied with news from home, after the event. Like when her father died. She missed the closeness. She wanted to be there, sharing the highs and lows with her family.

Then it dawned on her that Jess had been right all along about the minister's intentions. She felt guilty for not believing him, although deep down she still believed the minister to be a good man.

Megan thought she understood her brother's reasons for disliking the minister. Jess, as the oldest son, wanted to be regarded as the head of the Williams family. His mother's intended marriage had simply put his nose out of joint, but she was sure that he would come around once they were all settled in the manse. Megan had to smile to herself, fancy, her family living up at the manse. Now there's posh, isn't it?

Folding the letter into the envelope, she returned it to her pocket. No doubt she would read it again before the day was out.

"Hello, remember me?" It was Arthur Walters.

Megan was taken aback as he settled himself beside her. She noticed he was wearing the same pinstriped suit, but instead of a bow tie he sported a paisley patterned silk cravat. Her eyes were drawn to his black and white patent shoes, which gave him the appearance of a right dandy.

"I hope you don't mind me seeking you out? I wanted to thank you for the other night. You were a real sport. For a while there, I thought you might let the cat out of the bag. But you didn't even tell your cousin Lizzie."

"Really, Mr Walters. Your business is no one's but your own." She inched away from him. He was sitting far too close to her, making her feel uncomfortable.

"Call me Arthur, why don't you, I recognized you straight away the other night, but I thought it best to keep a low profile. You've done rather well for yourself, working for the Fothergills, haven't you?"

"Obviously not as well as you," she snapped. She thought him very cheeky.

"True. But then my change of luck is in the main part down to you."

"Me? How can that possibly be?"

"I can hardly believe it myself. You see, it all happened the day we met on the train station. If you remember I was on my way to the races."

Megan nodded.

"Anyway, I believe that the kiss from you had a lot to do with my change of luck."

Megan stayed silent, but her look spoke volumes.

"Don't look so surprised. When I tell you of my good fortune, you'll believe it too."

Seeing her embarrassment, he quickly continued.

"Well, it all happened just after I left you and boarded the train to Swindon. As the train pulled off I realized I needed to use the privy, it's always a good place to hide when you've no ticket. I do it often. Then once the guard has finished checking tickets, I take my seat."

Megan shook her head in disbelief.

He took a deep breath. He seemed intent on relating all. Megan sensed it was futile to try to stop him, and had to admit to being more than a little curious.

"Well, while I was in the lavatory, I found this wallet, bulging with fivers it was — over two hundred pounds. The answer to *my* prayers and to *your* lucky kiss."

"That's ridiculous. For one thing, I never gave you a kiss, you stole it!"

"True. But it make's no difference. Luck is luck!"

"You're mad! I really don't want you making me into some sort of accomplice to someone else's misfortune. I hope you handed the wallet to the guard?"

"And risk being prosecuted for travelling without a ticket? Don't be daft. My motto was, and still is, never to look a gift horse in the mouth. And talking about horses — after buying myself some classy clothes, I continued on to the races, where I more than doubled my money."

"*Your* money? So you're a hardened gambler?"

"No. Not any more. I'm not one to push my luck. I won a packet that day, over five hundred pounds.

Enough to purchase a small haulage business. I'm a respectable businessman now. I even transport goods for the Fothergill Tobacco Company. Harold Fothergill has even recommended me for membership at his gentlemen's club. And it's all thanks to you."

Megan was speechless. It was quite a story. This gambler and even worse, this thief, really believed she had been his saviour. She was about to give him a piece of her mind when she saw Sidney walking toward them.

"Hello, Sidney," she said as he came closer. She was pleased to see him and couldn't wait to tell him about the good news from home. He didn't answer. His eyes fixed on Arthur Walters. "This is Mr —" she attempted an introduction, but Sidney interrupted her.

"I know who he is. He's Lizzie's new fancy man."

Megan had never seen him so angry.

"Steady on now, old chap, let me explain," Arthur Walters said, reverting back to a false posh accent, conveniently dropped when speaking to her earlier.

Sidney was having none of it. "I'm talking to Megan and not you!" Sidney looked into Megan's eyes — she could tell he was hurting and reached out for his hand but he moved back to avoid her touch.

"I can see that you'll not be needing me to walk you back to the house today. So I'll not embarrass you any further."

Before Megan had time to stop him, Sidney turned and walked away.

Arthur Walters didn't seem a bit put out by Sidney's rude behaviour, but it had upset Megan, and she vowed to tackle him about it after tea. She stood up. It was time for her to head back.

"Don't worry, Megan, I'll be only to happy to walk you home." He offered her his arm.

"No, thank you, Mr Walters. I'm quite capable of finding my own way back to Redcliffe House. So I'll say goodbye." She left him standing at the bench with his mouth open.

"What conceit!" she thought. It was obvious he hadn't expected to be refused. Did he really believe she would take the arm of a man she did not know? Someone who, by his own admission, was a friend of Harold Fothergill. And another thing, who told him he could call her Megan?

She was still fuming when she reached the end of the downs and found herself reflecting on her day. First the news of her mother's marriage, then Arthur Walters's story, followed by Sidney's outburst. What a day!

CHAPTER
SIX

"Olive, can you tell me why the little ones are running around the house like wild animals?"

"They're excited, Jess, aren't you? *Duw*, I can't believe we're all going to be living here."

"No, I'm not the least bit excited. In fact, I'm dreading living in the same house as him. I just wish there could have been another way, and that Mam wasn't marrying him."

"All the same, Jess, I think you should have gone with her. I'm sure the minister's family from down the Gower will be at the Register Office."

"Mam understands. I just couldn't face witnessing her marriage to the minister Braithwaite. Anyway Gran, Uncle Jack, Maude and Auntie Margaret are all going to be there, so she'll not stand alone."

They stood in the kitchen of the manse awaiting the wedding party's return, knowing that from now on their mother would be addressed as Mrs Braithwaite.

Olive, sensing her brother's mood, attempted to lighten the conversation, "Have you seen all the food in the parlour? I think it was very kind of the reverend to organize a wedding breakfast for her. Mam said that all of his parishioners helped — which only goes to prove that he must be very well thought of."

"As we know from our own bitter experience, the reverend can be very persuasive. Our Mam didn't need much coaxing, did she?"

"Why are you being so nasty? You know Mam did it for us."

"Exactly! We all know Mam's reason. But something's niggling at me, and I'll not rest until I find out what's in it for him."

"Maybe he loves her. I don't suppose you've even considered that!" Olive snapped. She was getting a bit fed up with her brother's attitude toward the reverend. Why couldn't he just be happy about their good fortune? "Anyway, my deepest concern is what we're supposed to call him. Should we call him Dad, do you think?"

"I'll never call him Dad! And I don't think you should either! He may be Mam's husband, but I will never look upon him as my father, minister or not!" declared Jess.

"Well, we have to call him something?"

Before Jess could answer, the kitchen door flew open.

"Hello, son, daughter. Welcome to your new home," the minister's voice bellowed.

Elias Braithwaite was a tall man, standing nearly six feet, which seemed to exaggerate his slim build. His hair was light brown and hung limply around his gaunt face. A plain looking man with a long nose and protruding chin, he walked with his head bent, his chin

109

almost touching his chest, his eyes peering over half rimmed wire spectacles.

"I'm not . . ." Jess was about to tell him he was not, and never would be, his son, when he caught sight of his mother, standing behind the clergyman. Her eyes pleading with him to hold his tongue.

Jess thought how tiny she looked. Her face, once a picture of health, now thin and pale. Even the small amount of rouge strategically placed, failed to hide the greyness of her skin. She forced a smile, and Jess weakened. Ignoring the minister, he walked over to his mother and put his arms around her.

"Mam, you look lovely. The blue of that costume really suits you," Jess said, then whispered, "I'm sorry, Mam. I was being selfish. I should have been there for you today."

His mam, now Mary Braithwaite, squeezed his hand. "That be all right, son, I understand."

"Four whole guineas, that's what I gave your mother to buy her new outfit. Nothing but the best, I said. And she did well. You're right, *boy*, the suit fits her well and yet it's practical enough to keep for chapel on Sunday. From now on, I must insist that the whole family attend all three services — morning, afternoon and evening — each and every Sunday. We shall worship our Lord together." Elias Braithwaite spoke in a loud melodic voice, his arms outstretched as if giving a sermon. Slowly, he lowered his hands, clasping them behind his back to address them.

"Jess, I can hear the rest of the wedding party coming up the path. I want you to meet our guests at the front door, open it and escort them into the parlour. Olive, you gather the children, and for goodness' sake try to keep them under control. Children should be seen and not heard. Do I make myself clear?"

Olive simply nodded. Jess gently took his young sister's hand and led her from the room. Today for his mother's sake he vowed to stay silent, although it wasn't going to be easy. Earlier, when the minister had called him *boy*, he'd felt his hackles rise. Living with Elias Braithwaite was going to be even harder than he'd first thought!

"So you're the eldest of the brood then, are you?" a woman in her late forties asked Jess. He could tell she was some relation of the minister because she had the same lily-white skin and protruding chin. Her well-tailored clothes failed to enhance her plain appearance.

"Well, answer me, boy. Are you the eldest or not?"

"Yes, I am," Jess snapped. He wanted to be as rude to her as she was being to him . . . but for his mother's sake —

"There's one missing, isn't there. A girl. Where is she? In some sort of trouble no doubt."

Jess could feel his colour rising. This really was the last straw.

"Sadly, my daughter couldn't be here today," his mother answered. "She's in service, working for a well-established family in Bristol. We are all very proud of her."

Jess gave a sigh of relief.

"I see," the woman sniggered. "Let me congratulate you once again on your most fortunate betrothal." She held out her hand. "I'm Lilian Braithwaite, Elias's cousin. We did meet earlier, if somewhat briefly, outside the register office."

"Yes, I remember. Pleased to meet you again," Mary Braithwaite said, politely shaking the woman's hand.

"I must say, you've certainly made a fine catch. My cousin comes from a long line of great men. His father, himself a respected clergyman, is well known throughout the Gower Peninsular for his wonderful sermons. Elias has proved himself to be more than worthy for his chosen path through life. What other man would take on a woman and six children? Such benevolence!"

Jess watched as his mother meekly smiled and nodded her agreement. This was not the mother he knew. His mother had spirit. His mother was proud. She had been made to sacrifice all for the sake of her family. He turned away. He knew he couldn't stand much more of this, he had to get some fresh air or he would burst a blood vessel.

As always his mother sensed his mood.

"Jess, why don't you go outside and check on the little ones?" she said, gently placing a kiss on his cheek.

Once out in the garden Jess composed himself. It was a fine day. He looked up at the clear blue sky and hoped for once his father wasn't looking down on them, witnessing their humiliation. Jess walked along the stone path encircling the house. There could be no mistaking that it was certainly a fine house, boasting as it did a splendid view of the valley. The house stood alone, high above James Road — and their old terraced house. Under different circumstances Jess would have been more than happy to live here. For a while he stood and watched the children play ring-a-ring-a-rosy. They seemed happy enough and obviously didn't share his feeling of hopelessness.

Jess walked around to the back of the house, and as he passed the open window of the minister's study — a room which all the children had been told was strictly off limits — he heard mumbled voices. Although he knew it was wrong — "eavesdroppers seldom hear good news", his mother always said — something urged him to move closer. As he crouched down under the open window he could plainly hear a man's voice.

"Well, Elias, I cannot pretend that I was not bitterly disappointed when you informed me of your impending marriage. I had such high hopes for you. All the groundwork had been done, and the wheels well and truly in motion. I had spoken to all the right people, telling everyone of your most admirable calling to do the Lord's work among the less fortunate. It had always been my wish to do such work, but sadly, I was never given the opportunity. Whereas you, you only needed to wait another three months and you would have been on your way to the colonies. Once there you could have achieved great things and been awarded suitable recognition for the ultimate sacrifice. You will never achieve any of this, stuck here in this valley. I truly believed that your future lay in missionary work!"

"Oh, Father, so did I. But this woman and her family were so in need of salvation. Without my help they would most certainly have ended on the streets. Surely, it would not have been Christian of me to turn my back on them for self-gratification."

"I must say, to sacrifice one's own ambitions for the sake of others is indeed admirable. Will you kneel and join me in prayer? Together we can ask God to help me shake off my feeling of disappointment."

Jess didn't move. His mind was racing. So that was it! The minister had simply used them as a way to get out of being sent to the colonies! The crafty old bugger. Then making sure he was not discovered, he quietly made his way back around the house. Jess should have felt pleased with himself for finding out the truth, but all he could feel was a deep sadness in having to admit that such a clever, manipulative man had duped his family.

Megan hadn't spoken to Sidney in over a month. There had been no sign of him on the downs and he'd even stopped coming to the house for his tea. Cook had mentioned something about a big order at the brewery and him having to work overtime, but Megan doubted this to be reason. She was convinced he had been deliberately avoiding her. And if he was doing it to make her feel miserable, then he had succeeded.

"Alice, will you get a move on or we'll miss the charabanc," Megan called from the kitchen door.

For the last couple of Sundays Megan had accompanied Alice on a trip into town — not wanting

114

to face the downs on her own. With her family's change of circumstances, Megan didn't feel so guilty about spending a few coppers on herself.

"And about time too," Megan said, as she saw her friend making her way across the kitchen.

"Sorry, Megs. I've been having trouble with my hair irons. You don't know how lucky you are having natural curls. With my hair being as straight as pokers, it takes an age to get even the slightest kink. Still, I suppose needs must. It'll be well worth the effort when I catch myself a handsome fellow, eh?" Alice wiggled her bottom, making Megan laugh.

They hurried from the house and started running toward the Downs, reaching the charabanc with only minutes to spare.

Once in town they would hop on a tram, and for just tuppence get a tour of the city centre. It didn't matter to them that the shops were closed. They enjoyed just looking at the finery on display in the windows. Especially now, with it only being six weeks to Christmas.

Today, after the tram ride, they decided to visit the tearooms on the corner of Market Street, reasoning that a nice pot of tea and a sticky bun would help them ward off the cold.

"There's Sidney, look, I think he's coming over," Alice cried, pointing out of the window.

Megan wasn't sure she wanted to see him, at least not in a crowded tearoom. But as she watched him push open the entrance door and march towards their table, she knew she had no choice.

"Alice, I need to speak to Megan alone. Would you mind leaving us for a few minutes, please?" he asked and although addressing her friend, his eyes were firmly fixed on Megan.

He was visibly trembling. At this stage Megan wasn't sure if it was through nerves or temper.

"I need to visit the lav anyway," Alice said, as she stood up to leave.

"Thanks. It shouldn't take long." His eyes did not move from Megan.

With Alice gone, Sidney settled himself into her vacant seat.

"Don't I get a say in any of this?" Megan asked.

"I'm sorry, Megan, but I have to speak to you before I lose my nerve. I want to know why you've been avoiding me."

"Me! Avoiding you! Well, now that's rich, isn't it? I suppose it's me who's stopped having my meals up at the house then, is it?"

"No. But it's you who's stopped going to our bench."

Megan didn't answer. She looked down to the table, rubbing her finger along the rim of her empty teacup. The way he'd said "our bench" had worried her.

"I'm sorry, Megan. I know I'm being daft. It's just that I thought . . . you and that spiv were . . . were . . . well, you know?"

"No, Sidney. I don't know. Are you telling me you truly believed I had arranged to meet Arthur Walters that day?" Her voice had become raised, causing the couple on the next table to look around.

116

"Yes. I have to admit I did," Sidney whispered, aware that people were staring.

"Well, for your information, Sidney Partridge, I didn't. But even if I had, I'd like to know what it's got to do with you anyway?"

"I thought we were . . . I can see I was wrong." He looked hurt and began to raise himself out of the chair.

Megan caught his hand, he hesitated, then sat back down.

"Sidney, we're friends, that's all. Please don't spoil it. You have to understand, there's far too much going on in my life at the moment for me to think of anyone in — in that way. I'm sorry if I've misled you into thinking otherwise. But I'll not be made to feel guilty, just because someone stopped to speak to me." He stayed silent, his head bowed. "Sidney, I do miss our chats. I want us to be friends again."

He gave her hand a squeeze. "So do I, Megs. And it's me who should be sorry, for making two and two add up to more than four. I was never any good at sums." He gave her a smile. "As long as you regard me as your friend, that'll do me . . . for now, anyway."

She playfully slapped his shoulder, "I'll give you, 'for now', Sidney Partridge."

They were still laughing when Alice returned,

"Well, as pleased as I am to see the two of you on speaking terms again, if we don't get a move on soon, we're going to be late back and have to face Cook."

Sidney stood up. "Come on, I'll give you both a lift. I've got Samson and the cart tied up across the road. You see, Megan, I have been working."

Sidney helped them up on to the wagon, first Megan, and then Alice, making sure Megan was sitting next to him for the ride home. As he negotiated Samson out of the city he told them about the big order at the brewery. "Fifty new barrels we've got to find in less than three months. Me and the cooper have been working flat out, even on Sunday," he said, giving Megan a gentle nudge with his elbow. "Today I've had to pick up six barrels, all in need of repair, from the public house in Market Street. That's what me and Samson were doing when I spotted you in the tearooms."

"We don't want to get you into trouble. We can easily catch the charabanc back, honest," Megan said.

"Don't worry. I'll tell them at the depot that I had trouble getting the landlord to answer the door. They know that none of the pubs open on Sunday — well, not officially anyway!"

That night as Megan entered her bedroom, she felt happier than she had in a long while. After first lighting the candle on the shelf above her bed, she changed into her flannelette nightdress and settled down to read again her most recent letter from home.

It seemed that Jess had come to terms with the family's new situation, either that or he just wasn't saying. He assured her that everyone was well and how they liked living at the manse. Although they didn't much like having to accompany the reverend to chapel three times on Sunday.

Megan noticed how he always called him the reverend, and wondered what the others called him. Maybe she'd ask in her next letter. Megan read on: Jess told her how Olive enjoyed having a bedroom to herself and that Bryn had started work as an apprentice down the pit. Megan remembered how she had looked after him since the day he'd been born, even though she'd been not much more than a toddler herself. It was hard to believe that he was now thirteen and working alongside Jess.

Megan's eyes began to close, it was time to call it a night. Folding the letter she carefully placed it under her pillow. Then, after first licking her fingers, she reached up to extinguish the candle before snuggling under the blankets.

Sleep came quickly, but it was not restful. She felt afraid. Behind her heavy footsteps were getting closer . . . and closer. She stood precariously on a precipice. Below her black sea crashed against the rocks, she could here someone calling, "come to me, come to me". The footsteps were getting closer . . . she had to jump . . . she had to get away . . . here goes. one, two, three . . . off into the abyss . . .

"Come to me, my little sparrow," she heard a man's voice whisper in her ear.

Megan felt panic as she opened her eyes to complete darkness, yet aware of someone pulling at her bedcover, and trying to get at her body. She told herself this couldn't be happening, it had to be a bad dream. But when his heavy body fell on top of her, the reality of her situation became all too clear.

"I've got you now. You sweet little thing, you. Come on, you've kept me waiting far too long for a repeat performance."

Her mind raced as she struggled beneath him. How could this be happening? She was in her own bedroom. How had he found her? She began to scream out to alert Sally or Sadie or Alice. Their rooms were just down the hall, they would come to her, help her . . . But his hand reached up covering her mouth, preventing her from calling out.

"Shhhh, we'll have no screaming tonight. I'm going to take my hand away from your mouth. If you scream out, I'll have you put out of the house first thing in the morning, do you hear?" His voice sounded evil and she knew it was no idle threat.

She was helpless. She could do nothing to stop him. She couldn't fight him off, he was too big and strong. So, realizing how futile her efforts were, she stopped struggling, as he clumsily fumbled with his clothes in his eagerness to pleasure himself. She lay quiet and lifeless, only crying out as he roughly entered her. Her cry was soon muffled when his whisky mouth found hers. She felt tears sting her eyes and roll down her cheeks. How she hated this pig of a man. Under her breath she prayed to God that her ordeal would end quickly and questioned how *He* could allow an animal like this to go on living, and yet take a good, kind man like her father?

"There's a good girl. I'm glad to see you stopped playing hard to get. Given time you may even learn to enjoy it." He had finished with her. As he slid from the bed, she heard him adjusting his breeches.

A sob escaped in the darkness. Did he really believe she could ever enjoy such an act? She heard the rustle of paper and felt him press something into her hand — she knew it was yet another five pound note.

"Treat yourself to something special," he whispered.

Megan wondered how he could possibly believe that she would ever touch a penny of his filthy money. She would put it with the other one, in the Salvation Army box.

"Until the next time, my sweet," he said, as he brushed a wet kiss across her cheek.

Megan waited until she heard the door close behind him, then quickly jumped out of bed, only to fall to her knees as a violent shooting pain stabbed her — he had been so rough with her. With one hand holding her stomach, she crawled to the door, she had to make sure it was locked. In a little while, when she was sure the coast was clear, she would creep to the washroom and cleanse herself of him. She blamed herself — it was her own stupid fault. Why hadn't she locked the door in the first place?

The truth was, she had never dreamt he would come to the servants' quarters. She'd always felt so safe in her own little room, but not any more. As she turned the key in the lock, she vowed he would never enter her room again. From now on her door would stay locked at all times.

"No one sets foot up those stairs until all the work be done in readiness for the morning," Cook commanded. "Then, and only then, may you go and enjoy yourselves, for I know I shall get no work out of any of you after you've been drinking Mr Hutchins's mulled wine concoction."

This sent a ripple of laughter round the kitchen. Although they knew that Cook meant what she said, they also knew how much she, like everyone else, looked forward to the annual tradition of being asked above-stairs.

It was Christmas Eve — and Megan's first Christmas away from home. Cook had explained to her how every Christmas Eve the mistress, an accomplished pianist, entertained guests to an evening of buffet and music. Then, at around nine-thirty, the household staff would be summoned to the parlour to be presented with a small Christmas gift and a glass of mulled wine, and all would join together in singing Christmas carols.

Everyone was busy preparing for the festivities. Under the instruction of Mr Hutchins, the house was decorated with fragrant garlands of holly and ivy. Red candles were placed in every room and the piano shifted to a more central position in the parlour. While in the kitchen a wonderful smell wafted from the huge goose on the spit above the well-stoked fire in the grate and from the strategically placed basin below it which was already filling up with succulent goose-fat. Cook would allow no one else to turn the spit's handle every half hour or trust anyone with the glazed ham or the saddle of beef roasting in the oven.

122

Everyone had a list of jobs to do. Alice and Megan had been given the task of preparing the buffet for this evening and laying the table in the dining room, while the rest of the kitchen staff prepared vegetables and sauces to accompany each of the meats and cold pies. Mrs Partridge had made the numerous mince pies, plum puddings and glazed fruits months earlier and stored them in the huge larder off the kitchen.

Megan wondered what preparations her own family was making. She imagined Jess carrying a large capon in its baking tin to Tom *bara*'s. Like most of the people in the village, her family were always quick to take up the offer of using the baker's large coal-fired bread ovens, which could hold up to fifty baking tins at a time, to cook their Christmas fare. For this service there was a nominal charge of tuppence. She tried to remember the wonderful smell surrounding the bake-house on such an occasion. Three weeks earlier the same oven would have been offered to cook various sized Christmas cakes.

She sighed, and wondered if her family were missing her as much as she missed them.

"Remember, the more you do today the less you'll have to do tomorrow." Mrs Partridge's voice echoed around the kitchen. "If all goes well, the mistress may allow us to have a little Christmas party of our own tomorrow night."

The girls gave an excited scream, until a disapproving look from Cook soon silenced them.

As Megan changed into the parlour maid's uniform she couldn't help noticing what a perfect fit it had

123

become. She no longer had to rely on Mrs Partridge to pull in the apron strings to give her shape. She was pleased to have filled out and at last to have the figure of a seventeen year old as opposed to that of a child.

The guest list was much the same as the last dinner party, with the addition of the Reverend John Hopgood, who gave a Christmas prayer before the start of proceedings. His wife was a very large lady whose loud singing voice could be heard way above everyone else's. The mistress played the piano beautifully, managing to make even the flattest singing voice sound acceptable. At nine-thirty sharp all the staff gathered in the hall outside the parlour door, patiently waiting for Mr Hutchins's signal. When it came, they entered the room in single file and the mistress duly presented each of them with a gift.

As Megan stood in line behind Alice, the huge Christmas tree, practically filling the tall window on the opposite side of the room, instantly dazzled her. It was covered with brightly coloured baubles, all flickering as they each caught the light of the many candles clipped to the tree's branches. It was a magical sight and one, Megan knew, she would never forget.

As the mistress placed the small red box tied up with gold satin ribbon into her hand, Megan said a polite "Thank you, ma'am," and bobbed a small curtsy, before making way for the next member of staff. Cook had earlier instructed her on the procedure of such an occasion. As Megan watched her friends eagerly open their boxes, she followed suit. Inside was a small brooch in the shape of a flower. It was the prettiest thing she had ever owned and she knew she would treasure it always. After they had all opened their gifts — an assortment of brooches for the girls and a pair of gloves for Percy the scullery boy — Mr Hutchins handed each of them a cup of mulled wine, which probably had a lot to do with them all singing with such gusto when the mistress invited them to join in. They sang, "Oh Come All Ye Faithful", followed by "The First Noel" and finally "Silent Night".

At the end of the night, Megan had to admit that she, like everyone else, had thoroughly enjoyed the evening. And with Master Harold seeming inseparable from Miss Jane Arkwright, he hadn't even looked at Megan. When they were all singing, Arthur Walters had caught her eye, giving her a cheeky nod and a wink as if acknowledging her continued silence. Much to her surprise, even Lizzie had been nice to her, making Megan think there was a lot to be said for the Christmas spirit, or was it the effect of the mulled wine? Megan knew she would never be able to trust Lizzie ever again.

"Hasn't it been a great night?" Alice asked Megan, as they made their way up the stairs to bed. "Do you think the mistress will really let us have our very own party tomorrow?"

"I really don't know. It's possible I suppose." Megan felt suddenly weary — it had been a long day. She had reached her room. "Goodnight, Alice. See you tomorrow."

Megan entered her room, quickly locking the door behind her and flopping down on the bed fully clothed.

She closed her eyes, only to find that she felt suddenly nauseous. She opened her eyes, hoping it would go away . . . but the room was spinning . . . she was going to be sick. With no time to run down the hall to the washroom, she jumped off the bed and on to her knees, and made a quick grab for the chamber pot just in the nick of time. Later when Megan had washed and refreshed herself, she put her upset stomach down to the mulled wine — she wasn't used to drinking alcoholic beverages.

Christmas Day carried on like the day before with everyone happy and jolly. Megan was glad the sickness had not stayed with her. There had been a lot of work to get through this morning, Christmas or not, the fires still had to be cleaned and laid. Then she'd assisted Alice in the dining room serving the mistress's Christmas lunch.

"Just a small, intimate, family party," Mr Hutchins had said.

The party consisted of the mistress, her two sons and Miss Arkwright, and gave fuel to the rumour circulating below-stairs that there was soon to be an announcement regarding Master Harold's betrothal to Jane Arkwright. "The poor woman," Megan thought.

After lunch Cook was to give them good news indeed.

"The mistress has sent word that she will not be needing any of our services after seven o'clock this evening, as the family have all been invited to spend the night with the Arkwrights. And she has given us permission to have a staff party." The kitchen buzzed with excitement. "Quiet now. Let's all get on and finish our work. When we've done, we shall lay ourselves a proper party buffet and I think, for such an occasion, we should all dress in our Sunday best."

The rest of the day seemed to drag, with all of them simply going through the motions, getting on with their chores while anticipating the night ahead.

By the time they had all gathered, washed and changed into their best outfits, the atmosphere was very festive. Everyone was there, except Lizzie. She had actually volunteered to accompany the mistress to the Arkwrights'.

"It probably had a lot to do with that Arthur Walters also being invited to the Arkwrights. I can't see Lizzie offering her services, unless there was something in it for her," Megan overheard Alice gossiping to Sally.

"You must admit though, he's definitely a bit of all right. I wouldn't need much coaxing, I can tell you," Sally said, her gruff voice breaking into laughter.

Cook really went to town with the food and Mr Hutchins made the rum punch. Megan, after the result of the previous night's wine, decided she would stick with Cook's homemade lemonade. Mrs Jarvis surprised them all by bringing her phonogram to the party. Megan had never seen one before.

She watched spellbound as Mrs Jarvis turned the handle and the voice of a male singer came loudly from a large horn-like trumpet.

Sidney arrived to find Megan swaying to the music. All the other girls were either dancing in pairs or eating. There was much laughter with everyone in good spirits.

"Well, I'll risk a dance if you will?" Sidney joked as he stood beside Megan.

"Don't you think he has the loveliest voice you have ever heard?"

Sidney nodded in agreement. "His name is Al Jolson. He's in a film at the Roxy down town. We could go and see him if you like?"

"Really? I'd love to. Maybe I could swap my Sunday afternoon for an evening off instead."

"Leave it with me, I'll talk to Ma. But first — a dance." He held out his hand.

Mrs Jarvis's arm must have been getting tired from turning the handle of the music machine, because the music grew slower and slower and Al Jolson's voice grew deeper and deeper. This prompted everyone to break into laughter. Megan laughed so much she thought her sides would burst.

Later when she lay on her bed, she hoped her family had enjoyed Christmas as much as she had.

CHAPTER
SEVEN

Megan stood gripping the rail of Clifton Suspension Bridge. It was a cold and damp January afternoon. Since last Sunday, when Cook had told them all about the young man who had jumped from this very bridge, she had thought of nothing else. Megan cried for the young man as she tossed a small bunch of flowers into the air and watched them slowly float down into the fast moving muddy waters below. She felt so afraid. Some said that taking your own life was a coward's way out. But surely it was a final act of bravery for someone so desperate they could find no other way.

Well, she was certainly desperate. But was she brave enough to take her own life and in so doing, murder her unborn child? Even the knowledge that the child was Master Harold's couldn't make her hate the baby she was carrying. As the tears rolled down her cheeks she closed her eyes and prayed for the soul of the young lad who had died alone. Megan had prayed a lot over the past two weeks, since she'd realized why her monthly course had not appeared. At first she tried to convince herself that the sickness, sore breasts and swollen stomach were all in her imagination, but she could no longer fool herself. It had been nearly two months since Harold had come to her room. She hadn't wanted to believe that something so precious as a new life could be the outcome of such an evil act. But there was no doubting — she was indeed pregnant.

She wondered what was to become of her. So far, she had managed to hide her growing waistline by binding herself tightly with strips of calico cut from her petticoat. But it wouldn't be long before her pregnancy became evident to everyone and then the mistress would have no choice but to put her out on to the street. She felt such shame. Perhaps she could run away before anyone found out — but where would she go?

Megan let go of the rail, then turning away, slowly made her way in the direction of the downs. It was starting to rain. If she took her time walking back she might catch a chill and die, a sure way of escaping her problems.

"Whatever do you think you be doing, staying out in the rain all this time?" Cook rushed over as Megan walked into the kitchen soaked through. The rest of the staff, who were all seated around the kitchen table having tea, stopped and stared at her.

"Sorry I'm late back, Mrs Partridge." Megan felt guilty, she hadn't considered how worried Cook would be when she'd purposely taken her time walking home. Suddenly, she felt as cold as ice and couldn't stop shivering.

"Carry on with your tea, you lot, while I deal with Megan. Stop gawking at her. Haven't you seen anyone wet through before?" Cook spoke abruptly to the rest of the staff, but as she caught around Megan, her voice was tender. "Come here, child. Just wait until I see my Sidney. Keeping you out in such weather and letting you walk home alone."

"It wasn't Sidney's fault. You mustn't blame him," Megan pleaded. "He couldn't make it today, I was alone." The last thing Megan wanted was to get Sidney into trouble with his mother.

"Well, never mind that now, you get yourself off to your room and change out of those wet clothes. You look half froze to death." Cook ushered her across the kitchen and up the stairs. "When you return I'll have a nice cup of beef tea waiting for you."

"Thanks, Cook. I'm sorry if I worried you. It'll not happen again, I promise."

As Megan slowly made her way up to her room, she couldn't believe how difficult it was to move one foot in front of the other. She felt weak and uncomfortably hot, and yet for some reason she couldn't stop shivering.

The last thing Megan remembered was stepping out of her wet clothes and removing the binding from around her stomach. She must have collapsed on to the bed, for the next thing she knew Mrs Jarvis and Cook were standing over her.

Megan tried to lift her head but felt too weak and giddy, and the room appeared to be spinning.

"It's all right, Megan, lie still." Mrs Jarvis's voice sounded a long way away.

"Work . . . I have to do my work." Again Megan attempted to get up but failed.

"Don't you be worrying, child. Alice can do your work tonight. You just lie there while I go fetch some hot bricks for your bed." Cook lifted the end of her pinafore and patted the beads of perspiration from Megan's forehead. "I think you've gone and caught a terrible chill, child."

"Keep your eye on her tonight, Cook. If she's no better by morning I shall call in the doctor," Mrs Jarvis instructed, as she left the room.

"No! Please, no doctor — no doctor." Megan kept repeating these words as she tossed in her bed.

"Hush, child. Don't you go fretting yourself. Come on, try to sit up and drink this beef tea."

Megan felt as if she were floating away, perhaps her wish had come true and she really was going to die . . .

"Good morning. How are you feeling today? 'Tis about time you woke up. Proper worried about you, we've been." Mrs Partridge stood over her, smiling. "Poor lamb. You don't remember a thing do you? Well, you've had a fever. Two days you have laid there tossing and turning. A severe chill and high temperature the doctor said."

Megan felt sudden panic. "Doctor — what doctor? Did he —"

"Now, now. Don't you fret, you be fine," Cook interrupted Megan before she could ask if the doctor had mentioned the baby.

"Try and drink this tea. I have to go down to make the breakfasts, but I'll send Alice up to help you. 'Spect you would like to have a nice bath after all the

132

sweating? Still, I think you'd better wait until the doctor gives you the all clear. He'll be calling later this morning. The mistress insisted he called everyday."

As Megan sipped the sweet tea, she found it gave her a feeling of well being. She let her hand slide under the blanket to feel the bulge in her stomach, nothing had changed, except the way she now felt. For while she was still as frightened and desperate as the day she had walked in the rain, to her surprise, she felt so glad to be alive.

Megan had been back to work nearly a week, and everyone had been so kind to her, everyone that is, except Lizzie.

"You stupid fool, the mistress should have paid you off. Think yourself lucky you still have a job — for the time being anyway."

Megan gave her a questioning look. Surely she didn't know? The doctor had promised he wouldn't tell anyone. He'd been very kind, he'd even asked if she wanted him to be the one to tell Mistress Fothergill about the baby. "For told she will have to be — and soon."

Megan thanked him, but decided that, after all of her kindness, she owed it to the Mistress to tell her herself. Although how and when she planned to do this, she did not know.

"The mistress may not be so lenient next time, and it'll serve you right too, that's what I say. You had everyone waiting on you hand and foot for days," Lizzie complained as she went about her work.

Megan needed no reminder, and felt so guilty about her situation. She wondered what they would all think of her, when they knew the truth. That night she spent a restless night and pleaded for God's help . . .

The very next morning, be it by divine intervention or by coincidence, help was to come in a way Megan would never have believed possible.

"The mistress says you're to go upstairs to the parlour. You've got a visitor." Megan could tell Lizzie was annoyed at being the one to bring the message.

"Me, a visitor, are you sure?" Megan thought there had to be some mistake. Who would come to visit her?

"Are you accusing me of lying? 'Cause if you are, I'll have you know that liars don't become milady's maid."

Lizzie's sarcastic tone made Megan want to confront her. She'd had enough of her cousin talking down to her, and wanted to tell her that she, like most of the household staff, knew what Lizzie had willingly done to become milady's maid. She was a hypocrite and a liar and Megan longed to tell her so — but stopped herself. This was neither the time nor the place. Instead, she followed her upstairs to the parlour.

If Lizzie knew the identity of her visitor, she was not saying, and they walked in silence until they reached the parlour door. Lizzie gave it a gentle tap. Then, without waiting for a reply, opened the door and walked into the room.

"Megan Williams is here, ma'am." Lizzie spoke in a quiet, demure voice, as she gave a small bob by way of a curtsy.

134

Megan couldn't believe what a good actress her cousin had become. She could well understand how both the housekeeper and Mistress Fothergill had been taken in by her.

"Come in, Megan, you have a visitor." The mistress was seated in the big armchair beside the fireplace.

Megan slowly entered the room, the same room where *he* — By force of habit, she found herself glancing behind the door, making sure her attacker was not lurking in the shadows. but today she had nothing to fear. The mistress was there and the heavy brocade curtains were drawn back, allowing the bright daylight to shine in. The fire, which she'd so carefully laid earlier, was now lit and helped to make the room feel warm and, at least to everyone else, welcoming.

Megan looked around the room and in particular at the large man wearing a long black coat and knee breeches, sitting in the chair opposite the mistress. He had his back to the door, so Megan was unable to see his face. As she edged her way to the middle of the carpet, she watched him slowly raise himself from the chair and turn to face her.

She stared at this big man of stocky build with short brown wispy hair parted in the middle, and a heavily lined, grey-skinned face, but stare as she might, she was sure she did not know him. She was curious. If this was indeed her visitor, then who was he? And more to the point what did he want with her?

"Megan, my dear child. How good it is to meet you at last. I've heard so much about you," he said, walking toward her arms outstretched.

Mistress Fothergill must have notice the puzzled look on Megan's face and prompted recognition.

"Megan, your stepfather, Mr Braithwaite, has called to see you. A little while ago, he wrote to me explaining that he would be visiting the area, and asked if he could call to discuss a matter of some urgency. He asked me not to tell you until he himself had arrived," the mistress explained as quickly as she could.

Megan was trying to take it all in when the minister reached her, throwing his arms around her, embracing her. She felt herself pull away. This seemed to embarrass him and he gave a nervous cough. And once again the mistress came to the rescue.

"Come and sit by the fire, child. I am sure receiving such a distinguished visitor has come as a shock to you? No doubt you need time to gather yourself?"

Megan did as she was bid, eager to get away from the minister's strong arms. He might be her stepfather and a minister, but to her he was just another man to be feared.

"Lizzie, pour Megan a cup of tea. Then you can escort me to Mrs Jarvis's office. The housekeeper will need to be advised of today's developments."

Megan heard the mistress's words but didn't understand them. She was more worried about being left alone with this stranger.

Lizzie walked across the room and dutifully poured a cup of tea. As she laid it on the small table close to Megan, she gave her a look of contempt, it obviously peeved her to serve the likes of Megan — a mere kitchen maid. But she said nothing as she turned to face Mistress Fothergill, her face fixed with a false smile.

"Take as long as you like, Megan. No doubt you have a lot of family news to catch up on. And I know the minister has a surprise in store for you," the mistress said, as she left her chair and walked from the room with Lizzie dutifully following behind.

"Well, child, I must say it is good to see you looking so well and surrounded by such good people," Megan's stepfather said, taking the seat opposite her which the mistress had only just vacated.

Megan was glad he hadn't tried to put his arms around her again. She found it difficult to see this man as her mother's husband and her stepfather.

"You are probably wondering how I come to be in the area? Well, I was asked to pay a visit to the local Baptist church and I thought with me being so close it would be a good opportunity to call on your mistress and ask for her help, in order to fulfil your dear mother's greatest wish. For a while now she has spoken of nothing else but having you, her eldest and much loved daughter, return home. With this in mind, I decided to plead the case for your release from service, and I am pleased to tell you that Mistress Fothergill has agreed to let you go."

"You mean I am to return home to Wales? When? How?" Megan was so excited she jumped up from her chair.

The minister slowly waved the palm of his hand indicating she should sit down. And something in his eyes told her he would not give her any answers until she obeyed. She returned to the chair.

"I explained to Mrs Fothergill — such a kind lady — that since your dear mother agreed to marry me, your family's circumstances have greatly changed, I have to say for the better, and she wishes that her beloved Megan should rejoin the family." He stopped as if expecting Megan to say something, but she was speechless, half expecting to wake up at any moment and find out it was all a dream.

"Anyway," her stepfather continued, "I explained all this to your mistress and she has kindly agreed to release you from your duties. She in turn requested that you stay on for a further two weeks, during which time the housekeeper should have found a suitable replacement for your position. In the meantime, I shall return home and give your mother the good news."

Megan's eyes filled up, she felt tears run down her cheek, but they were tears of joy. She was going home to be with her mam and Jess and the rest of the brood. She instinctively touched her stomach. Perhaps there was hope after all.

Later that night Megan called to see Mrs Partridge, to tell her about her surprise visitor and share her good news.

"Well, we all heard you had a male visitor. You can imagine what a stir that made in the kitchen. They'll all be disappointed when they find out it was only your stepfather. Well, I'm very happy for you, child, although I shall be very sad to see you go. And I know that my

Sidney is going to miss you. There's no denying he has a soft spot for you."

"I know. And I shall miss you both. You have been so kind to me. I wondered if you could somehow let Sidney know before it becomes common knowledge."

Cook nodded, "I understand. I shall send Percy with a note to Sidney's lodgings, asking him to call to see me first thing in the morning. You're right, I think it's best he hears it from me, before one of the girls blurts it out."

"Thank you. I knew you'd understand."

"You're a good girl, Megan." Cook caught Megan's hand and gave it a gentle squeeze.

"I've known for a long time now that something be troubling you, child," she said, her soft brown eyes looking directly into Megan's.

Megan looked away, afraid her own eyes may give away too much. Cook had always been so kind to her. She wondered if she might confide in her, tell her . . . But she stopped herself. She didn't want to risk having to see Sidney's face when he found out she was . . .

"Don't worry, child, I shall not press you. I understand how much you need your family. A girl needs her mother at a time . . ." She didn't finish the sentence. Again their eyes met and for a while they just stood in silence. Megan wondered how much Cook really knew or if she had simply been fishing.

As if reading her thoughts, Cook smiled and patted her hand. "Go on, child, off to your bed. I have a letter to write."

The next morning Mrs Jarvis called to see Cook to inform her officially that Megan Williams would be leaving their employ on the fourth of February. The news travelled fast, and it wasn't long before it became the only topic of conversation below-stairs.

Everyone wished her luck and made her promise to keep in touch. Alice even joked that Megan could put in a good word for her with Jess. "Then maybe I'd end up being your sister-in-law."

The only person who didn't wish her luck was Lizzie. "You must be mad wanting to go back to the valley. I wouldn't care if I never saw the place again," she'd scoffed.

Megan believed her. She had never shown any signs of missing home or, for that matter, any of her family.

It was Sunday and the day before Megan was due to leave Bristol. After a busy morning going about her duties, she was summoned to the housekeeper's office.

"Come on in, my dear," Mrs Jarvis warmly greeted her. "Please, take a seat. So this is your last day with us?"

"Yes, Mrs Jarvis," was all Megan could think of to say. She couldn't pretend she didn't want to leave.

"Well, I have to say that I, like many of your fellow workers, will be sorry to see you go. But I know you have not been completely happy here, homesickness can be very painful and you are so very young." The housekeeper walked over to her desk. Taking her seat she slowly opened the drawer.

Megan stayed silent. There was no harm in letting her believe the homesickness story. It was much better than everyone knowing the true cause of her unhappiness, and she thanked God she was able to leave the house before her condition became obvious to one and all.

"Thank you for your understanding, Mrs Jarvis. I really am looking forward to seeing my family again."

"It gladdened me to hear about your family's change of circumstances. Here are your wages to date, which I am sure you will put to good use. You will as usual be allowed your afternoon off, no doubt to say your goodbyes. I shall just wish you luck." Mrs Jarvis touched Megan's elbow and escorted her to the door.

"Thank you again, Mrs Jarvis, and goodbye."

As Megan left the room it felt strange to be walking away from the housekeeper's office for the last time. There would be no more cleaning, no more scrubbing floors, no more waiting on table. And no more Harold.

She had arranged to meet Sidney as usual at the bench overlooking the suspension bridge. It was possibly her last visit to Clifton Downs.

"Megan, I know how much you want to go home and I truly am pleased for you, but that still don't make it any easier for me." He took her hand, "Megan, before you leave I must tell you how I feel about you. You really are the most wonderful person I have ever met. I don't just like you a lot, I —"

Megan put a hand to his mouth. "Please, Sidney, don't say another word. Don't complicate things."

He looked so sad, she felt the urge to hug him, but what good would that do? It would just be giving him false hope, for there could be nothing between them. It was best that she let him down gently, "Sidney, I really am fond of you, and what girl wouldn't be? You're such a kind man and so handsome, to boot!" she teased. "No, seriously, I'm so grateful to you, for I know that without your friendship I would never have been able to cope for as long as I have. Our Sunday afternoons have kept me sane. But now I'm going home, so please be happy for me."

Sidney squeezed her hand, "You'll let me and Samson take you to the station tomorrow? I promise not to have a long face, even though I shall be losing the best friend I've ever had."

The next day Megan and Sidney sat in silence as Samson pulled them slowly toward Temple Meads station. They both dreaded the final parting which was getting closer by the minute. Since arriving in Bristol Megan had prayed for this moment so many times, and yet now that the time had come to leave she had a strange feeling of sadness. It was as if all her dreams of doing something with her life were no longer possible. She was going home, but not in the way she had hoped.

Her dream had been to return home with enough money to support her family, and to make her family proud of her. As it turned out she had failed miserably. She had the intervention of the minister and the benevolence of the mistress to thank for making her return at all possible. And soon, when the truth was known of her condition, she would bring shame to them all.

Megan gave a deep sigh. This was the real world and seldom made out of dreams. She should thank her lucky stars that no one up at the big house had realised she was pregnant, enabling her to leave without everyone thinking ill of her. She reflected that in the eleven months that she had been up at the big house, it hadn't all been bad; she had made some good friends.

This morning before she left, Cook had given her a big hug. "Now you look after yourself, child. I've taken the liberty of packing you a bite to eat for the journey," she said, forcing a smile as she handed Megan a neatly wrapped food parcel. There had been no smiles from Alice and Sally as they gave her a final hug.

They actually cried and told her how much they would miss her. Sadie simply wished her well. Megan suspected that secretly she was pleased to see the back of her. She never liked sharing Alice's friendship. Percy shyly offered a handshake by way of a goodbye, expecting Megan to do the same. Instead she placed a tender kiss on his cheek, making him blush and bringing a cheer from all the girls.

Megan had been taken aback to find that Mistress Fothergill had taken the time to write Megan a glowing reference, saying how honest, trustworthy and hardworking she was.

As usual Lizzie was conspicuous by her absence. This came as no surprise to Megan, having finally worked out why Lizzie had been so keen for her to take up the position at the house. At first Megan didn't want to believe that her cousin deliberately set her up to be a plaything for Master Harold, but she now believed that Lizzie had planned it right from the start.

"Well, here we are," Sidney said, as he turned Samson toward the imposing entrance of Temple Meads station.

"Whoa, Samson." Sidney pulled the horse to a stop outside the large ornate stone archway leading to the platforms. "You go on in and get your ticket, I'll follow with your suitcase as soon as Samson's tied up."

As Sidney helped her down from the wagon, Megan gently patted Samson's mane. She was too choked up to speak, so instead she hastily walked away. Saying goodbye was going to be even more difficult than she'd imagined. By the time she had purchased her one-way ticket, Sidney had caught up with her, and together they made their way to Platform 14, where the train to Cardiff stood waiting for her to board.

"Will you write and let us know you got home safely?" Sidney shouted above the noise of the train's engine as it started up.

"Yes, of course I will. I'll write to your mother. I think that's best, don't you?" Megan saw the disappointment on Sidney's face, but she knew she had to be cruel to be kind. In her condition, she had to make a clean break. He would thank her in the end.

She boarded the train and Sidney slowly closed the carriage door behind her, then reaching through the open window he grabbed her hand, not wanting to let her go. It was then the finality of it all hit her. Why hadn't they said more on the journey to the station?

144

She suddenly realized how much they had left unsaid. She looked into his eyes and without having to say a word she knew that he felt the same. Lifting his hand, she brushed a kiss across his palm.

The engine noise grew louder and louder, indicating the train's immediate departure. As the train slowly began to move away from the platform, Sidney was forced to release her hand from his grasp.

"I'll never forget you," she called, as the train started to gather speed.

Sidney raised his arm in a final wave. "I love you," he shouted, and although she could not hear him she easily read his lips.

Megan didn't want to move from the window, she wanted to keep Sidney in her sight for as long as possible. If the circumstances were different, it would have been so easy to fall for him. As it was she must be content to love him like a brother.

"Please take your seat, miss. I need to secure all doors and windows." Reluctantly, Megan followed the guard's instructions.

On finding her seat she settled down for the long journey to Cardiff. Once there she would change trains before proceeding to Llan. She didn't want to think about Sidney, it was much too painful. So instead she looked forward to once again seeing her beloved brother Jess. In his last letter he had been so excited about her returning to the fold. He said the first thing they would do would be to walk together to the top of Carn Mountain like they always used to with Dad, and he promised that not even their step-father could stop him from meeting her at the train station.

She thought it a strange thing for him to say, but shrugged it off. The main thing was he had promised to meet her and take her *home*.

CHAPTER
EIGHT

Jess hurried from the colliery. He couldn't wait to get to the manse — if he lived there for the next twenty years he would never be able to call it home. But that didn't matter, in less than two hours his Megan would be arriving at Llan station. He had managed to bribe the foreman with a packet of baccy to let him leave the pit an hour early. A quick bath and a change of clothes, and he would be on his way to catch the now regular charabanc. What a difference this new service had made to the village folk. It was hard to believe that many of his fellow workers had never been further than Ponty, which was only a mile away.

Although Jess couldn't wait to see Megan, he really didn't want to be the one who had to bring her down to earth with a jolt. He knew that she truly believed that her speedy return was due to the family's change in circumstances and that all in the garden was rosy, but she was in for a rude awakening when she discovered the real reason she had been brought back.

He had found out the day after poor Olive, who had fallen sick with scarlet fever, had been taken away by ambulance to Blackmill Isolation Hospital. Jess had been about to enter the parlour when he heard the minister and his mother.

"Elias, may I speak with you?" he heard his mother meekly ask.

"Yes, but please make it brief. I have a sermon to write." The minister's voice sounded impatient.

"I have something to tell you: Elias, I am with child. We are going to have a baby."

Jess stepped back from the door. He felt sick. It had suited him to believe that his mother's marriage had been purely one of convenience. He didn't want to believe that they actually shared a marital bed. Now his worst fears had been confirmed.

"Well, praise be to God that he has seen fit to bless me with a true son, even if you, my dear, are not as ardent in the bedchamber as I could wish, often making me remind you of your wifely duties. You are such a cold bedfellow, it makes me wonder how you ever managed to give birth to six brats."

"I'm not getting any younger, Elias. I had thought that my days of childbearing were over. And to be honest, I do feel that I am not carrying this child as well as I did the others."

"Nonsense. You imagine it, woman. I hope you do not expect me to pay for help around the house. How untimely it is that Olive has been taken away to the infirmary. You shall have to make sure Phyllis does more to help you, and from now on you must look after yourself. I forbid you to do anything that may endanger the birth of my son."

148

"Maybe it would be a good idea to bring Megan back from Bristol." His mother's voice sounded shaky, as if frightened.

"Oh, not that old chestnut again . . . you keep on and on about your precious Megan. Haven't I got enough of you to feed and clothe already? Mind you, with Olive gone we do need someone to look after the house and keep those unruly little ones under control. And in the not too distant future, you shall have your work cut out giving *all* your attention to my son. Mmm, maybe it's not such a bad idea after all. I shall think about it."

A week later, just before the minister left for a chapel meeting in Bristol, he informed the family of his intention to call on the mistress of Redcliffe House and request Megan's return to the fold. While the rest of the family cheered, Jess said nothing, for he knew the truth: that Elias Braithwaite only wanted Megan in his house as yet another unpaid skivvy.

Jess's first instincts regarding the minister had been proved right, although he took no pleasure in the fact. On the contrary, he would have loved to have been proved wrong, but since the marriage the minister had shown his true colours. It was as if he were two people, a tyrant to his new family when at home and yet appearing so saintlike when taking service at his chapel. Recently the minister had been putting more and more work on to the little ones and it was obvious to Jess that they feared their stepfather. He also suspected that with the minister's uncontrollable temper, he might have been striking out at them, although this was something they fiercely denied whenever Jess questioned them, blaming their many visible bruises on silly accidents.

Jess had become very restless, helped no doubt by the knowledge that he was no longer the head of his family. In fact, just his presence in the same house as the minister had begun to cause tension between his mother and her new husband. With Jess looking so much like his dad, he was a constant reminder of the husband she had loved and lost.

At last Jess had arrived at the manse. He slowly opened the kitchen door and listened. He was in luck, there was no one at home. He didn't want his stepfather to know he had skived off work early to meet Megan, for it would surely lead to another argument. He rushed upstairs to the washroom. He usually liked a long hot soak but a quick bath would do today, as he didn't want to risk being late for his Megs.

As Jess undressed he caught sight of his reflection in the small mirror on the side of the bed. In the time Megan had been away, how he'd changed. Twelve months of wielding a heavy pick-axe underground had help build a strong, muscular, body and changed a boy into a man.

Dressed in his Sunday best he made his way downstairs but when he heard the minister's raised voice he sensed something amiss.

"Right, girl. It's the strap for you. You've been told time and time again. Well, let's see what effect a good hiding has on you." The minister's angry voice bellowed from the kitchen.

150

"I'll be a good girl, I p-promise. P-Please, not the strap, it really hurts."

As Jess burst open the kitchen door, his eyes went straight to young Phyllis cowering against the heavy wooden door leading to the hallway. The minister was slowly removing his thick leather belt from his waist and walking towards her.

"You leave her alone," Jess shouted at him, as he rushed across the room to his sister.

"I won't mitch from school again, honest, Jess." Phyllis looked up into Jess's face, her eyes pleading with him to help her.

He put his arm around her, "Don't worry, Sis. I'll not let him hurt you." He didn't care what she had done. In his mind, nothing warranted this man taking his belt to her. He turned to face the minister who had stopped about a foot away from them.

"Stand aside, son." The minister's voice had become quieter, almost persuasive. Jess suspected it to be a ploy, but he would not be moved.

"I'm not your son! I'd be ashamed to be related to you. Call yourself a man of God? You're such a hypocrite."

"The girl has done wrong. It'll be for her own good. I believe if you spare the rod, you spoil the child." His voice was almost melodic with its highs and lows. It was as if he were giving a sermon.

"I would rather believe my own father. He always said, 'In attempting to knock one devil out, you let a dozen more in.' So I'll thank you to put that belt down." Jess surprised himself, for, as he stood up to this large man, he felt no fear.

"Get out of my way or I'll give you some as well." The minister spat every word.

"I've stayed quiet for far too long, and so has my mam. Well, not any more! You lay one hand on her and I'll bloody well kill you. Do you hear?"

The minister answered by swiftly raising his belt in the air and bringing it down with force across the side of Jess's face.

"Jess! Jess!" Phyllis screamed.

Jess made a grab for the belt before it could be raised again, but the minister had other ideas and pulled it away.

"Think you're man enough to stand up to me then do you, *boy?*"

"Phyllis, go find Mam."

The young girl started to move but stopped when the minister screamed, "Don't you dare move. I'm the head of this house, so you *will* do as I say, do you hear?" His face had become bright red and distorted.

"Phyllis, don't listen to him. You go now! Find Mam. She's probably visiting Mamgu." Jess was relieved to see his sister open the kitchen door and run down the garden path.

"You-you upstart. Too big for your boots you're getting. I think it's time I taught you a lesson in obedience." The minister lunged at Jess, the hand holding the belt again raised and ready to strike. Jess put his arm up to protect himself from the blow, but too late . . . crack . . . the belt landed across his head

. . . crack . . . this time the belt hit his shoulder. Jess grabbed the minister's arms and struggled to fight him off, but there was no denying the minister was very strong. He pushed Jess, causing him to stumble backwards over the table . . . crack . . . the belt hit the table, only just missing the left side of his head. Jess hit out wildly with his fists catching the minister on the chin, making him momentarily lose his balance, and giving Jess just enough time to gather himself.

The minister collected himself, "I'll show you who's boss . . . when I've finished with you, you'll be screaming for mercy!"

He stood with the belt poised and Jess knew he somehow had to take man and belt if he were to have a chance of saving himself. Almost instinctively he lunged as if making a rugby tackle, so that they both fell heavily on to the flagstone floor. Jess heard a loud thud. The minister's head hit the hard surface. His whole body suddenly became still . . .

Jess, shaken by the heavy fall, lay on top of his stepfather for a while before raising himself up. He couldn't believe he'd actually knocked the minister out cold, and felt a sense of pride. It was then he noticed the pool of blood under the minister's head. The minister lay totally motionless — he had stopped breathing.

"What have you done, son?" He could hear his mother's voice, but could neither answer nor move his body. It was as if he were frozen to the spot. "Jess, *bach*. I think he be dead."

It was coming up to five o'clock and beginning to get dark when Megan's train arrived at Llan. As she made her way excitedly from the station and into the cold night air she gave a shiver. She had forgotten how much colder it was it Wales. In her letters to Jess she had often joked that the temperature was at least two overcoats warmer in Bristol, but she didn't mind the cold; it felt so good to be back that she would allow nothing to dampen her spirits — even when there was no sign of Jess she simply told herself that he must have been held up somehow, and that if she headed in the direction of home she was bound to meet up with him.

She hadn't walked far when she noticed about ten young lads standing on Llan square. As she approached, one of them turned to face her.

"Hello there. Just got off the train from Cardiff, have we? And here to visit someone up the valley, I don't doubt. What's your name, then? Maybe I can help."

Megan had missed the natural way everyone quizzed newcomers — it was a great feather in one's cap to find out the answers before the gossips got started.

Megan decided to oblige this inquisitive young lad.

"My name's Megan Williams. My family live in Nantgarw at the — the manse." It felt strange to give the manse as her home address.

"Then you must be Jess Williams's sister. The one who's been working away in Bristol, is it?"

"Yes, that's me."

"Well, indeed to goodness, Jess will be pleased to see you," the lad said, urgently shaking her hand, "We all know Jess, don't we lads? He works the same shift as us

154

down the Ffalldau. He's a great *buttie* to have I can tell you, and he's always telling everyone how proud he is of you, and I can see why. You're a real smasher."

With ten pairs of eyes staring at her, she suddenly felt embarrassed and looked away. She wondered if these lads, and more especially, her brother would change their attitude when they found out that she was with child. Up to now she'd managed to put her condition to the back of her mind, almost denying it, but she knew her family needed to know the truth of her predicament. And sooner rather than later. They deserved that much from her.

"Well, it's your lucky day, for there's a charabanc due any time now. It's well worth the thrupenny fare to save the long walk, I can tell you."

Jess had written, telling her about the new twice-weekly charabanc service to and from the valley.

"Thank you. I wasn't much looking forward to walking all the way in the dark."

"Where's Jess, then? I thought he would have been here to meet you."

"He must have been held up," she said, still not really put out by Jess's lateness. "Do you think, if I catch the charabanc, that we may cross?"

"Not if we all keep a look out for him, hey lads."

They all nodded their assurance.

It wasn't long before the charabanc arrived, not as grand as the ones in Bristol, but just as welcome. Megan boarded, then, after first handing the fare to the driver's assistant, made her way to a seat in the middle of the vehicle.

"Nantgarw Square is it?" the driver called out to her. "Visiting are we?"

Megan was about to answer him when the young lad she'd been speaking to earlier saved her the trouble.

"She's Jess Williams's sister. You know, his mother's not long married minister Braithwaite."

"Well now, there's a thing," They were talking about her as if she were not there. But she didn't object, it just made her smile to herself. "Well now, there's a thing," the driver repeated, as he turned to eye her from top to toe before moving off.

Megan was glad she'd worn her loose fitting overcoat. She had become expert at hiding her growing bulge, something she needed to continue doing for a little while longer if she didn't want the gossips to know yet. As the charabanc moved off a group of men seated at the back began to sing in unison, giving a haunting rendition of "Myfanwy", and with it, for Megan, a true welcome home. It had been so long since she'd heard any Welsh singing.

As the open charabanc gathered speed, brisk cold wind brushed across her face and through her hair, and she instinctively pulled the collar of her coat up to her chin. She wished it hadn't become so dark so soon. She had been so looking forward to seeing, once again, the true splendour of the Carn mountain and surrounding valley, but all she could see was blackness, periodically lit by gas lamps. Still, she told herself, there would be plenty of time for that. She was home now, home with Mam, with Jess and the little ones. Tomorrow, she and Jess would go for a long walk and he could tell her

156

more about this man who was her new stepfather. She frowned to herself, uneasy at the thought of living with a stranger. But now was not the time for such fears. She stared into the darkness. Where had Jess got to? It was so unlike him to let her down.

They had been travelling for about ten minutes when the charabanc stopped to pick up another passenger — a rather large lady who seemed to be having trouble getting on. Megan strained her eyes and could just make out the old chapel at Tylagwyn, which meant they were only three miles from Nantgarw.

"There we are, Mrs Griffith, sit yourself down by there," she heard the driver's assistant say, as he gently steered the lady towards the seat in front of Megan.

The lady sat down with a hard thump, her large backside taking most of the bench seat.

"Heard the news?" The lady wasn't speaking to anyone in particular, but her tone was that of someone with a juicy bit of gossip, and instantly drew everyone's attention. "There's been a fight up at the manse. My Trevor arrived home not thirty minutes since. Apparently both Doctor Lewis and Sergeant Price have been called. My boy was with Sergeant Price when he got the call . . . not that my Trevor has done anything wrong, you understand . . . just a little misunderstanding. Anyways, I got it first-hand that someone has been seriously hurt and there may even be need of my services."

Megan saw one of the passengers lean over and whisper in the old lady's ear, resulting in her quickly turning to face Megan. It was then that Megan recognized her. She was *the* Mrs Griffith — the lady who laid out the dead. Suddenly, every eye seemed to be on the two of them, and as Mrs Griffith smiled at her, Megan went cold.

"I shouldn't worry yourself, *bach*. My boy's probably got it all wrong, he's always been a bit fanciful, look you."

Megan wanted so much to believe her, even though part of her knew she was telling lies. But what if it were true and there had been a fight at the manse . . . who could have been involved? One thing was for sure, it had to be serious for the sergeant and the doctor to be called? Her mind started racing. Dear God, if Mrs Griffith was needed, then someone must be dead.

"Nantgarw Square," the driver called out.

Megan jumped from her seat and off the vehicle almost before it had time to stop, ran across the square, then up the hill passed Tom Bara's bakehouse and into James Road, where she used to live with her family. Along the familiar dimly lit street of terraced houses she saw some of her old neighbours standing on their doorsteps, all of them looking in the direction of the manse. Megan did the same, and saw the large stone building standing high on the mountainside. It looked even more imposing than Megan remembered. She found it hard to believe that this was her family's new home, it looked so inviting with every window lit by bright candlelight, although something told her that it was not normal for every room to be occupied. She had a sickening feeling of impending doom . . . that something terrible had happened up at the manse.

158

As she raced past the folk in the street, she heard her name mentioned.

"That's Megan. Mary Braithwaite's eldest daughter. She's in for a shock, that's for sure."

Someone called out, "Hello, Megan, love. Glad you've come home, your mam will be so glad to see you." She didn't stop to find out who it was, she was in too much of a hurry to get to her family. At the end of James Road, as she ran up the steep pathway leading to the manse, she saw two automobiles and a bicycle parked in the lane. Instantly she recognized all three vehicles: the bicycle belonged to Doctor Lewis, the little black boxcar to Sergeant Price and there could be no mistaking Tommy Bevan's big black hearse.

As she opened the front gate fear gripped every breath she took. Her feet raced up the garden path and then, as she drew nearer to the house, she slowed almost to a stop, afraid of what she would find . . .

Then the door opened and she came face to face with Sergeant Price. Behind him . . . her Jess.

"Megan . . . Oh Megs . . . What a homecoming! I'm so very sorry . . . please forgive me," her brother pleaded.

As Sergeant Price moved closer, she saw the shiny metal handcuffs joining him to Jess.

"Whatever's happened? Where are you taking him?" Megan stood in their path.

"Megan, I didn't mean to kill him, honest. He fell back and hit his head, *I* didn't do it!" Jess looked so big and strong and yet at the same time so vulnerable.

She threw her arms around him, "Jess, *bach* . . . Jess, *bach*," was all she could say.

"Stand aside, Megan. Go into the house, your mam needs you. The doctor is already with her." Sergeant Price took her arm and pulled her away from Jess. "I'm taking your brother to the station. Some people are coming up from Cardiff. They want to speak to him 'bout this matter, see. So it's best you let us be on our way."

"Go and see Mam, Megan . . . make sure she's all right. I'll be OK, I promise," Jess called, as the sergeant escorted him down the path and into his waiting car.

She stood frozen to the spot, watching the brother she had so been looking forward to seeing being driven away.

Only when the car was out of sight did Megan step into the house.

"Come on in, Megan." She heard the familiar voice of Doctor Lewis. "Not much of a homecoming for you, child, is it? Still, I'm glad you're here, I'm sure you'll be a great comfort to your mother. In the next few days you'll find that she's going to need your support more than ever."

"I'll be here for her, Doctor," Megan assured him. Then looking past him she saw the pale figure bending over the kitchen table, sobbing.

"Mam!" Megan cried out.

On hearing Megan's voice, Mary Braithwaite looked up, then with arms outstretched, she cried, "Megan! Oh, Megan love, have you heard what's happened? It's too terrible — I can't believe it. Elias is dead . . . and they have taken our Jess . . ."

Megan ran to her mother, throwing her arms around her. To her surprise she saw her mother was heavy with child. Her mother's sobs told her this was not the time for any questions, she just hugged her and said, "I know, Mam."

"The children are at *Mamgu*'s, Megan. I thought it best that they were out of the way whilst all this business is going on."

Megan just nodded her agreement to the doctor.

With that the parlour door opened and Tommy Bevan entered, leaving the door open just long enough for Megan to catch a glimpse of a large dark coffin on the table in the parlour. At that moment she thought of Mrs Griffith. No doubt, with the minister being so well off the doctor must have called the undertaker to see to the body; there would be no need of the old lady's services after all. Suddenly the whole house felt dark, dreary and almost . . . evil. Megan couldn't believe this was her new home.

That night Megan's mother was in a terrible state. She couldn't stop crying. Megan tried to comfort her, but how could you bring comfort to someone who had just lost her husband at the hands of her beloved son? Fortunately, Doctor Lewis had prescribed a mild sedative which sent her into a deep sleep. He was also able to explain her sister's absence. He told her that Olive had been struck down with scarlet fever and that a place had been found for her at the isolation hospital in Blackmill. Apparently, the fever had been rife throughout the valley, some of the elderly and very young had even died, "But your sister is going to be fine. We caught it in time," the doctor assured her.

She wondered why Jess hadn't written and told her about Olive or for that matter her mother's pregnancy, but she put it to the back of her mind. At present she had more than enough to worry about. She suddenly felt very tired. It had been a long day and, as much as she longed to see the children, she was glad they were staying the night at *Mamgu's*.

The next morning Megan stared at her mother hunched over the kitchen sink. She thought her to be about five to six months pregnant — about six weeks more than Megan herself. Megan understood how much of a shock last night's events had been to them all, which explained her mam's red-rimmed eyes and her pale complexion, but not how very ill she looked, nothing like the picture of health Megan remembered when Mam had been pregnant with Phyllis and Evan. She wondered how her mother was going to cope with the fact that in less than a week she would have the minister's funeral to deal with.

"Mam," she said softly. "Jess didn't mean it. He would never do such a thing to hurt you on purpose. It was an accident."

Her mother turned to face her, eyes fixed on Megan's with sudden doubt. "Was it? Was it really an accident? Can I believe him?"

"Mam, how can you say such a thing?"

Her mother shook her head. "You never saw them together. Megan, Jess hated my husband. I knew that

162

only too well from the start, but I had no choice. We needed a roof over our heads. You see, *cariad*, after your dad died . . ."

"I understand, Mam, it's all right."

Her mother's fist clenched into a ball of despair on top of her swollen belly. "Then why couldn't Jess understand? Why did he have to —?" Her voice broke, leaving the words unsaid.

Megan walked over to her mother and put a reassuring arm round her meagre shoulders. "Because he's a man, Mam."

Her mother rested her throbbing head against her daughter's cool cheek. "Thank the Lord you're here, Megan."

How Megan herself coped with the events following Jess being taken into police custody, she never knew. She blamed herself. If only she had heeded Jess's early doubts about the minister, or worked harder to send extra money home — perhaps then, her mother wouldn't have needed to marry anyone. Megan even wondered if she should have listened to Lizzie and encouraged Master Harold, for there was no doubting that he would have been more than generous, but she knew whatever the fate of her family, that was one thing she could never have done. No, now that she was back home she had to think positive and make amends the only way she knew how — by being there for her family.

Since Sergeant Price had taken Jess away from the house, the borough coroner had remanded him in custody pending an official inquest. Megan immediately applied to visit him but had been refused. There would be no visitors, family or otherwise, until after the inquest, scheduled to be heard the following week.

The next seven days seemed endless, yet life at the manse somehow managed to take on a strange normality; Bryn continued to work the night shift down the pit, while Megan and her mother went through the motions of cooking and cleaning, trying to act as normally as possible, each putting on a brave face for the sake of the children. It was strange how Phyllis and Evan, as if sensing the atmosphere, never once asked after Jess or their stepfather. They seemed quite happy to go along with the charade of pretending all was well. But when they were safely tucked up in bed it became a different matter. Then, Megan and her mother would sit in front of the kitchen fireplace to consider Jess's fate. They were both anxious about the inevitability of his committal for trial, and it was on one such night that Mary Braithwaite confided her innermost fears.

"Come here, child. I have something I must tell you," she said, taking Megan's hand and gently pulling her to sit beside her chair.

As Megan positioned herself on the floor she looked up into her mother's eyes, eyes so full of pain and anguish, encircled by dark rings and sunk back into a face so pale and drawn, and so different to the once smiling, rounded, healthy-looking face Megan so vividly remembered of old.

"Whatever's wrong, Mam, do you feel unwell? Is it the baby?" Megan lay her head on her mother's lap. As

164

she pressed her face softly against her stomach, she couldn't help but notice how small the bump was for a woman nearly six months gone, and so unlike all her mother's earlier pregnancies, when she had looked so healthy and the size of a small house.

"No, child, it not be the baba. It be me . . ." She hesitated as if not wanting to go on, then, "Oh Megan, love, your mam feels so ashamed. You see, I don't think I can face going to visit your brother. The thought of seeing him, or for that matter any other child of mine, locked up like some wild animal be too much for me to bear."

Megan made to raise her head, but her mother's hand stopped her, as if not wanting to meet her gaze.

"You don't have to tell me, child. I know I must find the courage from somewhere, he will expect me to be there, to help him, to give him hope. But how can I? When in truth I feel there be no hope at all . . ." She ended with a long sigh, removing her hand from Megan's head.

Megan responded by shifting on to her knees to face her mother, then, taking hold of her hand she kissed it long and hard.

"But Mam, there is no need for you to go fretting yourself. Doctor Lewis has already told me, with you being so far gone and all, that he thinks it best if you stay away from the gaol. And I agree with him. Anyway, our Jess is only allowed one visitor and I've already written to tell him to expect *me* as soon as I'm allowed."

Her mother simply nodded and gently patted Megan's hand. "You always were such a kind and considerate girl. It be so nice to have you home again. Together I be sure we will get through this ordeal, we have to!"

Megan caught around her mother's waist, "I love you, Mam." Megan clung to her mother and wanted so much to tell her about the baby she herself was carrying. She knew her mother needed to be told soon, but she also knew this was not the right time.

"I love you too, child," her mother whispered.

As expected the coroner's hearing established that there was indeed a criminal case to answer, and shortly afterwards Jess was officially charged with the murder of Elias Braithwaite. With the coroner's inquest completed, the minister's body was released for burial, which coincided with Megan hearing that she could visit Jess. Although she desperately wanted to see her brother, she felt it prudent to wait until after the funeral. Instead, she wrote him another letter, telling him that he was not alone in his ordeal and reassuring him of all the family's continued love and faith. She hoped it would give him the strength to face what she had been led to believe would be a long difficult trial.

As expected the minister's funeral was indeed a big one, with his relatives from down the Gower attending en masse, as did most of his congregation. Among the mourners the feelings toward Megan's mam were definitely mixed. It was obvious to all that many of the villagers pitied her, some even pitied Jess, but as for the minister's relatives they couldn't hide their contempt for Mary Braithwaite and what they called "her brood".

Weeks later, when it became known that the minister had left all his worldly possessions — worth quite a substantial amount of money — to his wife, his family's first reaction had been to contest the will immediately. But when the elders of the church heard about this they intervened, pointing out that to prevent his wife, who was after all carrying the minister's child, from receiving what was rightly hers by law would not be considered a Christian act — and they eventually backed down.

CHAPTER
NINE

"I'm here to see Jess Williams." Megan said. She kept her voice resolute, her head held high.

The police officer peered over his desk. "And you are?"

"Megan Williams, sir. I'm here to see my brother, Jess Williams," Megan repeated. She had never been in a police station before but she was determined not to let the grim surroundings intimidate her.

"Well, Megan Williams, you had better follow me." The guard's hand lifted a bunch of keys from a hook on the wall behind him, "This way, miss," he said, walking off. She followed the officer in silence down a dark narrow corridor, until he stopped outside a large metal door and turned to her.

"Your brother is due to be moved to Cardiff Gaol to await trial, but we haven't got a date yet. While your brother is held here at Bridgend police station, he will be allowed one visitor for one hour a week. Other than his counsel, Mr Charles Joseph, that is."

"His counsel? I don't understand. We can't afford —"

"Don't worry, miss. Mr Joseph has been appointed by the courts to act on your brother's behalf and a lucky man he is too, having such a fine solicitor fighting his corner."

"I'm sure my brother doesn't think himself at all *lucky*," Megan snapped.

"Quite. Anyway, in you go, miss," he said, noisily unlocking the door, "I shall return in an hour."

As she entered, Jess walked towards her arms outstretched, his shirt-sleeves rolled up showing strong, sun-tanned arms. Megan couldn't believe how much he had changed since she had been away. He stood at least a foot taller than herself. Her beloved Jess was no longer a boy but a fine strong-willed young man.

He flung his arms around her, embracing her. "Megs, Megs, it's so good to see you."

"Oh, Jess, I'm so sorry. I should have been there for you, I should have listened . . ."

Jess released her. "I didn't mean to kill him. I only wanted to stop him hitting Phyllis," he spoke softly, his eyes intent on hers. She realized that while his overall appearance might have changed, deep down he was still the same sensitive young boy she had left behind.

"I know, Jess, *bach*. Even before Mam told me all about it, I knew it must have been an accident. I believe you, and so will the court, you'll see."

He swallowed hard.

They stood for a while just staring at each other, so relieved to see each other once again.

"Shall we sit?" Jess eventually asked, leading her over to a small table in the corner of the small, box-like room. "We haven't got long and there's so much I want to know." He had composed himself, but she could tell it was just an act put on for her benefit.

"Mam sends her love, she's holding up well. She wanted to come but in her condition . . ." Megan instantly touched the front of her coat, hoping her own bulge was not showing. She had to keep it hidden, at least, until she found a way to tell her mother.

"The police officer told me that you have a solicitor working for you."

"I don't know about working for me. It seems to me that Mr Joseph is working for the court. He says I should plead guilty to wilful murd — but it was an accident. We had a fight."

"What did you fight about, Jess?"

"Oh Megs, you didn't know him. He was a lying, vicious bully who was knocking the little ones about." His face hardened and Megan flinched at the sight of such bitterness in his eyes. "It *was* an accident, Megan. I honestly didn't mean to kill the man. But by God, he deserved to die."

"And does Mam deserve to lose her husband, her eldest son and maybe even her unborn baba?"

Jess dropped his head in his hands, but said nothing.

She gently touched his dark hair. "How are they treating you here?"

With a visible effort, he composed himself once again. "If I'm honest, it's really not too bad here. The officers are friendly enough. Although I've been told it'll be different if . . . when I'm sent to a proper prison." He gave a shiver as if the very thought was more than he could bear.

"How do you manage to sleep in such a small bed?" Megan asked pointing to the iron framed bed up against the opposite wall. She didn't want to consider the prospect of her brother maybe spending years locked up in prison. "Why, that bed is even smaller than the one I had at Redcliffe House."

"Oh, Megs, there's selfish I've been. I haven't even asked how you are. How awful for you, having to come home to this lot. I bet you were so looking forward to being home, and all. Tell me, how is Olive? Is she still at Blackmill?"

"Yes, she's still at the infirmary but she's on the mend. With a bit of luck she'll be home soon. As for me I am very glad to be home. It means I can at least be here for you, Mam and the little ones."

"It doesn't seem fair, Megs. You shouldn't have to look after us all. I so wanted to be the one who looked after the family."

"I know, Jess. But we'll be fine, you'll see."

The door behind her opened. "Time's up, miss. I'm afraid you'll have to go."

They both stood up. Megan hugged her brother and after placing a soft kiss on his cheek, whispered in his ear, "Try to be strong. You can get through this. Just remember that we all love you."

As she turned to leave, she saw him straighten his broad shoulders and her heart went out to him. She managed to stay strong long enough to thank the constable for looking after her brother, and only when she was well clear of the police station did she finally give way to tears.

Three days later Jess was brought up on remand before the stipendiary magistrate, Sir Edward Rees-Jones.

Jess pleaded not guilty.

The magistrate committed him to trial at the Summer Assizes to be held on 20 July 1920 on the charge of murder. No bail order was issued. Jess would be held in custody at Cardiff Gaol, "for his own safety". The police feared, if he were allowed out on bail, the minister's many followers might attempt to take the law into their own hands. On hearing this news, Mary Braithwaite went into premature labour and gave birth to a baby boy. Sadly he was stillborn.

In the days that followed Mary Braithwaite, by way of coping with her loss, kept herself busy — which wasn't difficult, with the family once again on the move. It had come as no surprise when two of the chapel elders had called to see her. They apologized for having to call and hoped she wouldn't think they were at all unsympathetic, with her losing the baby . . .

"And having, er, such a worry r-regarding your, er, eldest s-son, look y-you," Idris Lloyd stammered.

The way he couldn't even bring himself to mention Jess by name wounded Mary Braithwaite. It was as if to speak his name would be an admittance of how well he knew him — with Jess having practically grown up with his son John. For years John Lloyd and Jess had been inseparable, until Jess had to leave school to go work down the pit. John, on the other hand, with his father a teacher at the school, managed to stay on and continue his education and had even gone on to university.

"What Idris is trying to say, Mrs Braithwaite, is that the chapel has managed to find a replacement for your husband, a young man, newly ordained and married with a young family. As I am sure you will understand, he is keen to take up residence at the manse, and therefore it is with great regret that we have to ask you to vacate, and hope you won't find it too difficult to find other accommodation." Dai Morgan rubbed his hands nervously.

Mary Braithwaite was tempted to let them sweat for a bit. They were such weak men. The irony of her situation was not lost to her. Once again, for whatever reason, her family was being evicted. At least with her new-found wealth she could make sure it never happened again. With this in mind she decided to put her visitors out of their misery.

"Now, don't you gentlemen go fretting yourself. I quite understand the position and I have already made arrangements to move out this coming Saturday."

The look of relief on both men's faces spoke volumes.

"So, what do you all think then?" Mary Braithwaite stood behind the counter of her newly purchased drapery shop just a mile away in Oxford Street, Ponty.

"Is it really ours?" Bryn asked, as Phyllis and Evan went exploring at the back of the shop.

"It certainly is — lock, stock and barrel. I'm sorry I couldn't mention it sooner. I thought it best to wait until it was all signed and sealed. A case of not counting chickens . . . well, anyways, it's ours. And we move in on Saturday. There's a huge flat above the shop where we're all going to live, and this time no one can ever move us out! Come on, you lot, Megan's upstairs waiting to show you all around."

"I wish she'd bought a sweet shop," Evan whispered.

"Me too," agreed Phyllis.

The decision to purchase the drapery shop had not been taken lightly. After many nights of discussion, Megan, Mamgu Williams and Mary Braithwaite all came to the conclusion that the time was right for change. With Phyllis and Evan both at school, Bryn working full time down the pit, Olive soon to be released from Blackmill Hospital with a clean bill of health, which meant she would soon be able to take on light duties around the flat, this would leave Megan free to help in the shop, and with Mary Braithwaite's natural skill as a seamstress, it made good business sense for her to undertake personally all of the customers' sewing needs. Added to this she hoped that, with all the family busy concentrating on the new venture, it would take their minds off Jess's wretched predicament.

It was Sunday morning in early June. Megan stood looking out of the kitchen window on to Oxford Street. With all the shops closed there was an eerie yet enjoyable silence. So far "flaming June" was more than living up to its name. With temperatures well up in the seventies there could be no mistaking, summer had definitely arrived. She felt hot and uncomfortable, not helped by the woollen cardigan she was wearing to

174

cover her now large stomach. She glanced across to her mother who was at the sink, busy preparing lemonade in readiness for Bryn, Phyllis and Evan's return, who, with it being so warm and all, had decided to go for a paddle up in the mountain brook. Olive had gone to see Mamgu. So there was no excuse, she had her mother to herself . . . there would never be a better time.

"Mam," she said, taking a deep breath, "I've got something to tell you."

"You have, have you? Could it be you've finally decided to tell me about the baba you be carrying?" Her mother turned to face her.

Megan looked to the floor, feeling embarrassed and ashamed.

"Did you really believe that I wouldn't notice that great bump of yours? The truth be I've known since the day you first arrived back home. I said naught, waiting for you to tell me. I was beginning to think I'd have to wait until the actual birth."

"I'm sorry, Mam. I wanted to tell you, honest. I kept waiting for the right time. The truth is I've been afraid to tell you, afraid you might hate me for bringing you shame . . . Mam, I'm so sorry," she sobbed, as her mother's arms went around her, hugging her.

"You daft ha'peth. How could I ever hate or be ashamed of you? Why, you be carrying my first grandchild and I shall be as proud as punch to show him or her off to all the valley."

"Mam, I'm going to be the talk of the valley."

175

"So what? It'll be nothing but a nine days' wonder. And what I say is, while they be talking about you they shall be giving some other poor bugger a rest."

This made Megan smile, especially as she had never heard her mother utter a swear word before.

"That's more like it. No more tears. You're my daughter, I be proud of all my children and that's a fact."

Megan kissed her mother gently on the cheek, "Thank you, Mam. And thank you for not asking about the baby's father."

"Seems to me, if you wanted me to know you'd have told me long before now." Her mother's voice held not a hint of reproach, she simply continued stirring the lemonade.

As had been expected, the valley gossips did indeed have a field day at the family's expense, with much speculation as to who had fathered Megan's unborn child.

Lizzie slowly opened the small dirty-brown envelope, instantly recognizing the untidy scrawl on the front as that of her mother's. Lizzie wanted desperately to disassociate herself from her family in Wales and her humble beginnings, they didn't feature in any of her plans for the future. Normally, her mother's letters were tedious and full of trivia about her boring family, but this letter was different, the content almost unbelievable . . . First, there was the news that her cousin Jess had been arrested for the murder of his stepfather, and to prove it, her mother had enclosed a cutting from a back issue of the *Cardiff Times*;

On Tuesday, the magistrate formally committed Jess Williams, who gave his address as: The Manse, Higher James road, Nantgarw, for trial at the Assizes, on a charge of murder.

The magistrate added that the accused could be offered bail immediately the proceedings had concluded. Superintendent Ivor Thomas, who along with Detective Inspector Harris had been present all through the hearing, told the court that he would apply for the prisoner to be remanded until the Summer Assizes and would be making an appeal against bail for the prisoner's own safety.

While Lizzie tried to take in the full implications of Jess's arrest, she read on. The second bit of news had her grabbing for the nearest chair. Megan was pregnant! Of course Lizzie's mother had nothing but sympathy for Megan, and hoped that the father of the child would do his duty by her, if only to put a stop to all the gossips.

Lizzie wasn't so benevolent. As far as she was concerned, it served her cousin right. She was always acting sweet and innocent, making out her side of the family was somehow superior to Lizzie's. Now, with her brother on a charge of murder and she a fallen woman, Megan would have to climb down off her high horse. With the letter safely in her pocket, Lizzie made her way to the kitchen, she couldn't wait to tell everyone below-stairs.

As she entered the room, she found them all sitting around the kitchen table. They seemed surprised to see her.

"Look who's decided to grace us with her presence then," Alice said, with a wry look on her face.

Ignoring her sarcasm, Lizzie took the letter from her pocket. Then, not bothering to tell them about Jess's arrest — that could wait until later — she excitedly blurted out the news about Megan's state of health. If she expected the room to erupt with disapproval regarding her cousin's morals, she had been greatly mistaken.

To her surprise the room fell silent. Mrs Partridge's only reaction had been to grab Sidney's hand. He sat with his head bowed, preventing Lizzie, or anyone else for that matter, from seeing the look on his face.

"Well, who'd have thought it, that's what I say. Still, I always knew she was a good actress, always pretending to be what she so obviously wasn't." Lizzie's spiteful tone brought an unprecedented outburst from Sidney.

"Don't you dare talk about Megan in that way! Why, you're not fit to lick her boots. And if you're all wondering — as I suspect you are — who the father is? Well, wonder no more . . . it's me!"

Cook was quickly to her feet. "It's time you all went about your work and I shall tell you only once: if I hear anyone gossiping about what you've just heard there'll be trouble. And as for you — you young madam.

178

People in glass houses shouldn't throw stones. Now should they?" Cook glared at Lizzie who knew better than to enter into an argument with her.

"Well!" was all she said. Then, with a deep defiant grunt, she turned and left the room.

All of the kitchen staff left the table and busied themselves, as Cook had ordered.

Rose Partridge gently touched her son's shoulder as she bent over to whisper in his ear, "I think we should have a private little chat later, don't you?"

Sidney simply nodded his head. Their eyes met, and for a while they just stared at each other, he, wondering if his mother had believed him, and she, feeling proud that her son had lied to defend young Megan.

Lizzie hadn't for one minute believed Sidney Partridge's confession. After all, she was sure she knew the true identity of the culprit, but she was not about to let on. No, her knowledge of Master Harold's involvement she must keep close to her chest until she could decide how best to use it. This could well be the way to rid herself of him once and for all.

Since Megan's return to Wales, Harold had again turned to Lizzie for his pleasures. He, for some inexplicable reason, had expected her to welcome him with open arms — nothing could have been further from the truth. For the last six months she had been walking out with Arthur Walters and didn't want to risk him finding out about her past involvement with Harold. She had too much to lose. Arthur was such a good catch, a respected business man, a man with prospects and a man who she knew wanted her like crazy. She was in no doubt that, if she played her cards right, she could end up becoming Mrs Arthur Walters.

"Well, Ma, I've heard from the brewery in Bridgend, and they have a place for me. I've written to Megan telling her that I should be with her by the end of the month."

"And has she accepted your offer of marriage, Sidney lad?"

"Not yet, Ma, but I'll not take no for an answer. I know she be fond of me and I can be satisfied with that."

"You're one in a million lad. Mind you, I have to say I've a notion who be to blame for her predicament." Rose Partridge well remembered the night Megan had come home soaking wet and had taken to her bed, delirious, and how she called out Harold's name, over and over again. She was obviously terrified of him. She also remembered the episode with young Agnes. "I know one thing, lad, Megan was not to blame. She's a good girl and I shall be more than pleased to have her as a daughter-in-law. I only hope the true culprit gets what he deserves one day."

"I really don't care about him, although I have my suspicions as well. My regret is that I didn't press her to confide in me when I had the chance. She should never have had to shoulder such a burden alone." Sidney vowed never to reproach Megan about her involvement with that blackguard Arthur Walters, although he did have the urge to seek him out and knock him senseless for forcing himself on someone as trusting as Megan. Of course he knew it was out of the question; what

180

good would it do for him to be arrested for assault? His first priority had to be to go to Megan.

"So, you're to leave in under two weeks. Well, Son, I shall miss you, but in my heart I believe you are doing the right thing, and it's not as if you're going a million miles away, is it?"

Sidney walked over to his mother and tenderly placed a kiss on the top of her head.

"Ma, I shall never be far from you, for you will always be in my thoughts."

CHAPTER
TEN

Megan sat patiently waiting for Sidney to arrive. She looked at the clock on the mantelpiece. The charabanc would be reaching Ponty anytime now. So he wouldn't be long.

Her mother was fussing over the tea table, rearranging all the food they had both so carefully laid out over an hour earlier. It was only four-thirty. Olive had offered to stay on in the shop until closing and Bryn had taken the little ones to see Mamgu, promising not to return with them until after six. The plan was to give Megan, Mam and Sidney, time to get acquainted.

"Mam, the table looks fine, honest."

"Well, with his mam being a cook at the big house, and all, I'm sure he be used to a nice spread."

Megan knew Sidney wouldn't care what he had for tea. The only thing he wanted was an answer to the question he had repeatedly asked in his many letters — since cousin Lizzie had chosen to inform all and sundry about her condition — would she marry him? At first she was sure she couldn't — it just wouldn't be fair to him. She wrote back pleading with him not to change his job and move to Wales, but he would not budge. He told her his mind was made up, and if she was honest with herself, she was secretly glad he hadn't listened to her. She was so very fond of him and had really missed his friendship — but marriage?

The knock on the door made her jump.

"That'll be your visitor, no doubt."

Megan needed no prompting from her mother. She was already heading across the small hallway and towards the side door of the apartment. She was pleased they had a private entrance at the side of the shop. She didn't want him to be met with a tirade of nosy questions from the customers in the shop. She opened the door.

The shocked look on Sidney's face said it all.

"Not quite what you were expecting, eh? Don't be embarrassed. I'm used to everyone trying to pretend this bump doesn't exist. I even tried it myself for a while." She gave Sidney a warm smile and patted her rather large stomach. "I know I'm big, apparently Mam was like this on her first, so I s'pose it's only to be expected. Anyway, how was your trip? And how's your mother? Are you OK staying at the Wyndham Hotel? When do you start your new job? What do you think of Wales then?" She knew she was rambling on, but seeing him standing there in his Sunday best suit, looking so attractive, suddenly made her feel very nervous.

"For goodness sake, *cariad*, stop interrogating the lad and ask him in," her mother called from inside.

"Sorry," Megan said, as she stepped back from the door, "please, do come in."

"That's OK. There's going to be plenty of time for me to answer all of your questions. But first you have to answer one."

She didn't know why, but as he walked passed her she had the sudden urge to give him a peck on the cheek. He reacted as if it were the most normal thing for her to do, putting his arms around her and returning her kiss. But his was on her lips.

They stood for a while, just holding on to each other.

"Are you going to bring the lad in to meet your mam, or what?"

"Coming, Mam," Megan answered, taking Sidney's hand and leading him down the hall.

The kitchen was the largest room in the apartment above the shop. It was here that all the family usually converged. The parlour was much smaller, as were the four bedrooms, with the smallest room, the fully equipped bathroom, to be found at the end of the narrow hallway running the length of the apartment and linking every room.

"So you're Sidney?" She was eyeing him from top to toe. "What I know for a fact is that my Megan speaks well of you — but I would still like to know why you should want to marry her?"

"Mam," Megan protested.

"I believe in plain speaking. Call a spade a spade, that's what I say. Sit yourself down, lad." She waited until Sidney did as she asked. "Now, I know you be not the father of Megan's unborn child. So why are you offering to marry her?"

"Mam, please! I —"

184

Sidney interrupted her, "It's all right, Megan. Your mother has the right to know the truth. And the truth is, Mrs Braithwaite, I love Megan — I think I have always loved her. And yes, I do know the baby is not mine, I only wish it were. But if Megan would do me the honour of becoming my wife, I promise to treat the baby as my own. Megan has been wronged by an evil man. I offer marriage, not out of pity, but because I want to protect her and I hope to make her happy." Although addressing Mary Braithwaite, he stared into Megan's tearful eyes.

"Well, you seem to be better informed than the rest of us. Megan has chosen not to name the father — and that be her privilege." Mary Braithwaite stood up, "I shall leave you two alone for a while. We shall eat in about half an hour. Meanwhile, I'll go and give Olive a hand downstairs." As she reached the door leading to the shop, she turned and said, "Megan, I think you have found a good 'un there." And with that she was gone.

"Sorry about that," Megan spoke quietly. "I had no idea she was going to put you on the spot like that. Still you seem to have won her vote anyway."

"But it's your vote I want," Sidney said, taking hold of her hands.

"Sidney? I need to know how you found out about Harold. Is it common knowledge below-stairs?" Embarrassed, Megan fixed her eyes down to his hands, clasped tightly around hers.

"Harold? Master Harold?" He was glad she couldn't see his look of surprise. What a fool he'd been. Of course, it had to have been Harold — the bastard. He quickly composed himself; she would never forgive him if she knew how he'd jumped to the wrong conclusion regarding Arthur Walters.

"I just guessed," he answered. It was better to tell a little white lie than admit to his initial mistake. "Think back. Remember Agnes, the girl you replaced?"

Megan nodded, still unable to look at him.

"Well, I know for a fact she left because of Harold. Why else do you think the mistress gave her money — and not only the train fare home either. It was a large sum by all accounts. I overheard Agnes tell my mother." He wondered why he hadn't remembered it before.

Megan looked up. "I didn't know about Agnes and Harold. Sidney, I'd have done anything for this not to have happened. I feel so ashamed."

"Megan, you have to believe me when I say it wasn't your fault. You were so helpless . . . so alone. Those bloody Fothergills!"

"Oh please, don't blame them all. The mistress has been so kind to me, and I'm sure if she'd known — and if it hadn't been for Master Robert Fothergill —"

"Master Robert? What has he to do with it?"

Megan knew she had come too far to stop now, after all, hadn't Sidney earned the right to know the truth?

"It-it happened my first night alone above-stairs. Harold was hiding in the darkness. He pounced on me taking me by surprise. I tried to fight him off —"

"Megan, you don't need to do this —"

186

"I want you to know. I need to explain about that night. You see, it was Robert Fothergill who came to my rescue, he even fought with his own brother . . . he wasn't to know that Harold would try again . . . and the next time —"

"If I ever get my hands on that bastard Harold, I swear I'll bloody throttle him."

"And what good will that do? You can't change things. What's done is done, and venting your temper is never the answer. Look what it's done for my brother Jess?"

"I'm sorry, Megan. You've already enough to bear. I wasn't thinking."

"Sidney, I need you to believe that I don't hate *all* of the Fothergills."

"No, you're right. The mistress has always done well by everyone and as for Robert Fothergill, if I didn't know it before, I know now, that he truly is a good man. Megan, I meant what I said earlier, I really do love you."

"But Sidney, I —"

"It's OK, I know you don't love *me*. Although I do believe you are fond of me, and that's good enough for me. If you agree to marry me I swear you'll never regret it." He slid from the chair and knelt down beside her. "Megan Williams, will you do me the honour of becoming my wife?"

Megan looked into Sidney's bright blue eyes. Suddenly it became so clear to her. She was being given a second chance at life. Sidney was such a good man.

With him it would be so easy to have a happy and contented marriage.

"Yes, Sidney. I'll be proud to become your wife."

He jumped up off the floor, throwing his arms around her and lifting her off her feet. "I'll go and arrange a special licence first thing in the morning. We'll have to rush if we're to be married before the babe arrives. By the way, I have a request. Would it be all right with you if we let everyone believe that the baby is mine — I so wish it were. This way, I can at least pretend."

Megan put her arms around his neck and kissed him. "Sidney Partridge, you're a man in a million."

For a long while they clung to each other, neither able to believe their good fortune.

"Sorry, Sis. I tried to keep them away longer but they couldn't be persuaded," Bryn apologized, as he entered the kitchen. The young ones rushed past him, crossing the room to where she stood with Sidney.

"Megan, is this your boyfriend, then?" Phyllis giggled.

"Are you going to marry him?" Evan asked.

Before Megan could answer, Phyllis butted in, "Can we come to the wedding then?"

"Yes, yes and yes." Megan answered all three questions at once.

"Congratulations!" Bryn said, taking hold of Sidney's hand and giving it a bold shake. "It's about time this family had something to celebrate."

"Yippee! Mam, Olive, Megan's going to get married, and she said we can all go to the wedding," Phyllis excitedly greeted her mother and sister as they entered the room. Then added, "Can I have a new dress?"

"Does this mean I'll have to have another bath? If so, I don't want to go," Evan informed them all.

Olive and her mother hugged Megan. They didn't need to say a word. Megan could tell by the warmth of their embrace how happy they were for her.

"Bryn, lad, get out that bottle of sherry from the cabinet — tea can wait. We shall all have a glass to toast the happy couple. There be a bottle of Corona pop in the larder for the young ones."

From then on the noise in the room became deafening, with everyone talking at the same time.

Megan took hold of Sidney's hand. "Do you remember the first day we met, when you told me how you could never imagine having such a large family — well this is it. Welcome to the madhouse!"

Two weeks later, on Saturday, 27 June, 1920, at Bridgend Register Office, Megan and Sidney were married. It was a quiet affair with just the close family in attendance and after the ceremony they returned to the flat above the shop for a modest spread. Megan felt it best to keep it simple. She wished Jess could have been there. He had recently been moved to Cardiff Gaol where visiting was restricted to two visitors per inmate for two hours on the first Wednesday of every month. How he must hate it there. Next week she would take Sidney along to meet him and together they would give him the good news.

"Come on, you lot, get a move on. It's time we left the newlyweds alone."

Mary Braithwaite didn't need to ask twice. For the last hour Phyllis and Evan had been eager to leave, excited by the prospect of spending a few nights away at Mamgu's.

"So long, Megs, so long, Sidney," they called as they rushed down the stairs.

"It's been a great day. Pity our Jess couldn't be here, hey?" Bryn said, giving Megan a brotherly hug.

"Don't you worry, Megs. When Jess is released we'll have the party of all parties to celebrate his homecoming. Everyone knows it was an accident, now don't they?" It was Olive's turn to hug her sister.

"I hope so."

"Look after her," Olive said, turning to Sidney.

"I promise, I will."

"Right then, that's that. With tomorrow being Sunday we've all got the day off, so I'll be here first thing Monday morning to open up, you can have the kettle on ready for a brew, if you like." Mary Braithwaite stood with arms outstretched.

"Come here, and give your mother a kiss."

Megan took her mother's hands, "I love you, Mam."

"And I, you. Be happy. It's what your dad would have wanted. He always favoured you, you know. He'd be pleased to know that, like me, you found a good man."

Megan smiled, and nodded in agreement.

Sidney stood up from the table; up to now their wedding evening had gone to plan. While he understood why Megan might feel uncomfortable with the idea of sleeping with him, surely she didn't think he'd be anything like . . . Harold. There, he'd said it. As much as he didn't want to think about his Megan and that bastard, the images, conjured up in his head, just would not go away. He wondered if Megan had somehow read his mind. For the last hour they had hardly spoken, they'd gone through the motion of having a bite to eat, nothing elaborate, just a plate of bread and cheese and some fruit, both only managing to eat a small amount. They spoke only pleasantries, like a pair of strangers, until he could stand it no more.

"It's getting late, love. It's been a long day. Why don't you turn in for the night? I'll clear away the supper dishes and join you shortly."

Megan made her way to the bedroom feeling sick. The time had come, there could be no avoiding what she knew was expected of her. He was her husband, he had the right to lie with her . . . she prayed to God that he would at least be gentle with her.

When Sidney entered the bedroom he found Megan undressed and in bed, tightly clutching the bedclothes around her. "Megan, what's wrong? Are you cold? You're shivering." He didn't undress, but lay beside her, taking her in his arms. Pulling her close, he hugged her.

"Oh, Sidney — I'm so sorry. I'm — acting like — a child."

"Trust me, you're no child. You're a beautiful woman who I have to say I want like mad . . . but I can wait. Did you really believe I was about to demand my conjugal rights? Shame on you. I think too much of the baby you're carrying, I wouldn't do anything to hurt him — or her, or you. You must know that."

She turned her face to his and kissed him, a tender kiss, which he eagerly returned, lingering on her lips for what seemed like minutes.

"Now, Mrs Partridge. While my heart and head wish to keep the promise I just made, I have to tell you, that my body is saying something totally different. And who can blame it. God, I want you — how long, did you say, before this baby's born?"

Megan giggled, she felt so relaxed, so comfortable, and so safe from harm in the arms of this caring, loving man. A man she was so happy to have as her husband.

Megan and Sidney followed the guard, a large rugged faced man, down the long, dark, foul-smelling corridor. Megan grabbed for Sidney's hand. She had spent many a sleepless night wondering what Cardiff Gaol would be like. It was even worse than she had thought: a truly dismal place, dark, damp, dirty and very noisy, with iron doors constantly clanging and banging, and inmates rattling on the bars while shouting obscenities to one another.

"Hey, Fingers, is your missus visiting you today? I hear she's been got at by one of them foreign sailors. If I were you, I should check on the brat's colour when it pops out," one inmate shouted.

"You'd better shut your filthy bloody mouth, or I'm going to shut it for you," came an angry reply.

"I'm due out next week," someone else shouted. "If his missus is so accommodating, maybe I should pay her a visit. Any chance of you putting in a good word for me, Fingers?"

"I recognize your voice, Shaky. If you go anywhere near my wife I'll kill you, you bastard!"

"Shut up the lot of you, or I'll put you on report. A few hours in the hole will soon silence you," the guard warned.

"OK, Boss, we hear you," Fingers answered.

"Good. Now get ready for your visitors before I change my mind."

He ushered Megan and Sidney into a large room filled with lines of chairs set out in front of a long table divided into individual small booths. They were led to the one on the end.

"Sit yourselves down. There is to be no physical contact, and you must speak up at all times," the guard ordered. "Do you understand?"

Megan and Sidney nodded their agreement.

Satisfied, the guard moved to usher other visitors to their designated places.

Jess sat on the other side of the booth, head bent. He looked up, and while his lips forced a smile, his eyes were unable to hide his pain and suffering.

"A bit different to the police station, eh Megs? There's no privacy here, here everyone hears everyone else's business."

"Don't you let that worry you. I'm sure everyone's got better things to do than listen to us. I'm just so happy to see you. How are you? How are they treating you?" She made to reach out, to touch his hand.

The guard coughed. Jess shook his head and pulled away.

"Sorry, Sis, no contact allowed. Anyway, who's this?" he asked looking directly at Sidney.

"Jess. This is Sidney Partridge . . . my-my husband. We were married last Saturday. I'm sorry to spring it on you like this. It all happened so fast . . ."

"And not before bloody time, by the looks of it," Jess said, staring at her open coat.

Megan had given up trying to hide the bulge which seemed to have doubled in size in the month since her last visit.

At first he looked hurt. "You could have told me about the baby." Then, getting to his feet, the look changed to anger. "And where the hell have you been until now?" he spat at Sidney.

"Sit down," the guard ordered. Jess reluctantly obeyed but continued to glare at Sidney.

"Please, Jess. It wasn't his fault. Like you, *he* didn't know. He only found out from Lizzie a few weeks ago. You see he's —"

Sidney quickly interrupted, "Your daft sister thought I would feel trapped and wouldn't want to marry her, when the truth is, I've been in love with her from the very first day I set eyes on her. I want you to know that by becoming my wife Megan has made me the happiest man alive, and I promise you, Jess, that I *will* take good care of her. I know how much she thinks of you, and

194

how much she needs your approval." He caught Megan's hand and gave it a gentle squeeze.

Megan responded with a warm smile, grateful for his timely intervention.

"I'm glad to hear it. If you, or anyone else, ever hurts her, you'll answer to me," Jess snapped.

Megan looked to the floor, afraid her eyes might give away the truth.

"Well, brother-in-law, knowing how stubborn my sister can be, I'm prepared to give you the benefit of the doubt and I wish you both every happiness."

Megan gave a sigh of relief.

"Megan tells me your trial date is set for the twenty-sixth of July. I just want to say that no matter what, we'll be there to give our support, won't we Megs?"

"Of course, every day, for as long as it takes."

"Thanks. It'll be good to see a friendly face. Will Mam be there, Megs?"

"I'm not sure. The thing is she's not been feeling her best since the . . . funeral . . . losing the baby, and all." Megan felt it best to conceal the truth regarding the doubts her mother had about Jess's motives, regarding his stepfather's death.

Jess thumped the table, sending a loud thud around the visiting room. "And it's all my fault! Why did I have to go lose my temper like that, mun? I shouldn't be in here. I should be at home looking after you, Mam and the family."

"And I'm sure, when the court hears the full details of how you were only protecting Phyllis, and how, if the

195

minister hadn't fallen and hit his head on the flag-stoned floor —"

"Megan's right. You've got to keep your spirits up. I'm sure your counsel will put a good case forward," Sidney enthused.

"I'm not so sure. When the bugger first took the case he wanted me to plead guilty! But I told him straight that I wasn't having any of it!"

The court was full to bursting. Most of the people in the public gallery were strangers. Megan wondered what made some people so interested in the trials of others.

Megan, Sidney and her mother sat in the front of the gallery.

"Mam. You've got to go. Jess will be looking to see you there showing your support." Megan had pleaded.

"I know, and, for that reason, on the first day of the trial I intend to be there for him. But, Megs, I really can't sit through days of them going over and over what happened that day."

"I understand. I'm sure Jess will too."

On the second row of the gallery sat the Braithwaite family. The two families didn't acknowledge one another.

Below the gallery, barristers paraded in white wigs and black gowns and what seemed like an army of court officials all talking in low whispers, their conversations hidden by loud excited chatter coming from the majority of those in the public gallery.

As the door opened, Jess was led into the court, surrounded by four prison guards and placed in the dock. He felt everyone's eyes upon him, and he visibly trembled. Suddenly he felt very small.

A court official stood facing the gallery and in a loud voice announced, "Court One — Prisoner at the Bar: Jess Williams. Glamorgan Summer Assizes at Cardiff. Mr Justice Waring. Please rise."

As the judge entered the court everyone stood up and only when the judge duly took his place did the rest of the court sit down.

Jess looked around the court, straight away finding Megan and Sidney and then, eventually, he saw his mother. He'd had to look twice, she looked so different: greyer, thinner . . . older. He caught his breath — he'd done this to her. The fact that he wasn't guilty made not a scrap of difference — he *was* responsible for putting her through this ordeal. He decided to talk to Megan and tell her not to bring Mam to court any more.

He averted his eyes, as he felt the eyes of the judge upon him. Then, to his ears came the distant rumble of a voice full of bitter reproving.

"Jess Albert Williams. You have been charged with the wilful murder of the Reverend Elias Braithwaite. How do you plead?"

Only a long drawn-out sob broke the deadly silence of the court. Jess instinctively knew the sound had come from his mother.

Jess found himself grasping for the wooden rail. Then, slowly he lifted his face and taking a deep breath he stood upright and looked into the stern gaze of the judge. Without hesitation, in a strong voice he declared, "Not guilty."

That first day was to be the only time Mary Braithwaite attended the court. From then on, it was left to Megan and Sidney to make the long journey each day. The case lasted two weeks. And for all Jess's initial doubts, he had to admit that his counsel, Mr Charles Joseph, pleaded his case well. In the end, after hours of deliberation, the jury believed that Jess had not set out intentionally to kill Elias Braithwaite and unanimously agreed on a verdict of manslaughter. Jess was duly sentenced to five years' imprisonment and immediately taken back to Cardiff Gaol.

CHAPTER
ELEVEN

Lizzie cautiously walked towards the large oak tree overlooking Clifton suspension bridge. Her eyes darted nervously about her, straining to see through the blanket of morning mist covering Clifton Downs. She needed to make sure she had not been followed, that Harold had not tricked her. To her great relief there were only a few keen dog walkers far away on the other side of the downs. She could barely make them out so it followed that they would have the same difficulty in seeing her.

With renewed confidence Lizzie bent down to retrieve the small, brown-paper package concealed in the grass at the base of the tree's trunk. The grass glistened with droplets of morning dew, the package felt cold and damp. She tore eagerly at the paper, holding her breath when she saw the contents — a neat pile of large white notes. As her fingers fumbled to count them, she could hardly contain her excitement. There were ten crisp new five pound notes, *fifty pounds*, and it was all hers. She felt quite light-headed and made a grab for the tree to steady herself. She couldn't believe her plan had actually worked, a plan which had been

199

spurred on by the announcement of Master Harold's engagement to Jane Arkwright.

After the announcement the Redcliffe House had simply buzzed with the news of the couple's betrothal. Everyone looked forward to the forthcoming wedding and the party which would no doubt follow ... everyone that was, except Lizzie. All she could feel was hate, with so much venom that it made her stomach churn. She hated Harold for using her, treating her no better than a common whore, like a bug to be swatted away or stepped on at any time. She hated Jane Arkwright for being born upper class, a lady and an undeniable snob, always walking around with her nose held so high in the air it was a surprise she ever managed to see where she was going. Lizzie wondered what gave her the right to look down her nose at anyone? Surely it was only a mere accident of birth which separated Jane from the likes of her, a fact Lizzie found totally unfair, and she vowed somehow to get back at both Harold and Jane.

It wasn't long before Lizzie's devious mind began working overtime, and she realized that with her knowledge of Harold, and especially Megan and her *little secret*, there was money to be made. Surely Harold would give anything to prevent his fiancée finding out about Megan, and the fact that she was carrying his child. Lizzie began to forge the plan to send him an anonymous letter, threatening to tell all unless he agreed to pay cash in return for silence. How she savoured the thought of watching him squirm. To remove herself from suspicion she cleverly sent the

200

anonymous letter inside a food parcel to her mother in Wales, requesting she redirect it. Her unsuspecting mother, believing it to be part of a harmless prank, duly forwarded the sealed letter addressed to: Harold Fothergill, Esquire, The Sportsman Club, Bristol. Lizzie hoped that by sending it from Wales, Harold would suspect Megan. A thought which pleased Lizzie immensely.

The downs had started to grow busy. With the brown-paper package and contents safely hidden beneath her coat Lizzie made her way back to Redcliffe House. She needed to put the money in a safe place away from prying eyes and for the time being her bedroom would just have to do. On her next day off she planned to open a savings account at the bank, for she was sure there was a lot more where this came from, but next time she would demand a hundred pounds. Why not? Harold could afford it.

Harold pondered his predicament. How he wished he'd taken more care concerning his dalliance with that young chit of a parlour maid. For while he had to admit to having enjoyed the planting, he certainly had not bargained on harvesting any fruit! He had been shocked when he read the letter awaiting him at his club, informing him of Megan's state of health, threatening him . . . Demanding money. Of course, with his forthcoming marriage, he had had no choice but to pay up, as he dared not risk a scandal. He would never have believed that such a sweet young girl like

Megan would end up so vindictive. All of his other slip ups had simply asked for help with an abortion.

"Are you all right, my love? You seem preoccupied," Jane Arkwright meekly asked.

"Yes, of course, my sweet," Harold lied, as he reached up to take her hand which was busy fingering a loose blonde curl.

Harold found Jane's childlike practice of incessantly playing with her hair most annoying. Of course, he made sure not to show it; time enough for that when they were safely married.

"I was just thinking what a lucky man I am and what a beautiful bride you'll make," he said, placing a hard wet kiss on the back of her lily white hand.

Harold was in no doubt that Megan had sent the letter. He also realised that she must have an accomplice in Bristol — someone to pick up the money. He wondered who hated him enough to help *her*. He had thought of employing a private detective, but did not want to risk the consequence of not complying fully with the blackmailer's instructions.

"I can think of no one but you, my darling Jane," he lied again, moving his lips slowly up her arm to the nape of her neck.

The ever gullible Jane Arkwright simply gave a soft sigh of contentment.

Harold knew he needed to be patient with his intended bride. Despite the fact that she was almost thirty years of age, she was obviously inexperienced around men and most definitely a virgin. He was convinced she would make a perfect wife, and one with such an influential father . . . a man highly regarded in the world of banking . . . a man who naturally worshipped his only child and could prove to be a great ally to his future son-in-law. For Harold this had been reason enough to restrain his sexual urges. With Jane there could be no going at it like a rampant bull — well at least not until *after* their marriage. With this thought in mind he allowed himself a self-satisfied smirk in anticipation of things to come. On reflection, he decided that fifty pounds blackmail money was a cheap price to pay.

As Lizzie was now walking out with Arthur Walters, she no longer wanted Harold coming to her bed whenever it pleased him. Somehow she needed to convince him that it would be better for *him* if he arranged to visit her on specific nights.

"That way, I could be ready and waiting for you, freshly bathed and smelling of rose-petal bath salts, with skin as soft and naked as the day I was born," she'd whispered, softly brushing her lips across his large naked stomach, while simultaneously sliding her hand down towards his manhood.

"I must say, the thought of you lying naked —" He stopped, his growing excitement making his breathing laboured. He reached out, roughly pulling her on top of him.

Lizzie had become an expert at pretending to enjoy his sexual advances — such a good actress, when in truth — with his pot belly and his breath always reeking of beer — he disgusted her. She told herself it was not for much longer. Little did he know it, but, thanks to him, her nest egg was growing. So far he had paid her a total of five hundred pounds for her silence — blackmail was such an ugly word. Soon she would have enough money to leave her employ at Redcliffe House and start a new life with Arthur.

She smiled to herself when Harold, aroused by her sensuous proposition, announced that from now on he would come to her every Monday and Wednesday night. The rest of the week he would stay at his club, where rumour had it he would drink and gamble into the early hours; once again her ploy had worked.

"By the way, I've decide to move house," Arthur announced to Lizzie on one of their now regular nights together. "No more rent for me. I've decided to buy my own premises. As from next week I'll be the proud owner of a small apartment on Docks Road, although, if I'm honest, I don't intend to stay there long. It's just a way of getting my foot on to the property ladder." His voice sounded so determined, it was hard not to be impressed.

At first Lizzie had been pleased with the move. It was a lot more lively on Docks Road than up with the toffs. The new apartment was situated in the middle of a busy, cobbled market street, a lively place where hawkers noisily vied for customers while competing with loud music from the public house at the end of the parade — and so different from the quiet of Fairfield Road. This evening, with it being the middle of summer, the small studio apartment felt very stuffy and she reached up to open the small window, as far as the sash cord would allow, and immediately heard robust singing voices, accompanied by someone playing a honky-tonk piano coming from the King's Head pub down the road. How she longed to be there. It seemed ages since she'd enjoyed a good old sing-song. She was bored. They'd been sitting around Arthur's stuffy apartment all day. What a way to spend my day off, she thought. And how things had changed. In the beginning they'd had so much fun, with Arthur taking her to such lively places: public houses, restaurants and even the Gaiety Theatre. Now he seemed content to stay at home with his head buried in some boring accounts book.

Over the past year Lizzie had become a regular visitor, not only to Arthur's apartment, but also to his bed. In him she saw a respectable way to leave the Redcliffe House — marriage to Arthur would allow her to end her employment without any suspicion regarding her newly acquired wealth. But she was growing impatient with Arthur's obvious reluctance to pop the question. Lizzie's despondent mood had not been helped by the news from home, telling her that Sidney Partridge had actually gone and married Megan. It seemed ironic that even when pregnant by another man, her cousin had managed to make a fine catch, while she, readily available with no encumbrances, and well off to boot, was without an offer of marriage.

She looked across at Arthur, sitting on the high feather bed on the opposite side of the room, engrossed in one of his ledgers, his white cotton shirt opened to the waist, revealing an athletic physique. He wore no trousers, just tight fitting underpants which left little to the imagination. He was undeniably a fine figure of a man, and one she fancied like mad. She smiled to herself, maybe he could be persuaded to take her out after all.

Lizzie walked towards the bed and knelt down beside him. "How would you like to take your girl for a night on the town? We wouldn't have to go far, the pub on the corner would do. Somewhere where we could maybe have a sing-song and a few drinks. I promise, I'll be ever so grateful . . ." She pouted her lips, gently kissing his mouth . . . then his neck . . . then his chest . . . then his stomach . . . her hands expertly removing his underpants.

"Well, I suppose I could be persuaded," he chuckled, dropping the accounts ledger to the floor.

Lizzie knew she'd won and that they would indeed be going out, but first she needed to satisfy his and now her own sexual arousal. He always had this effect on her. And now that she had Arthur's undivided attention, she began to undress, taking her time, sensually removing each item of clothing before discarding it on to the floor . . . titillating . . . teasing . . . edging closer to him . . . Then, she felt his strong arms about her, lifting her on to the bed, urgently covering her naked body with kisses before moving to lie on top of her.

She couldn't believe the conceit of men. They truly believed that everything revolved around their sexual prowess, when in truth it only made them easier to manipulate, though having sex with Arthur was never a chore. He was always an ardent lover and tonight proved no exception — passionate, satisfying and exhausting, so much so that Arthur was now slumped beside her fast asleep.

"Money . . . I must find the money . . . I must . . . money . . . money." Arthur was talking in his sleep, his head tossing back and forth on his pillow, with beads of perspiration covering his forehead. He was obviously distressed about something.

Lizzie took hold of his shoulders and gave them a hard shake. "Arthur, Arthur . . . wake up. You're having a bad dream. Arthur!"

His eyes shot open.

"Sorry . . . I'm all right. Honestly . . . I'm fine."

He looked embarrassed. She was puzzled. Maybe his business was not doing as well as he'd have her believe. "Arthur, are you in some sort of trouble? With the business, I mean."

"Whatever makes you ask that?" he asked, turning his head away. As if not wishing to meet her gaze.

"In your sleep . . . you mentioned something about needing money."

He gave a nervous laugh. "A bit of a cash-flow problem, that's all. It's bound to happen from time to time. There's nothing for you to concern yourself with. It's just that my partner is considering selling his share of the business."

It was then that Lizzie had an idea: what if she were to become Arthur's new partner? It would certainly be a way out of the Redcliffe House and still keep — as it were — her sleeping partner.

"How much money would it take? I have some money saved," Lizzie boasted.

"I doubt if you could find the kind of money I'm looking for, or are you just masquerading as a lady's maid, when in truth you're an heiress?" he teased.

"I'll have you know I have five hundred pounds in my own private bank account!"

Arthur sat bolt upright. "You've got five . . . hundred . . . pounds? Where on earth did you get that sort of money?"

"It doesn't matter how or where I got it. The fact is, *I* could become your new partner."

He rubbed his chin, obviously puzzled. But Lizzie dared not enlighten him regarding her nest egg, although part of her wanted to show him how clever she'd been. But Arthur and Harold were members of the same drinking men's club, so she dared not risk the chance that he might, in drink, talk out of turn. That would never do.

"Well?" she prompted.

"You'll have to give me a few days to consider it. As I said, my partner's only thinking about — Five . . . hundred . . . pounds, you say? Well I never."

"Megan, love, what's wrong? Is it the baby?" Sidney was shocked to find his wife kneeling beside the bed, obviously in pain.

"Please, Sidney, go get Mam. Tell her that my waters have broken and the baby's coming."

"I'm on my way. Get Mam. Yes . . . that's what I'll do." He turned to leave the room.

"Sidney? Help me on to the bed first, eh! I don't want to have this baby on the floor, now do I?"

He turned back. "Right — help you on to bed — get Mam — waters broke," Sidney nervously mumbled as he lifted her on to the bed.

"Sidney, will you stop repeating everything I say and get a move on?"

"But what if there's no time to get Mam? What will you do if the baby comes and you're all alone?"

"There's plenty of time *if* you go now," Megan replied, trying to stay calm.

"I'll go. But first I'll call next door to see Mrs Thomas and ask her to sit with you until I get back, OK?"

"Yes — yes, anything you say. Only *please* go get my mam!"

Sidney reluctantly left her in their cosy three bedroomed terrace house in Ponty. They had been so lucky to get it, and had only heard about it through Sidney's job at the brewery — the house belonged to one of his managers. Up to now, with Sidney's regular wage coming in, they'd had no trouble paying the two shillings and six pence a week rent. The house was clean and comfortably furnished, thanks mainly to his mam's generous wedding present of fifty pounds. Megan's mam had given them a bale of bed linen and they considered themselves very fortunate. Unfortunately, the house had no bathroom, so, twice a week, Megan would take the mile walk to her mother's flat for a long hot soak in the large white enamel indoor bath. Sidney, on the other hand, seemed to enjoy the novelty of bathing in a tin bath by the fire in their small back-kitchen.

"It's a girl — and she's a beauty!" the midwife announced as she slapped the baby's bottom, appearing pleased with the resulting pitiful little cry.

After what seemed like an age attending to the baby in the far corner of the bedroom, the midwife finally handed Megan the new arrival, wrapped up so tightly in cotton sheets that only a pink wrinkled chubby face was visible.

"There we are, your new daughter. She weighs seven pounds and four ounces, it's a good weight for a first child," the midwife said, removing her rubber apron. "I'm afraid I have to go, I need to attend to Gwen Perkins up the Garw. That one shouldn't take long though, with it being her sixth baby in six years, and all." She paused to roll down her tunic sleeves, expertly buttoning them at the cuff. "For Gwen it's a bit like shelling peas." She chuckled at her own joke. "On my way out I shall put the proud father out of his misery. On my last trip to the kitchen for hot water, he had practically worn a track in the oilcloth with his pacing up and down — new fathers!" She was still laughing when she left the room.

"Is the baby all right, Mam?"

"The baba's fine. All her bits be in the right place. So don't you go fretting yourself."

Megan gave a sigh of relief. For a while the room fell silent as both women closed their eyes in a prayer of thanks. The silence was soon broken when the door burst open and Sidney came running in and straight across the room to his wife's bedside. He knelt down to embrace Megan and the baby. The look of love in his eyes spoke volumes and dispelled any doubts that Megan might have had.

"Megan, she's beautiful . . . just like her mother. Do you think I could hold her?"

Megan held the baby out to him. She watched as he gently took her in his arms, his lips lightly brushing against her small pink cheeks. Then, speaking directly to the small bundle, he murmured, "Hello, now aren't you the pretty one? Do you see that little lady lying in the bed over there? Well, she's your mother. And me? Well I'm your dad. And your name is —?" He looked to Megan for an answer.

Megan quickly obliged. "Her name's Mary-Rose. As we agreed if we had a girl, after both our mothers."

"Well, Mary-Rose, we welcome you and love you very much." Sidney caught hold of Megan's hand, both unable to control their tears of joy.

"Come on, give the baba to me. It's time Megan had a rest." Mam took the baby from Sidney with the confidence you would expect, having brought up six children of her own. "This little one will be due for a feed shortly, and it'll be no place for a man." Gently she placed Mary-Rose in the tiny wooden crib at the bottom of the bed. "I'll give you a few minutes alone, then I shall be back to shoo you out. Do you hear?" She stood at the door waiting for an answer.

"Yes, Mam, and thank you," he said, and he genuinely meant it. He liked his mother-in-law, even if her tongue was sometimes a bit rough.

As the door closed behind her Sidney reached over the bed to place a tender kiss on Megan's lips.

"The baby's lovely, isn't she?" Megan asked.

"She's beautiful, you're so clever. But are *you* OK? Was it very bad?"

Megan felt embarrassed, he had obviously heard her screams during labour. "When I see her looking so perfect? I can honestly say it was well worth the pain."

Sidney took her hand in his, giving it a gentle squeeze. "Well, she certainly took her time coming into the world. I was so worried about you, Megan, love. The delivery seemed to go on forever. I really thought that once Nurse Jones, the midwife, arrived, it wouldn't take long. And yet you were another six hours in labour."

"Poor love." She reached up to brush away wisps of his hair from his forehead.

"I felt so helpless. At one time I actually tried to look into the bedroom. Needless to say Nurse Jones sent me away with a flea in my ear, "This is woman's work and no place for the likes of you, so be off with you." Sidney mimicked the midwife's squeaky voice perfectly.

"Oh, don't make me laugh. It really hurts."

It didn't take long after the birth of Megan's baby, for the gossips in the village to move on to someone else. Mary Braithwaite had been so right when she'd said it would only be a nine days wonder, the same as when Jess was sent to prison — the gossips always

212

found better fodder. Whatever the reason, Megan was glad they were, at last, leaving her family alone.

Megan and Sidney settled easily into married life. The joy of having Mary-Rose helped them over the initial awkwardness they had both felt in the early days of their marriage. It also helped Megan to put behind her the painful memories of the way her child was conceived. Sidney, true to his word, never once questioned her about what happened up at Redcliffe House. Her husband was truly a good man and everyday she thanked God for bringing him to her. He was a good husband and father, and worked hard to provide for his ready-made family. His love for them was never in question.

Megan told herself that the deep affection and respect she felt for Sidney was a lot healthier than the intense and sometimes foolish behaviour of women in love. In her own way she did love him — he adored her and was always sensitive to her feelings. She in turn always tried to be a good wife, in every sense of the word. Sidney proved to be a gentle lover, often respecting her wish just to be cuddled. She knew how much he wanted a son and longed to please him. Maybe she wanted it too much, because try as they might there was no sign of another baby.

CHAPTER
TWELVE

1922

It was Mary-Rose's second birthday. Megan and her mother were busy baking in Megan's kitchen in preparation for a special family tea party. The birthday girl was fast asleep in the parlour taking her regular afternoon nap, allowing them to get on without the help of an inquisitive two-year-old.

The party was set for four o'clock, and Megan's younger brothers and sisters were all eager to take part. Evan, the baby of the family, had recently moved up to the infant school and, at six years of age, could be trusted to walk the half mile home with his schoolmates. He had suggested having the day off, but Mary Braithwaite would hear none of it. Bryn was working afternoons and consequently would miss all the fun, but he made Mary-Rose promise to keep him a piece of cake. Phyllis, who at thirteen had recently left school, offered to help Olive look after the shop, thus allowing their Mam time off to help Megan. They planned to join the party after they closed the shop.

It was hard to believe that two years had passed since the birth of Mary-Rose. It had gone by so quickly —

214

although Megan doubted her brother Jess would agree with her. Megan still visited him every month without fail, visits made easier now that Sidney accompanied her, and it pleased her that Jess and Sidney got on so well. Jess had taken a long time to adjust to prison life and was, understandably, subject to many mood swings. It was as if in Sidney he felt he had found a friend, someone who would see the facts as they were, be objective, not biased like Megan. With Sidney he could talk man to man.

Megan suddenly became aware that her mother had stopped cooking and was staring at her.

"What's wrong, Mam?"

"Got anything to tell your mother then?"

"Tell you? Tell you what?"

"Seen the way you look too many times before. So there be no use in denying it."

"Mam, will you stop talking in riddles. What look?"

"The *look*. It be what all women get when they are with child."

Megan immediately stopped what she was doing. "What? You think I'm pregnant?" Although Megan questioned her mother, suddenly it all made sense. For weeks now she had been feeling a little off colour. Her periods had been irregular since the birth of Mary-Rose — well, everyone knew this happened when you breastfed for a long time, and Mary-Rose had been eighteen-months-old before being weaned.

"I'd say that you were about two-to-three months gone. In fact, I would put money on it."

"You'd put money on what, Mam?" Sidney asked, as he walked across the room casually picking up one of the freshly baked fairy cakes from the plate on the table.

"I would put money on your wife being pregnant," she repeated.

Sidney dropped the cake he was about to put into his mouth.

"Really? Megan, is it true? When? Give me that mixing bowl, sit yourself down."

"Now, stop fussing. We don't know for sure. It could be that Mam's got it wrong. First thing tomorrow I'll go to the new clinic. Now, don't you go getting your hopes up, do you hear?"

His arms went around her, tenderly pulling her to him, "I believe Mam, she's seldom wrong about these things."

Megan laughed and rested her head on his shoulders. More than anything in the world she longed to give him a child, a son. She kissed her husband's cheek and murmured, "We'll see."

The next morning the nurse at the clinic confirmed that she was indeed three months pregnant. Megan and Sidney were so happy at the prospect of having a brother or sister for Mary-Rose; nothing or no one could spoil their joy . . . or so they believed.

Megan was almost seven months into her pregnancy when Sidney — who had been coughing and not feeling well for the last few weeks — decided to pay a visit to Doctor Lewis's weekly surgery, though the last thing he needed right now was a doctor's bill. Megan wanted to go along with him but he would not hear of it.

"There's nothing for you to worry about. I've probably caught a chill that's all," he insisted.

But he had lost so much weight that Megan felt worried. She knew that for some weeks now, he'd been finding the work at the brewery a lot harder than usual, arriving home later and later, wearier and wearier. When she suggested he took a day off, he wouldn't hear of it. Since they'd been together, Sidney had always prided himself on bringing home a full week's wage.

It all seemed to happen so suddenly. No long illness like her dad. That would have at least given her time to get used to the idea that he was really sick. Only four short weeks after being diagnosed with tuberculosis, Sidney was dead and buried, just a month before the birth of his son — Thomas Sidney Partridge — who weighed in a strapping seven pounds ten ounces, with a captivating smile exactly like his dad's.

Months after the birth Megan still suffered terrible depressions. She missed Sidney unbearably, his cheerful smile when she was feeling down and his gentle warmth at night. The fact that the baby looked so much like his dad only made it worse, knowing how much Sidney would have loved him.

She had an overwhelming desire to hit out, to blame someone, but who? She wanted to scream out: "Why? Why? Why?" She wanted to, but her grief was far too raw. Black days were to follow, days when her depression left her not wanting to continue. What was the point? Without Sidney she could see nothing but a bleak future for herself and her two children. She felt angry with God. Why, when there were so many evil people in the world, had God chosen to take her Sidney, a gentle and good man who wouldn't harm a soul? The very same God had taken her father and locked up her beloved brother Jess, whose only sin had been to stand up and defend a helpless child. It was all so unfair.

Added to this was the underlying feeling that she had let everyone down. She was racked with guilt for not being able to love Sidney in the same way he'd loved her and for not listening to Jess when he had his doubts about the minister. Perhaps God was, after all, punishing her for her inadequacies. In her troubled mind these events were somehow connected.

"Don't you think it's time you pulled yourself together? You'll not be the first woman to lose a man, you know?"

"Mam, I miss him so much. With Sidney, I felt so secure, so loved. Now that he's gone I have to think of the practicality of looking after two small children. How am I going to pay the rent, when I can't even go out to work? And before you say anything, it's not right for us to keep relying on your help. The truth is, Mam, I'm at my wits end."

"Well, I think I may have a solution." Mam stopped in mid-sentence, and taking Megan's hand she led her across the room to sit with her on the old brown sofa. "Listen, you know our Olive be walking out with the Jenkins lad?"

Megan nodded. For the past few months her sister and Dewi Jenkins had been inseparable. She doubted there could be anyone in the valley who didn't know they were courting.

"Well, last night they told me that as soon as they can find somewhere to live they intend to fix a wedding date and —"

Megan interrupted, the last thing she wanted to hear was about someone else's — even her sister's — happiness. "I'm very pleased for them, Mam. Dewi is a nice lad and I think they're very well suited. But —"

"Let me finish. As I was saying, they need somewhere to live, so why not let them move in with you? Many folk have to share smaller houses. Maybe they could have the two rooms upstairs and you could live, private like, in the three rooms downstairs. That way, the children would have easy access to the garden and you would only need to share the kitchen. Surely, with no stairs to climb it would make life a lot easier for you, and they would pay you half the rent." She took a deep breath, "And there's another thing: for weeks I've been toying with the idea of taking someone on to help with the alterations in the shop. If you took the job you could work from home. What do you think?"

Megan smiled for the first time in a long while. "I think you've missed your vocation, Mam. Why, with all the planning you've been doing you could easily have been a politician. Maybe someone should warn Nancy Astor."

Although Megan mocked her mother, secretly she knew it all made sense. This way everyone had something to gain. She would need to talk with Olive and Dewi, but if they agreed that half the rent was a fair price, and if Mam would agree to treat her like any other employee — paid on results, then maybe it would seem less like charity.

"Well, are you in agreement?" her mother pressed for an answer.

"Mam, first, I'd like to have a family meeting to hear what Olive and Dewi have to say."

"I took the liberty of asking them around to see you this evening. They should be here in about half an hour."

Megan gave another smile as she bent over to kiss her mother's forehead.

Rose Partridge was to hear of her son's death in a letter from Megan. At first she was sure there had to be a mistake. Why, only last month Sidney had written, telling her of his intention to come visit soon. With the birth of his baby only a couple of months away, he promised that once Megan felt well enough to travel they intended to bring the children to meet their English grandmother. There had been no mention of his feeling unwell. He had written about his Megan, the pregnancy, Mary-Rose, their new home and how well he was getting on at the brewery. He'd even mentioned promotion. He sounded so happy and so full of life. There *had* to be a mistake. But with realization of truth, came despair. There was a gaping wound, so ugly she wanted to hide herself away — away from having to face a life without her beloved son. She was no newcomer to grief. She'd had to cope with the loss of her dear husband — he, too, had been a young man in the prime of life. She had coped then for the sake of her child, a son she had watched mature from boy to man, a man so honest and kind and loving. It just did not seem fair.

Mistress Fothergill had been one of the first to come to offer her condolence. She also offered Rose the time off to attend Sidney's funeral in Wales. Rose declined. She had no wish to see her only child being lowered into the ground. A mother never expected to outlive her children . . . it was far too cruel!

Those first days following her sad news Rose Partridge was so overcome with grief the doctor had to be called. He duly prescribed a sedative and complete rest, informing Mistress Fothergill that her trusted employee was tottering on the edge of complete breakdown and could quite easily fall into the abyss. The mistress gave orders that all of the staff were to do everything in their power to help Cook, by taking away any worry she might have over her household duties. Everyone below-stairs was more than pleased to oblige, to make sure the kitchen ran smoothly. They needed Cook to know how much they sympathized and that they were there for her as she had always been there for them.

A few days later Mrs Jarvis complimented them on their efficiency in the kitchen. Sally in particular had surprised everyone by offering to take over all of the cooking duties, duties which she performed exception- ally well. The housekeeper felt it wise not to mention this to Rose Partridge and in fact she planned to tell her quite the opposite; a little white lie was more than justified, if it spurred her dear friend out of despair and back to work.

Rose sat in her room alone with her thoughts, her memories and her grief. In the distance she heard a tap on the door and sensed that someone had entered.

"Hello, Cook. Do you mind if I come in for a little chat?" It was Mrs Jarvis.

Rose did not answer, simply shrugged her shoulders as if she did not care one way or another.

"I've just come from a meeting with the mistress . . . Cook, please look at me."

Rose did as she asked.

"That's better. I wanted you to be the first to hear my news, after all we've worked together a good many years."

"Seventeen — seventeen years, my Sidney was only five years old when I came to work here." Rose smiled. "He was such a boisterous toddler, a proper boy, do you remember?"

For the first time in days, Mrs Jarvis saw her friend's eyes light up, "I do indeed. They were good times, good memories . . . memories no one can ever take away. I know that I, for one, shall cherish them when I move on."

"Move on? Move on where?" Rose sat up straight, at last paying attention.

"That's what I came to tell you. I've just resigned my position as housekeeper and plan to leave at the end of the month."

Rose looked shocked. "Whatever made you do such a thing? Where will you go?"

"It's my mother. She's eighty-three, and of late has become noticeably frail. I talked it over with my brother and we both agree she really shouldn't be living alone. It's difficult for him. He has a small business and a wife and family of his own whereas I —"

"I see. What does the mistress say?" Rose asked with genuine concern.

"Oh, she was very kind. She said she understood all about family commitments. Mind you, I must say I was surprised when she told me she would not be looking to replace me. It appears that she intends to take over the role of housekeeper herself."

"The mistress said that! How on earth would she manage?" Rose stood up and began pacing the floor.

The housekeeper smiled to herself, her visit was having the effect she'd hoped, but she couldn't stop here, one extra push should do the trick.

"I don't know I'm sure. Especially with her already shouldering the burden of not having *you* in the kitchen running things, controlling the staff and all. Look, I know it's none of my business, and I'm sure you'll return to work in your own good time, but, I have to say, things are really starting to fall behind below-stairs. I'll say no more, for I'm sure I have said too much already. I just thought you should be told."

Rose sat back in her chair. "Thank you, Mrs Jarvis." Even after years of working side by side they always addressed each other formally — for them it showed a mark of a respect. "I shall bid you good day. If it's all

223

right with you, I'll come again before I leave the house for good?"

"I would like that," Rose said, and meant it.

As the door slowly closed behind her Rose knew the time had come to return to her work. Her time for mourning was over. She would always grieve for her loss, but nothing could bring her son back to her. Soon she would have a new grandchild, a part of Sidney, and something to live for. Megan and the children needed her, the mistress needed her, and in work she hoped to find solace.

"Good morning, Cook. Please, do come in."

The mistress sat across the room on the large brocade sofa in front of the fireplace. She looked splendid, dressed in a pale grey taffeta dress, a strategically placed cameo brooch accentuating its high neckline. Her light grey hair, swept off her face, was groomed into a high chignon. Her overall appearance left no doubt that she was indeed a very handsome woman.

"I've taken the liberty of ordering us some tea. Please, join me." Mistress Fothergill gently patted the sofa, beckoning for Rose to sit next to her.

With trepidation Rose slowly crossed the room to the sofa. Ever since Mrs Jarvis's sudden departure, the mistress had taken to meeting Rose every Monday morning to discuss the menus for the week. But today was Friday, so Rose suspected this meeting to be of a more personal nature. There had been much gossip below-stairs regarding . . . Fothergill Tobacco Company.

Rumour had it that they were in trouble, due in the main part to Master Harold's gambling debts, and that Master Robert, now in better health, had offered to step in and help, in the short term, with the day-to-day running of the company. This offer Harold had adamantly refused, claiming the company to be solely *his*. There had been much talk about a cutback of staff. Rose feared that she might be one of the first to go.

"I hear from Hutchins that congratulations are in order; another grandchild, and this time a little boy. Tell me, how is your daughter-in-law, it must be very difficult for her?"

Rose felt strangely uncomfortable, it was obvious that the mistress believed Sidney to be the father of Megan's first-born. It had been what Sidney had wanted.

"Megan, like me, copes as best she can, ma'am. We both know it's what Sidney would have expected, for the sake of the children. It's fortunate they be too young to understand fully."

"A small blessing, I suppose." The mistress stopped to pour the tea, handing Rose a delicately decorated fine china cup and saucer before continuing, "It must be difficult for you, with them living so far away?"

"Thank you, ma'am," Rose said, reluctantly taking the hot tea. It didn't seem right for the mistress to be serving her. "We manage to keep in touch with regular correspondence. Megan is very good with her writing, whereas I have to enlist the help of Mr Hutchins."

"Rose? Don't you think it's about time you had things a little easier? What would you say to a few days off each week? A few days away from this house where you could maybe start to live something of a normal life?"

Rose was overcome with panic, her hands visibly shaking. She quickly placed the cup and saucer on the small table to the side of her before she dropped it. This was the first time the mistress had ever called her Rose, a sure sign that something was amiss.

"Ma'am, if it be all right with you, I would much rather stay as I am. The truth is, I have nowhere else to go. This is my home." Rose was near to tears, surely the mistress wouldn't put her out on to the streets, not after all these years?

"I'm sorry, Rose. I did not explain myself well. I'd like you to move into the cottage at Cumberland Way. For many years, as you know, it was occupied by old Nanny Tomlinson. Would you believe she was nearly ninety when she died? Anyway, the cottage has been empty for far too long and I would like you to have it — rent free of course. I am sure with just a few homely touches, it could be made most comfortable. What do you say?"

Rose knew the cottage well. She had been a frequent visitor when, under instruction from the mistress, she had delivered Nanny Tomlinson her daily meals. Rose always chose to take it herself rather than send one of the staff. She enjoyed spending the odd hour with Nanny, reminiscing over old times — times when Nanny Tomlinson used to live up at the house.

"That be very generous of you, ma'am, and it does sound very tempting, I must say. But who would do the cooking and keep the household staff in check? No mistress, my place is here."

"As I suggested earlier, if you were to come into work three days a week, and if on these days you were to prepare the meals for the rest of the week, then I'm sure Sally would be more than capable of completing the cooking in your absence. I hear she did a fine job when you were . . . indisposed. A splendid reflection on your excellent training."

Rose felt an inward shiver. What was going on here? She wasn't blind, she had eyes in her head and could see that this was the beginning of the end, not just for her but also for Mistress Fothergill. Was money really that tight for the family then? But at the same time Rose had to admit to herself that something about the idea did appeal to her. And yes, Sally could do it . . . so had she become dispensable after all?

As if reading her thoughts the mistress quickly added, "Of course, should we at any time decide to have a dinner party, we would most certainly need you. I would however give you plenty of notice of any such arrangement."

"I don't know what to say."

"Why not take a few days to think it over?"

CHAPTER
THIRTEEN

Olive Williams and Dewi Jenkins were married on Saturday, 16 June 1923. A quiet register office wedding, followed by a small family celebration in the flat above the shop. Although everyone tried to make Olive's day a special one, the tragedy of Sidney's death hung over the proceedings, casting a shadow over an otherwise happy event.

"Olive, love, congratulations," Megan said warmly. "I really am so happy for you both. Dewi is a good man, you make a lovely couple. In a minute I shall go find him and tell him how lucky he is to have *you* — and I shall mean it to."

Olive flung her arms around Megan, "Oh, Megs. I feel so guilty. I know I'm being selfish. I have no right to feel this happy when you are obviously feeling so wretched."

"Don't be daft. Today should be the happiest day of your life. I won't let you spoil it worrying about me. I'm OK, I promise," Megan lied. It was hard to pretend all was well when today's celebration brought back such vivid memories of her own wedding to Sidney only a few short years before.

"Thanks, Megs. And thank you for letting me and Dewi move in with you. It's going to be great. I can't believe how well you and Mam managed to transform our upstairs rooms, and in such a short time."

"It wasn't just us. You and Dewi worked just as hard. Mind you, I must say at one stage I had grave doubt that your settee would even make it up the stairs, never mind into the bedroom — sorry, parlour."

Olive had chosen Megan and Sidney's old bedroom as a parlour. This pleased Megan more than she would have believed. She knew she was being silly but she would not have liked to think of the newlyweds using it as a bedroom. She wondered if her mother had sensed this and had had words with Olive. Anyway a parlour it was, and Megan and her mother soon set about sewing new covers and curtains.

"Evening, Megan. I must say, you be looking more like your old self. Why, you've even got a bit of colour in your cheeks."

Megan did not have the heart to tell her mother that her flush of colour was simply a touch of rouge, although the fact that Megan felt the need to touch up her appearance was proof enough that she was indeed feeling better. Having Olive and Dewi living with her, albeit upstairs, was working well. She quite liked living on the bottom floor with the children, and far from being an intrusion it was made all the better for having shared kitchen facilities. Olive, who had always helped her mother, had been determined to cook for her new husband. Unfortunately, without her mother's guidance, she proved a hopeless cook, but, much to Megan's surprise, every one of her culinary disasters resulted in a good deal of light-hearted banter between the newlyweds, their laughter filling the house with such a genuine feeling of love and happiness that Megan found it hard not to be warmed by it.

"I've brought you today's alterations. I'm afraid there's not many. The shop has gone a lot quieter this past week," Mary Braithwaite called out as she laid the garments down on the kitchen table. She had taken to dropping off any work for Megan at the end of her trading day in the shop. Up to now the arrangement had worked well, with her mother staying true to her word and paying only a fair price on results.

"I can't grumble. It's been a busy enough summer. I don't expect trade to pick up again until folk start thinking of their winter coats. Where be the babas?" her mother asked, peering into the parlour.

"I've just put them up to bed. It's been a long day. Luckily, with the nights starting to draw in, Mary-Rose thinks it's later than it is."

"I'll just go pop my head around the door. I'll not disturb them, I promise."

She returned a few minutes later. "They're both out for the count. I'll put the kettle on for a brew, shall I?" Mary Braithwaite did not wait for an answer, she simply walked over to the fireplace and lifted the black cast iron kettle on to the hot coals.

"Mam? What do you think of me taking the children to Bristol for a visit? I received another letter from

Sidney's mam today. Now that she's settled into her new cottage she desperately wants to see us. I thought with the shop quieter . . ."

"Of course you should go. I dread to think what that poor woman's been going through, losing her only son so sudden, like. I might have lost my Jess to prison but at least he be still alive. I don't think I could have coped if he'd been —" Mary Braithwaite checked herself. "You must go to see her. I doubt that the shop will get busy until the end of October so there be no need for you to rush back, do you hear?"

"Thanks, Mam. I shall start making arrangements to go next week after my monthly prison visit to see Jess. In fact I shall write a letter to Mrs Partridge tonight telling her of my plans."

"Sit yourself down. No physical contact. Speak up. No whispering," the guard ordered.

Megan nodded. How many times had she heard the same well practised, tedious list of rules and regulations? How she missed Sidney not being there supporting her, loving her. In his love she had found the inner strength to cope with seeing her brother in such a dreadful place. All around her the sounds of iron doors opening and closing accompanied her to the visitors' room. It was such a dismal place.

Jess sat facing her. There was a bruise low on his cheek and sullen lines round his mouth. He had already been in trouble more than once for fighting other inmates.

"Hello, *browd*. I don't have to ask what you've been up to. Jess, you really must try to curb that temper of yours."

"Don't you lecture me as well, Megs. I've enough of being told what I should or shouldn't do." He leaned toward her, his hand motioning for her to move closer, "Megs, since Sidney's death I've began to give up on God." He whispered it, as if by way of keeping his doubts secret even from the Almighty.

"Speak up!" the guard shouted, causing them to sit bolt upright.

Megan quickly composed herself. "It's a surprise to me that you can still believe there is a God. I tell you for nothing, over the last few years my faith has been tested to the limit." She spoke the truth. How many times in the past four years had she pleaded with God to protect her from evil? To provide for her family, to help her brother and more recently to save Sidney — all to no avail.

"But surely without our faith in God, we have nothing?" he said, shaking his head. "Megs, you have to remember all the things He's already done for us. Like bringing you home safely from Bristol. Or making sure Mam had the funds to start a new life after — And don't forget how He saved my life. There were many who thought that I should have had the death penalty. After all I did take a man's life, and no ordinary man — a man of the cloth."

Megan was quite taken aback. This was the first time Jess had mentioned the act that had brought him to prison. She had deliberately given the subject a wide

232

berth, believing it better to look to the future than dwell on the past.

"Now, now, *browd*, remember what our mam always says?"

He nodded. "The only thing thee get from looking back be a crick in the neck," they recited in unison, each mimicking their mother's voice.

They both laughed. A short laugh but the first in a long while.

"That's better. But you're right. We do have a lot to be thankful for and we have to think positively. In a way I've already made a start. Tomorrow I plan to take the children to visit Sidney's mother in Bristol."

"Will you be OK travelling on your own, like?" He shook his head. "Look at me, still treating you like a little girl. The truth is I find it hard to think of you as a grown woman with babas. *Duw*, I wish I could see them."

"You will see them, and soon. I've heard the authorities have started this new system. You can apply to the court to have time knocked off your sentence" — she looked pointedly at the bruise on his face — "as a reward for good behaviour."

"That lets me out then, doesn't it?" His mouth hardened into a resigned line of defeat that caught at Megan's heart.

"No," she said firmly. "No, Jess. OK, so you've been in a few fights in the last three years. But nothing serious. It's still worth trying. While I'm away in Bristol I shall set about drafting a letter to the court. What do you say to that?"

Jess forced a smile.

It was time for her to leave. As the guard escorted her out she turned in time to catch Jess raising a hand to his lips to blow her a kiss. The thought of leaving him for another month made her want to cry, but there had been enough tears. It was time to move on, think positively — for Jess, for her children, but mainly for herself.

The train journey to Bristol brought back many memories, so much had happened in the years since she had first left home with such hope for the future.

"Mammy, look, moo-cows." Mary-Rose was bursting with excitement on this her first train journey. So far the only trains she had seen were the ones carrying coal to and from the pit. Little Thomas was sound asleep, held secure in a shawl draped the Welsh way, with one end of the shawl wrapped tightly around the baby and cradled in the left arm, leaving Megan's right arm free to hold on to Mary-Rose.

"Yes, my love, I can see all the cows, and the sheep, and the horses. It's a shame that Tom is missing it all. Look, he's fast asleep."

She was relieved that the baby had slept most of the journey, but the pains in her breast told her it would not be long before he awoke in need of a feed. She hoped there were no delays. By her reckoning they should be arriving at Bristol Temple Meads in about half an hour. Her mother-in-law had written to tell her how pleased she was that they were coming to stay, and informing her that Mistress Fothergill had kindly given

Hutchins permission to use the car to pick up Megan and her children from the station. Megan wondered what the mistress would do if she found out that one of the children was in fact her own grandchild. Megan gave a shiver — it did not bear thinking of. One thing for sure, the mistress would never find out from her.

The train arrived at Bristol on time. With a large suitcase, a baby in arms and a very tired three year old holding on to her skirt she was expecting a struggle. As it turned out, a sympathetic railway guard offered his assistance and carried her suitcase not only off the train but to the end of the platform. Only after she assured him that someone was indeed coming to meet her, did he doff his cap and bid her good day. It partly restored her faith in her fellow man.

Megan looked around. There was no sign of Mr Hutchins. She wondered if she should make her own way to her mother-in-law's house, as the baby had began to whimper, a sure sign that it was nearly time for his feed. She needed to get to her destination — and quickly.

"Mrs Partridge?"

Megan span round to face quite a tall man, dressed in a long, grey tweed overcoat and black bowler hat.

"Y-yes. I'm Mrs Partridge, and who wants to know?" she asked, rather taken aback.

"I'm sorry if I startled you. Robert Fothergill at your service, ma'am," he said, politely removing his hat.

For a while she just stared at him. He had changed. His skin no longer the grey previously remembered.

Gone were the dark rings around his eyes. Instead he looked healthy and vibrant and quite . . . handsome.

"You don't remember me, do you?"

"Yes, of course I do but —?" She hesitated, feeling embarrassed, as she remembered the night he had saved her, and puzzled as to why he was here now. "I-I don't understand?"

"Please, let me help you. Hutchins is waiting in the car. I'll explain as we go along, shall I?"

Not waiting for an answer he picked up her suitcase and led the way out of the station. She fell in behind him, after first making sure Mary-Rose was tightly holding on to the baby's shawl.

"I do hope you haven't been waiting long? I'm afraid the delay in meeting you is all down to my brother Harold's forthcoming marriage. With it being just two weeks away my dear mother insisted I attend today's rehearsal at the church. I'm afraid it ran on longer than I expected. There was no time for Hutchins to take me home. I suggested, to save time, that I came along to pick you up. I really don't wish to intrude on your visit. It just seemed the best thing to do."

Although she could hear him chattering on, she had stopped listening. She was still taking in the news about Harold. Even his name made her feel as if someone was walking over her grave. So, he was getting married — how she pitied his intended bride.

"Are you all right, Mrs Partridge? You've gone as white as a sheet,"

"Yes-yes, I'm fine, thank you," then, quickly composing herself, "it's very kind of you to put yourself

236

out like this." Megan hoped her voice sounded genuine, for she truly meant it.

"I'd like to take full credit. But in truth I didn't fancy facing Cook — sorry, your mother-in-law — if we kept you and her grandchildren waiting at the station too long."

They both laughed. They had reached the car. Hutchins stood, holding the door open.

"It's all right, Hutchins. If you just put the suitcase in the boot, I'll make sure Mrs Partridge and this big girl here are comfortably seated." Captain Fothergill turned to pick up Mary-Rose in one arm, and with the other gently supported Megan's elbow as she entered the big black saloon car. His touch made her tingle, sending a shiver down her spine. She felt embarrassed and strangely uncomfortable, and breathed a sigh of relief when he called out, "I'll travel up front with you, Hutchins."

Hutchins was as professional as ever. He didn't seem at all put out by her arrival. Megan wondered if he secretly objected to picking up a former kitchen maid. She hoped not. She had always respected him, and hoped he didn't think ill of her. Megan's thoughts could not have been further from the truth. For nearly a year Mr Hutchins and Mrs Partridge senior had been walking out, something her mother-in-law had failed to mention in her many letters to Megan.

"I shall tell her face-to-face, woman to woman like," Rose Partridge had told Mr Hutchins.

It was the first time Megan had travelled in an automobile. She was impressed by the speed and ease with which the car held the road, especially when going up Park Street. She remembered her first sight of the big hill and how she had held on to Sydney for grim death, worried that Samson would not make it. She felt ashamed for ever doubting the faithful dray horse.

The baby stirred letting out a little cry. Megan knew Tom would not be comforted until fed. "There, there, *bachen*. Not long now," she whispered, lifting him up to her face. She looked across to Mary-Rose, who had fallen fast asleep.

"We're nearly there. I must say, for one so tiny, he's certainly got a good pair of lungs," Captain Robert called from the front of the car.

"I'm sorry about the noise. You see he's well overdue for his feed, and I'm afraid he's not very patient."

"Quite — I-I understand."

Not surprisingly, Tom's crying woke Mary-Rose. "Are we there yet, Mammy?" she asked rubbing her eyes.

Before Megan could answer Captain Fothergill announced, "We're here. Look, there's your grandmother pacing the pavement."

As the car pulled to a stop Rose Partridge's face appeared at the car window, tears of joy streaming down her cheeks. Hutchins rushed around to open the car door for Megan, but she had already opened it. Instead he helped her out, by which time Captain Robert was already out of the car and lifting Mary-Rose from the back seat.

Rose Partridge threw her arms around Megan squeezing both her and the baby so hard it took her breath away. "I can't believe you are actually here. I've waited so long to see you and the babies. Why, I be that excited —" She paused as she spotted Robert Fothergill coming toward her carrying Mary-Rose, "Master Robert. Whatever you be doing here?" she asked, reaching out to take the child from his arms.

"It's a long story and one I'm sure your daughter-in-law will explain. The main thing is that we managed to get her here more or less on time." Then turning to Megan, "I hope you enjoy your stay, Mrs Partridge. I shall leave you now. Somehow I think the little one has finally reached the end of his patience." He smiled as he made his way back to the car covering both ears with his hands as Tom's cries reached an even higher octave.

"Come on, let's go inside. You can feed the babe, while I spoil young Mary-Rose." As she ushered them into her comfortable terraced cottage she muttered in disbelief, "Fancy, Master Robert escorting you from the station. Well I never!"

The week that followed was one of mixed emotions. For Rose Partridge there was the joy of seeing Megan again, getting to know Mary-Rose, holding Tom — his eyes and smile, so like his father's and grandfather's before him. There was the sadness for Megan, hearing first-hand how full of life and hope Sidney had been when he'd left Bristol for Wales. Then Megan had to relate every detail of their married life together before it was cut short. It hurt her to remember but she did it for Rose knowing it would help her with her grief.

It was during this time that Rose plucked up the courage to tell Megan of her intention to marry Mr Hutchins. She blushed like a schoolgirl. "I 'spect you think that, at our age, we're being foolish? But we truly are very fond of each other."

"Not at all. I think it's wonderful. And I'm sure Sidney would have thought so too. He always liked Mr Hutchins."

"I like to think so . . ." For a while Rose's mind seemed elsewhere, "Anyways, I do hope you and the little ones will come to the wedding — you be all the family Victor and I have now."

"We wouldn't miss it for the world. When do you think it will be?" Megan meant what she said. She and the children would be there, but she hoped it wouldn't clash with her visits to see Jess.

"Oh, not until after Christmas. Victor says that Mistress Fothergill has arranged to go to her cottage in Devon for a month's holiday in January. She has already told him that his services will not be needed, so it would be an ideal time to get wed. We've talked about having a small gathering at the Register Office in town, then maybe go on for high tea at the Sefton Hotel. What do you think?"

"It sounds perfect," Megan enthused, as she placed a kiss on Rose's cheek.

In the days that passed, Megan told her mother-in-law all about her brother, Jess. Rose listened with interest as Megan outlined her plan.

"Do you really believe there's a chance your Jess could get an early release?"

240

"Well, I'm not sure, but it's worth a try, don't you agree?" Megan didn't need an answer, she already knew she could rely on Rose for support. "I really need someone who could give me practical help. Someone able to draft a letter to the courts, a letter with the right wording, to make those in authority sit up and take notice." Megan pondered for a while. Then, "Mr Hutchins! Do you think he could do it?"

"Mr Hutchins — Victor? Well I know he's good with his reading and writing, but I'm not so sure he would know 'bout the workings of the court ... whereas Master Robert ... of course ... Master Robert. He's the one we have to ask."

"Mammy, there's someone at the door."

"I know, *cariad*. Let me put your brother into his pram and we'll go see who it can be."

Having just fed the baby, Megan checked the buttons of her blouse making sure she was decent before opening the front door.

"Hello, Mrs Partridge. I hope this is a good time, only Cook, sorry your mother-in-law, mentioned something about you needing help with regards to writing a letter."

Megan was speechless, taken aback to find Captain Fothergill standing on the door step.

"If it's not a good time —?"

"No — I mean — yes. How very kind of you. Please, won't you come in?"

"Thank you," he said as he stepped into the hallway.

"Hello, my name's Mary-Rose."

"Well, hello, Mary-Rose," he said, bending down to shake the toddler's hand. "My name is Robert. I must say how very nice it is to see you again, and how very pretty you look in that dress."

Mary-Rose's face beamed with pride as she held on to his hand and led him into the parlour leaving Megan to follow.

"Mammy's taking me to the park later. Do you want to come?"

"I —" He hesitated as if not sure what to say.

Megan quickly came to his rescue. "I'm sure Captain Fothergill is far too busy to join us in the park today — maybe another time? Now you go play with your building blocks while I make our visitor some tea, there's a good girl."

This seemed to satisfy the child, and she set about dragging her box of wooden bricks across the floor positioning herself and them at the feet of Robert Fothergill. "What are we going to build then?" she asked, her big brown eyes looking up into his face.

Megan left them both delving into the box. She smiled to herself. Her daughter had definitely taken a shine to Captain Fothergill, and much to Megan's surprise he, in turn, obviously felt comfortable with the presumptuous little three-year-old.

Over tea Megan outlined her brother's predicament. Robert Fothergill listened attentively, his dark brown eyes focused on hers, an occasional question probing for further details. By the time she'd finished, his brows were drawn down in a heavy frown and his voice was thoughtful as he said, "It's not been easy for you,

Megan." Then he stood up to leave. "I shall get on to it straight away. I feel the sooner you begin the fight the better."

"You think it'll be a struggle then?"

"Who can say? But I certainly believe it to be worth a try."

The fact that he sounded so enthusiastic gave her some hope. In Captain Fothergill she had found a definite ally, and for some reason this thought warmed her greatly.

"Mrs Partridge, I shall leave you now. But, if it's all right with you, I shall return tomorrow with a draft of a letter for your approval."

"Captain Fothergill, I really can't thank you enough. And I'd feel a lot happier if you called me Megan."

"Only if you call me Robert."

Megan nodded her agreement. "Very well, Robert." She was surprised to find how easy it was for her to address a Fothergill so informally.

That afternoon, as promised, Megan took the children first to the park and then on to the downs. She loved being back on the downs, to look out once again over Clifton Suspension Bridge. It seemed a lifetime ago since she and Sidney had shared the very bench where she now sat watching her daughter at play with the baby gurgling contentedly in his pram.

"Mary, love. Don't you go too far with that ball now, do you hear?"

"Yes, Mammy," her daughter answered, racing along the grass chasing after her brightly coloured ball — a recent gift from Mr Hutchins — Victor. It had surprised Megan how easily he accepted them as part of his family.

Although the day was bright the cold wind gave notice that summer had definitely passed. She was glad she'd dressed the children in their new woollen cardigans with matching hats, lovingly knitted by their Granny Rose.

The baby stirred, Megan peered into the pram to find Tom's bright-blue eyes staring up at her. And then, on seeing his mother's face, he began blowing bubbles and writhing his arms and legs excitedly. He looked so much like his father, except that was for his rosy red cheeks, confirming his good health. The possibility that Sidney might have unwittingly passed on tuberculosis to his son had been a constant worry to her, but up to now, thank God, there had been no sign of it. Megan looked up to see a woman wearing a smart black two-piece walking towards her, waving her hands and smiling. Megan returned the wave when she realized it was her friend, Alice, from up at Redcliffe House. Once face-to-face they hugged and kissed each other.

"How lovely to see you. You haven't changed a bit. I was so pleased when Mam Partridge said you wanted to meet with me," Megan said.

"I couldn't come until today — my day off. It's as mad as ever up at the house. Gosh, I'm so glad to see you looking so well. I have wondered about you, and how you've been coping. I was so sorry to hear about Sidney . . . he was a good 'un," Alice said, giving Megan yet another hug. "Did you get my note? 'Fraid

I'm not very good with writing and such." Alice had eventually released her hold on Megan.

"Yes, I did. And thank you. It meant a lot to know you were all thinking of me. I'm sorry I didn't write back only I wasn't myself for a long time after . . ."

"That's all right. I understand. It must have been such a terrible shock for you," then, noticing Megan's eyes well up with tears, she quickly changed the subject. "Enough of that, tell me, who's the little beauty."

"Mary-Rose, stop playing with the ball and come and meet my friend. Alice, this is my daughter."

Mary-Rose offered her hand, which Alice gently kissed as she knelt to give the child a friendly hug.

"Mary-Rose, love. Do you think that, while I sit and have a chat to Alice, you could rock the baby's pram — you know how it always manages to send little Tom to sleep?"

"Yes, Mammy," she beamed.

Megan knew how much her little daughter loved being treated like a big girl.

"How old is the baby?" Alice asked, taking a seat.

"Nearly eight months. He's no trouble. I've been very lucky in that respect. They're both as good as gold."

"I can see the baby favours Sidney. Whereas Mary-Rose, with her dark curls and big brown eyes, obviously takes after you."

Megan nodded and smiled, while thanking God that her daughter bore no resemblance to her birth father. Instantly shaking herself from such thoughts, she said,

"Mam Partridge tells me there have been a lot of changes since I left Redcliffe House."

"Yeah, and not all for the better either. Mind you, as much as we miss Cook being there every day, it has to be said that Sally does a grand job in her place, though none of us can get used to Mistress Fothergill doing the houskeeper's job. It just doesn't seem fit and proper. Mind you, the one good thing is that Lizzie can no longer queen it like she used to. There's too much to do with Harold's wedding and all. By the way, did Cook tell you about Sadie marrying the butcher boy? He's a bit young and still living in lodgings so she's keeping her job on. Between you and me, I've been thinking of leaving. There's a job going in the lingerie department at Lewis's. I quite fancy myself among all that finery. I always did like pretty knickers."

This made them both laugh aloud. Alice's laugh was so infectious that Mary-Rose joined in as well. Megan raised her eyes to the sky and wondered if Sidney was looking down on her and, if he was, would he forgive her for feeling happier than she had in a long time?

The next day, true to his word, the captain called with a letter.

"Do you approve?" he'd asked, when she had finished reading it.

"Approve? Captain Fothergill . . . I mean Robert, it's . . . it's wonderful. You truly have pleaded Jess's case well. I'm sure those in authority will not fail to be impressed. I really can't thank you enough."

"No thanks needed. And maybe it is I who should be thanking you. It has been a long time since I've felt this much use to anyone. Only please, don't set your hopes too high. This may be the first of many such letters before we achieve any results."

At that precise moment Rose Partridge entered with a tray of tea. "I've left the little ones playing in the garden. The gate is closed so they be quite safe. I couldn't help overhearing what you said about maybe writing more letters. While I, like Megan, appreciate your help, Master Robert. I know you won't mind if I talk open and frank-like."

"Please do," he urged.

Megan wondered what on earth her mother-in-law was up to.

"The thing is, if you and Megan are planning to meet regular, like, and even though I know it be on Jess's behalf, I think it best if you arrange to meet on my days off, when I be at home. It wouldn't do to start tongues wagging, now would it?"

Megan blushed a fierce scarlet but Robert Fothergill appeared not to notice and took the suggestion in his stride.

"Of course," he said, "I really hadn't thought. And yes, you are right. In future I shall check with you before I call on Megan."

Megan could not believe what her mother-in-law had suggested. The thought that anyone might think that she and Captain Fothergill were — Well it was just too ludicrous to think about.

CHAPTER
FOURTEEN

Lizzie entered the kitchen, letting the door slam behind her. "It just isn't fair. I'm supposed to be milady's maid. Do this, fetch that. How many pair of hands does she think I've got? Well not for much longer —" she muttered under her breath.

She was definitely not happy. First, Mrs Jarvis had left. Then Cook was reduced to working part-time. Now, to cap it all, Alice had given in her notice and the mistress had just told her that she, Lizzie Williams, milady's maid, would have to take on Alice's parlour maid's duties as well as her own! Since becoming milady's maid Lizzie had become used to having quite an easy time with the added bonus of having one and a half days off, leaving her plenty of time to visit Arthur or, to be more exact, Arthur's bed. Now, with her extra duties all of this would have to stop.

Lizzie banged the mistress's breakfast tray on to the kitchen table and turned to leave. She was sure that by now Alice would have told them all below-stairs of her leaving and who was expected to do her duties.

"Lizzie, have you heard the news?"

Lizzie took a deep breath, getting ready to answer any attempt to ridicule her.

"Megan and the children have come to visit me and I thought that, with you being family and all, you might like to call around to the cottage for tea one evening."

Lizzie felt sick in her stomach. She was in no mood for yet another shock. This was just too much . . . I bet she has only come to gloat over me, she thought. After all, hadn't Megan managed to return to Wales, marry a man who obviously loved her enough to take on another man's child, and against all odds return to Bristol with two healthy children as Mrs Partridge, the respectable widow. What was she living off, Lizzie wondered? She could not but help compare her own achievements: *she* was still unmarried, a lady's maid-cum-parlour maid, albeit one with a secret nest egg she could *never* boast about.

"Well, you thought wrong! I couldn't care less if I never set eyes on Megan again. And I'd be pleased if you would tell her as much," she said, glaring defiantly at Cook before marching out of the kitchen.

Lizzie rushed to her bedroom. She needed to be alone. The news about her cousin had only strengthened her resolve to find a way of leaving the house for good — determined to show that bloody Megan!

Later, when calmed down, Lizzie realized how Megan's timely visit, so close to Harold's impending wedding, might have played right into her hands. Personally she couldn't wait for him to marry the silly, prim banker's daughter and move away from Redcliffe House — everyone knew that his soon to be father-in-law had recently purchased a large house on

Clifton Road as a wedding gift for the happy couple. Lizzie hoped that once married, Harold would have no need of her. But until then, and with tonight being Wednesday, she would tell him of Megan's visit. She knew it wouldn't take much to convince him that her cousin had returned with the sole purpose of causing him trouble.

"Damn woman! Well, if she thinks she's going to get any more money out of me she's got another thing coming."

Harold Fothergill had been drinking heavily with his friends most of the night, a sort of pre-wedding send off, but by now most of them had fallen by the wayside.

"Can't take the pace, eh? Serious drinking's for men not boys," Harold had boasted as one by one his friends left the party. In the end only Arthur Walters remained, and even he admitted to feeling rather the worse for wear.

"What woman? Who are you mumblin' on about?" Arthur asked, slurring his words.

"That little vixen from Wales. Her, that Megan Williams. Such a sweet piece of meat . . . but a woman scorned and all that? Another drink over here!" Harold called to the barman.

"Are you trying to tell me that you and Megan were —?" Arthur suddenly didn't feel so drunk. "I don't believe it."

"Believe it! It's true. She even had my bastard child . . . a girl I believe. If she needed help she only had to ask. I'm sure we could have come to some

250

arrangement. Why, I would have been willing to set her up with an apartment of her own, had she been more . . . amiable. There was no need for blackmail," he shrugged his shoulders, "Well I don't know what she's up to, but she'll not get another penny! Five hundred pounds is enough of anyone's money. I'll show her."

Arthur was puzzled. He remembered Megan well. He'd liked her a lot and it had surprised him how much he'd missed her when she first left Bristol. Who knows? If she had stayed they might have become friends even . . . He stopped himself. Who was he kidding? Megan would never have been interested in the likes of him, which made it all the more unbelievable that she would have willingly given herself to Harold . . . and blackmail? Harold had mentioned five hundred pounds, the exact amount that Lizzie said she had in her bank account. Surely, it was too much of a coincidence.

"What do you mean, you'll show her?" Arthur asked, suddenly worried for Megan's welfare.

"That's only for me to know. Anyway, why are you so bloody interested all of a sudden?"

Arthur knew he must back off. This was a tricky situation and he would have to think carefully about his next course of action.

"Only wanted to help, that's all," he lied. "You know if there's anything I can do to help . . ." Arthur knew he needed to stay in Harold's confidence if he wanted to find out the truth.

"It's good to know that I have a friend. And yes, I may need your help. But not until after I'm married.

Then I'll show her, I —" Before he could finish the sentence he passed out, falling on the floor.

With the help of an obliging barman, who was probably glad to see the back of them, they managed to carry Harold outside to his waiting car and the ever patient chauffeur.

"Take him home, Hutchins. He'll have a sore head in the morning, that's for sure."

"Certainly, Sir. Can I drop you somewhere, Mr Walters?"

"No, thank you, Hutchins, I need the walk." Arthur watched the car drive away. He needed to think, there was so much going on in his head, and maybe the long walk home would make him see things more clearly.

Unfortunately, the walk didn't help him at all. He had so many questions: should he confront Lizzie with his suspicions, and would she come clean? What did Harold intend to do? Whatever it was, it most certainly involved Megan in some way. He wondered if he should try to warn her, but what proof did he have? It was certainly a dilemma and one that could not easily be resolved.

"Well, aren't you going to ask me in?"

Megan was surprised to see Lizzie standing at the door. In the three weeks since her return to Bristol she had seen nothing of her cousin, not that she had expected to, especially after Rose Partridge had told her how adamant Lizzie had been about not wanting to see either Megan or the children. For a while she just stared in disbelief at Lizzie's changed appearance —

252

gone was her mass of brown curly hair, in its place a short bob smoothed with brilliantine giving a sleek sheen. Her face was heavily powdered, hiding her natural high complexion, which was replaced by the pink rouge obviously chosen to match her bright glossy lipstick.

"Do you intend to keep me standing here all day?"

"No, of course not. Please, come in."

As Lizzie stepped into the hall she brushed Megan's arm. Her soft woollen coat felt soft and luxurious. It was a smart coat with beaver fur trim around both the collar and at the new length short hemline, adding a touch of elegance, so different from the new coat Megan had recently purchased from her mother's shop. Hers was made of a dark-brown barathea, hard wearing and practical.

"I'm sorry I haven't called sooner. It's been so hectic up at the house."

Megan knew this to be true. Mam Partridge had kept her up to date on all the recent staff changes, although Megan didn't believe it to be the reason Lizzie hadn't called on her.

"You look ever so tired, and I have to say, a lot older. Still, I suppose it must be hard for you having two small children and no husband, and, of course, all that trouble with Jess. Who'd have believed that our Jess would have had the backbone to actually kill someone?" Lizzie retorted.

"For your information, our Jess never *meant* to kill anyone. As was proven in court —" Megan was about to elaborate but stopped herself, realizing how futile it would be. Lizzie was not at all interested in anyone but herself. She had proved this when she had failed to send a letter of condolence when Sidney died. Megan felt the anger well up inside her and could contain herself no longer,

"Why have you come, Lizzie? And please don't insult me by saying you care. The truth is we both know there's no love lost between us — although God knows I've tried."

Lizzie walked towards her, her face fixed with a false smile. "I've upset you. I'm so sorry. I didn't mean to come on so strong about Jess. Of course, I know he didn't mean to do it. Come on, let's at least try and be friends, we're family after all. Why, only today I received a letter from my mother asking about you and the children. It made me feel so very guilty that I hadn't found time to visit you. As I said before, it really has been so busy up at the house, what with the wedding and all," Lizzie said, by way of explanation.

Although she sounded genuine, something told Megan not to trust her. One thing for sure, Megan was not about to be drawn on the subject of Harold's wedding.

"Where are the children? I was so hoping to meet them."

Megan decided, if only for her Auntie's sake in Wales, to bite her tongue. She motioned for Lizzie to take a seat.

"They've gone for a walk with their Granny Partridge," Megan answered. She was wondering when the small talk would end and the true reason for

Lizzie's visit emerge. She knew her cousin too well to believe there was no ulterior motive.

"What a pity. Still, there's always next time," Lizzie said, losing the fixed smile, her eyes staring into Megan's. "Anyway perhaps it's for the best. I've got something to tell you . . . and it's really not for their ears." Her voice now lowered to a whisper, "I thought it only right that you should know about the rumours up at the big house — as they concern you."

"Rumours, about me? I don't believe you. Rose would have told me if —"

"Maybe she didn't want you to find out how you and Captain Robert have become the butt of everyones jokes!" Lizzie seemed pleased with herself.

So that's it, Megan thought, the real reason for her visit was to fuel the gossips.

Megan stood up and walked over to the parlour door, then, holding it open, said, "Lizzie, I think you'd better leave."

"Come now, cousin dear! Don't play the innocent with me. Why it's common knowledge that Master Robert regularly calls on you. I'm not pointing a finger, you understand. On the contrary, I'm all for having a bit of fun. After all, he is so good looking and such a good catch, although you must know that his type will never marry the likes of you," she scoffed, making no attempt to move off the sofa.

Megan was furious, "How dare you imply that Captain Fothergill is anything but a gentleman. Although I doubt that you would understand . . . he's a friend, and nothing more. Now will you please leave?"

"A friend you say. Well, there are friends . . . and there are friends. I should be very careful that this friend doesn't make you pregnant, like the last *friend*. Talk about keeping it in the family —" she sniggered and smiled triumphantly.

Megan could not hide her shock. Did her cousin really know the true identity of Mary-Rose's father or was she merely guessing? Megan composed herself. She reasoned that if Lizzie had known the truth, surely she would have found some way to use it against her long before now.

"Hello, we're home," Rose Partridge called from the hallway.

Mary-Rose came running into the parlour, "Mammy, look, a new dolly, a present from Mr Hutch —" Seeing Lizzie she stopped in mid-sentence.

"Hello. You must be Mary-Rose? I've heard so much about you. I'm your Auntie Lizzie. What a lovely dolly. Won't you bring her over to show me?" Then delving into her handbag, "Somewhere in this bag, there's a shiny new threepenny bit I've been saving just for you."

Mary-Rose, a friendly little thing, made her way across the room while at the same time looking to her mother for reassurance. Megan smiled and nodded her approval, although inside she seethed with anger to think that Lizzie would resort to bribery in order to win the child over.

Rose Partridge, having left the pram in the hallway, entered carrying Tom in her arms, and was somewhat taken aback when she saw they had a visitor.

"Lizzie, what —?"

"Lizzie was just leaving. Weren't you?" Megan spoke with such authority in her voice that she even surprised herself.

"Yes. I really must make a move. It was so nice to see you again, Megan. And I did enjoy our little chat. Maybe we can do it again sometime soon?" she said, straightening her coat as she stood up.

Megan didn't answer. She led the way down the hall. She could not wait to be rid of her cousin — not to mention her evil accusations.

"What did that young madam want?" her mother-in-law asked.

"As usual, she was just out to cause trouble. I'll explain later when the children are in bed."

There was to be no escaping the build up to Harold's wedding, especially when Rose Partridge arrived home from Redcliffe House with the news that on the actual day of the wedding the mistress had given all staff the afternoon and night off, as all the family would be away. "And she says it be alright for us to arrange our own party below-stairs. I've had a word with the others, and they all insist you and the children be invited," Rose proudly announced.

Megan would rather not have been asked. She had no wish to return to the house, even as a guest, but felt her refusal would have led to awkward questions, so she accepted gracefully. For days, the party arrangements were all Rose could talk about.

"Won't it be grand to have us all together again?" she'd said.

Megan had hoped that a visit from Robert would change the subject. Yet he, too, seemed preoccupied with the wedding, although for different reasons.

"All this fuss, it's a sham. Left to me, I would not attend. No doubt I shall have to grin and bear it, if only for my mother's sake."

While Megan totally agreed with him, she thought it best to make light of his uncharacteristic outburst.

"I thought everyone enjoyed a wedding. And I'm sure your mother will be as proud as punch to see her first born married to such a fine lady," she said, forcing a smile.

"As would I, if I didn't consider the whole event such a farce. I hate to admit it but my brother is not an honourable man . . . you of all people should know that?"

Megan froze. This was the first time he had given any indication that he remembered the circumstances of their first meeting.

"I'm sorry, I've embarrassed you. I shall take my leave," he said, making for the door. Then by way of changing the subject, "I'm afraid there's been no news as yet regarding Jess's application. Still, no news is good news, as they say. As soon as I hear anything I'll be in touch." And with that he was gone.

Harold James Fothergill, Esquire, and Miss Jane Elizabeth Arkwright were married on Saturday, 20 October 1923, with a reception at the Sefton Hotel. It was a grand affair, where guests were expected to party well into the night, and with this in mind the bride's parents had generously booked accommodation for themselves and all of their guests to stay the night at the hotel. The bride and groom were to spend their wedding night at the Arkwrights' spacious family home, with a full contingence of household staff at their disposal before travelling up to London the next day to spend a few days' honeymoon, thus giving the decorators ample time to put the final touches to their new home.

"We shall take a cruise on the Queen Mary later in the year, my dear, by way of a belated honeymoon," Harold had promised, knowing full well that by then her own healthy bank account would have been in corporated with his, making such a trip easily affordable.

"Whatever you say, dearest," Jane meekly agreed.

Gertrude Fothergill had gratefully accepted the Arkwrights' kind invitation to stay the night at the Sefton Hotel, and offered Lizzie the night off.

"I believe Cook is planning a staff party. I thought you might like to join them all below-stairs. I can assure you it will cause me no hardship, I'm sure the hotel will be only too pleased to supply me with a maid for the night."

"Oh no, m'lady! It just wouldn't seem right for you to be looked after by a stranger. I really would rather accompany you." Lizzie had sounded so convincing; she didn't want her mistress to suspect her ulterior motive.

"Very well, if you're sure," was all the mistress said, but Lizzie knew that she was secretly pleased.

Lizzie couldn't wait to tell Arthur, who, as a close friend of Harold's, had been invited to the wedding and also to stay the night. Which meant that, as she was accompanying the mistress, they could, for the first time spend a whole night together.

The familiar kitchen felt so warm and welcoming and, with everyone so genuinely pleased to see her and the children, Megan's initial feeling of foreboding quickly disappeared. To her surprise, she soon found herself actually enjoying being there. Rose had been right, it was nice to see all of her old friends again. Sally, Sadie, Percy, Mr Hutchins and Alice — who appeared to be treating it as her own private leaving party.

"Look at all the lovely food, Mummy. And Granny Rose says she's made a big cake," Mary-Rose squealed with excitement.

Megan's biggest surprise of all was seeing Mrs Jarvis — not the fact that she had been invited, but at how different she looked. Megan remembered her always dressed in long black sombre clothes with her hair tied back in a tight bun. Today she stood before Megan dressed in an elegant aqua-green costume, her hair falling softly around her face in a flattering pageboy style. She looked much younger. She had put on a little weight, and it suited her.

"Hello, Megan. How nice it is to see you again, and with two such beautiful children," Mrs Jarvis said, taking Megan's hand and gently patting it before continuing, "I often wondered what became of you. I was so sad to hear about Sidney . . . I remember him as such a kind young man. I'm sure he made a good husband and father."

"Yes, he did, and thank you. Although our time together was far too short, I do consider myself lucky to have shared so much with him." Megan was overcome by a feeling of relief. This was the first time she had been able to think of Sidney without the pain, the hurt . . . the guilt.

"I hope we can talk again, later perhaps?"

"I'd like that. And Mrs Jarvis . . . thank you again."

It seemed strange to Megan how no one even mentioned Harold or his new bride all day. Although they did raise a glass — a choice of sherry or beer — in a toast, "To Mistress Fothergill!" As the day progressed it led to much singing and dancing with everyone in general good spirits. It reminded Megan of her first staff Christmas party, and of how much she and Sidney had enjoyed themselves.

"Come on, Mammy, come dance with me." Megan smiled at her daughter. Then after checking on baby Tom, who was happily gurgling away in his pram near the fireplace, the same fireplace she had so proudly cleaned to perfection, she allowed Mary-Rose to lead her into the centre of the kitchen floor where the rest of the staff were already dancing to the sound of Al Jolson coming from Mr Hutchins's phonograph.

Around five-thirty, Megan stood watching Mary-Rose as she attempted to dance with Percy who, it had to be said, had two left feet. Rose was dancing with Mr Hutchins. Sadie and Alice danced together, while Sadie's adoring husband looked on.

Megan had thought it was nearly time to leave and take the children home, but seeing Mary-Rose enjoying herself, and the fact that, despite all the noise, baby Tom had fallen fast asleep in his pram, she decided to stay a little longer, at least until the huge fruit cake was cut.

With so much going on no one noticed Captain Fothergill enter the room carrying a case of champagne under his arm.

"Hello, Megan."

"Why, Captain . . . Robert . . . what are you doing here? Shouldn't you be with the wedding party?"

"Do you think anyone would mind if I gatecrashed this one? I have come bearing gifts."

He need not have worried. Everyone was pleased to see him, and not just because of the champagne either. They genuinely liked him. It seemed the rigid divide she remembered between above and below-stairs was slowly disappearing and in its place had come a kind of mutual respect — no doubt a sign of the changing times.

"Well, what's going on here? I hope you've saved a dance for me," Robert teased, as he bent down taking Mary-Rose's hand. She had just finished dancing with Percy and was eagerly biting into a large piece of fruit cake, but still managed to let out a little squeal of pleasure.

"I'll take that as a yes then, shall I?" he joked. "And do you think, if I ask her nicely, your mother might dance with me too?"

262

As Mary-Rose excitedly nodded her head in approval, he looked towards Megan, who suddenly felt extremely embarrassed.

A few dances later he stood holding out his hand to her, "May I have this dance?"

Nervously, Megan stepped forward, as if in a dream. The dance, a slow waltz, she knew would stay in her memory forever. As he held her to him, his arm warm and firm around her waist, her whole being tingled. Her hand visibly shook as she placed it loosely around his neck. She was so glad her gaze was directed over his shoulder — for if at that very moment he had been able to look into her eyes he would have plainly seen the love she felt for him.

Robert, aware they were being watched by the rest of the party, strove to hold her at a respectable distance. Cook had told him about Lizzie's visit and what she had said regarding certain rumours, so he understood the need for propriety — he didn't want to compromise Megan in any way. And in order not to be seen to single her out, he intended to ask every other woman in the room for a dance before the evening was over. With his arm around Megan's waist he felt the urge to pull her to him, to feel her soft face against his, to kiss her tenderly and tell her how much he loved her. Of course he resisted. It was neither the time nor the place. He wondered if there would ever be a "right time" for him and Megan.

CHAPTER
FIFTEEN

Megan had planned to return to Wales with the children a few days before Monday, the fifth of November — the date scheduled for her next visit with Jess.

"Couldn't you stay a little longer?" Rose Partridge pleaded, "I dread the day you have to leave. It's been such a joy having you and the children here at the cottage."

It was strange how Megan also felt the need to stay on, at least for a little while longer. Before committing herself she wrote to her mother to find out if she was needed back at the shop. Her mother quickly replied saying that although she missed having her and the children around, it was only fair to let them get to know their Granny Rose. And as for the shop, Phyllis had recently started serving at the counter and was doing very well, leaving Olive free to take on the alterations, so there was no need for her to rush back.

With this assurance she decided to extend her visit. Needless to say, Rose was thrilled.

"I still intend to go and see Jess. I couldn't let him down. I know how he looks forward to my visits. I'm sure it's the only thing that keeps him going in that dreadful place."

"Of course you must go. The children can stay with me. We shall have great fun."

"Thank you. It will make life a lot easier if I travel alone. I thought I'd go up and back in a day. If I take the early train I would arrive in Cardiff well in time for my one o'clock visit. I plan to return on the six o'clock."

"All that travelling. Are you sure it be wise?"

"It's worth it just to see Jess. I only wish I was going armed with some good news for him."

Although they had received two letters from the court, both were non-committal. The first politely acknowledged her application on her brother's behalf. The second, with its many legal references, might as well have been written in a foreign language for all the sense it made to her. She had simply handed it to Robert. He assured her that Jess's early release was being seriously considered.

"There's still time before your visit. Tonight I shall pray even harder," Rose encouraged.

Megan smiled and nodded, "You're right. There's still time."

The very next morning Robert stood at the door frantically waving a letter in his hand.

"Megan, we've done it; Jess's case is being reviewed as we speak. This letter confirms it. The Lord Chief Justice has promised to seek advice from the Governor of Cardiff Prison. If the report on Jess's behaviour during his incarceration is favourable, he could be released within the next couple of months."

Without thinking, Megan flung her arms around his neck. "Oh thank you, thank you, this is all your doing. I can't wait to tell Jess —" Then she quickly released her hold on him. "I'm so sorry . . . what must you think of me?"

"Please, don't apologize, I quite enjoyed it," he joked. Then seeing her blush, "Look, don't give it another thought. Although you must realize that while the news is good, we still have to play a waiting game."

If Lizzie believed Harold's marriage would end his visits to her bedroom, she had been greatly mistaken, for only a few days after returning from honeymoon he began staying at Redcliffe House on Wednesday and Friday nights. He told his gullible bride that he needed to stay to discuss family business with his mother, and of course, being a considerate husband, he did not want to disturb his darling wife by arriving home at a late hour. No, it would be much better for him to stay in his old room. Of course, in truth, he would be in Lizzie's bed.

This arrangement puzzled his mother. She wondered why he felt the need to spend time away from his new wife. Whatever the reason, she was sure it had nothing to do with the business, as these days Harold seldom entered into any sort of conversation with her, least of all about the Fothergill Tobacco Company. The last time they had spoken on the subject was after one of her charity luncheons, where she'd overheard whispers suggesting that "the Fothergill company was in serious trouble". On arriving home she confronted Harold who became very angry.

"Gossips! I can't believe you would listen to silly gossips."

Although not wishing to upset him, yet needing to know the truth, she pressed him further. "If we were in trouble, you would tell me, dear, wouldn't you?"

Harold changed tactic, believing the best form of defence to be in attack.

"Is all this because I told you to cut back on the household staff? I only suggested cutting back, thinking it was what you wanted. You said it didn't seem right keeping such a large staff for so few, especially when I was soon to be married and have a home of my home. Or have things changed now that Robert's been discharged from the funny farm?"

"Your brother was at a military hospital, and you would do well to remember what he has been through. As for him living in this house, this is his home, and like you, he is welcome to stay as long as it pleases him."

Although surprised by her outburst, he cursed himself. He should have known she would rear up to defend *her* Robert. He decided to try a different approach.

"I understand. The invalid needs looking after so you require extra staff to help you, is that it?"

"Your brother is no invalid. He just needed time to adjust to civilian life. And no, I do not require extra staff. On the contrary, since Mrs Jarvis chose to leave, I've enjoyed running the household. It makes me feel

. . . useful. All I want is your assurance that all is well within the company."

Harold knew he had won. "Now, don't you go giving it another thought, Mother dear. I assure you, everything is fine." He bent down and placed a kiss on her forehead.

Harold truly believed that the problem with the business was just a hiccup. Before long he was bound to have a turn of luck at the tables. Failing that, there was always his wife. What was the point of marrying a banker's daughter if she could not secure funds from her doting father?

Harold slid in alongside Lizzie, pleased at having what seemed to be the best of both worlds. He had married well, although he had hoped that what his wife lacked in good looks she would more than make up for in the bedroom. Unfortunately, it was not to be. While she, ever mindful of her duties as a wife, allowed him to take her at will, it soon became obvious that she had no inclination for the pleasures of the flesh, never responding, lying almost lifeless until the act was over. Thank God for his Lizzie. Now *she* knew how to please a man. Aroused at the mere thought of what pleasures lay in store for him he began to perspire.

Harold lay alongside Lizzie feeling both satisfied and exhausted. Once again she had not disappointed him — he could always rely on her, which strengthened his belief in her as an ally in his plan to get back at Megan Partridge, especially since the new development. It had happened the very day he returned from his honeymoon. After spending a week in the sole company of his wife, he'd felt the need for male company and headed for his club. There, waiting for his return was a letter or, to be precise, a *blackmail* letter. It was then that he decided that enough was enough. Now that he was safely married he was determined not to give that bitch another penny. The time had come for revenge.

"Lizzie, how would you like to earn yourself fifty pounds?" Harold asked, lighting a cigarette, which always seemed to taste so much better after sex.

"Are you joking?" Lizzie laughed.

"No, I'm serious. I need you to look after something for me for a few days. It would mean you having to take time off from the house?"

"But how can I do that? What excuse would I give the mistress, and where am I to stay?"

"Just tell her that your poor mother's ill and you need to visit her in Wales. You know my mother. She's a soft touch for a sob story. And don't worry, I've rented rooms down by the docks. You can stay there. Mind you, no gadding about, you'll have to keep your head down."

"What do you want me to look after?"

"You'll know soon enough. It's to be our little secret. Well, will you do it?" Harold had thought it best not to reveal too much of his plan at this stage.

Lizzie didn't answer. She watched as he trembled with excitement. It was obvious he was up to something, but what?

Harold took her silence as a sign of indecision, "One hundred pounds. I'll give you one hundred pounds. What do you say?"

"All right. I'll do it." Lizzie couldn't believe he had doubled the amount. She would have done it for fifty pounds.

The next morning Lizzie sneaked out of the house and made her way to Arthur's apartment. The sooner she prepared him for her trip away the better.

She found him sitting on the sofa surrounded by official-looking documents. As she entered the room he quickly gathered them up — almost as if he didn't want her to see them.

Lizzie smiled to herself. She was being paranoid, suspecting everyone of conspiracy.

"Arthur, love, I've received a letter from home. Apparently my mam's not very well. I've been to see the mistress and she suggested that I go home for a few days."

"I'm sorry to hear that. Of course, you must go."

"I thought I'd go the day after tomorrow," she said, trying to sound casual.

"Do you need a lift to the station?"

"No!" Lizzie answered, rather too sharply.

Arthur threw her a look of surprise.

She quickly added, "Thank you, but Hutchins said he would give me a lift." Lizzie hoped she had covered herself. It wouldn't do if Arthur became suspicious.

For once she was telling the truth. Harold had already arranged for Hutchins to drop her off at the station on Monday morning. From there she was to take a cab to the docks. He still hadn't told her what he was up to. She expected it to be something shady — why else would he have offered her one hundred pounds?

She walked over to the sofa draping herself across Arthur's lap, planting a passionate kiss on his mouth. She felt her nipples harden with desire — he always managed to affect her that way.

"Don't you worry, I'll not stay away any longer than I need to," Lizzie said, as she slowly undid the top of her dress, revealing her full breasts.

Arthur was not at all worried. In fact he was quite pleased she was going away for a while. He had begun to tire of her. He guessed she wanted marriage. Her offer of five hundred pounds — money he now believed to be the fruits of her blackmail — had been a simple ploy to make him beholden to her. If she became his partner in business then it would be easy to become a partner in marriage. For Arthur, both were out of the question.

In the beginning his relationship with Lizzie had been fun, and it had to be said, he would miss her shameless lovemaking, but the time had come to move on. While she was away visiting her mother he would make serious enquiries with regards to his plans for the future. Since the loss of the lucrative contract from the Fothergill Tobacco Company Arthur's transport business had taken a nosedive. Although Harold had assured him it was purely a temporary arrangement, Arthur didn't believe him. It was obvious that Harold was not interested in working for a living, he preferred spending his time drinking and gambling at his club, or else in some woman's bed.

Anyway, Arthur had become restless. He had long decided to cut his losses and make a new start, while he could still afford a stake in a new and exciting venture. America seemed favourite. Everywhere you looked, billboards boasted it to be a land of freedom and opportunity.

On Monday morning, Hutchins, as requested, took Lizzie armed with a small valise to the train station. Before taking his leave, he conveyed his good wishes for her mother's health then bid her good day. With Hutchins safely out of the way she hailed a cab to take her to an address on the docks. At first, she wondered if it wasn't a little too close for comfort to Arthur's apartment, which was only about half a mile away, but she soon dismissed any fears, telling herself Arthur had no business on the actual docks, a place he seldom visited. The apartment Harold had taken for her was situated on a narrow cobbled street above a shop. Its entrance was through a small gap between premises and up a flight of iron steps. She let herself in with the key Harold had given her, promising to visit later and explain all. She was beginning to find the intrigue quite exciting. One thing for sure, it was better than working for a living and certainly better paid!

The rooms of her secret dwelling consisted of a small, comfortably furnished parlour, a double bedroom, a bath and water closet and a kitchen, which she found to be well stocked. Harold obviously expected her to take all her meals on the premises. With so much food, it entered her mind that maybe Harold intended to join her and that he'd rented the apartment as a kind of love nest — but surely he wouldn't have offered her so much money just to spend a few days alone with her? No, he had definitely asked her to look after something for him.

After spending a boring hour on her own, Lizzie was glad when Harold finally arrived carrying a bottle of wine.

"Well done, Lizzie. I'm glad to see you made it. Let me pour us a drink and I'll tell you of my plan. We've got until Wednesday evening to rehearse it. We shall only have the one chance so we have to get it right."

"What's happening on Wednesday?" Lizzie asked.

"I have it on good authority that on Wednesday your dear cousin intends to go to Cardiff to visit her convict of a brother." Harold had overheard Robert telling his mother about some good news regarding Megan.

"Megan! You mean all this has to do with Megan?"

Harold made a grab for her wrist, squeezing it hard, "What I'm about to tell you must go no further, do you hear?"

"Master Harold, you're hurting me!" she cried.

"It's nothing to what I'll do if you let me down." Slowly he released his grip. "Now, don't pretend there's any love lost between you and your cousin. And from what I've seen I can't say I blame you. For more than three years, ever since that bitch left Bristol, she's been holding me to ransom, threatening to tell the world that her brat of a daughter is my child."

Lizzie caught her breath, pretending to be shocked. Afraid her face might give the game away. From now on she would need to be an even better actress.

"I don't believe it."

"Believe it. And believe this. On Wednesday evening I intend to borrow my father-in-law's horse and carriage and take the child from her grandmother's house in Clifton."

"Oh, Master Harold! Is that wise?" Lizzie wasn't at all sure she wanted any part of this.

"For days now I've been secretly watching Cook's cottage, and around four o'clock every day the child is left to play alone in the garden. All it needs is for me to pull the carriage up near the back gate, then you can creep into the garden, grab the child and bring her to me. Within minutes we shall be on our way."

"But what makes you think she'll come with me? She really doesn't know me that well — and what if Cook was to catch me?"

"You're her auntie, surely the child trusts you. And in the unlikely event of you being caught, all you have to say is that you decided to call and visit. After all you are family; what could be more normal?"

He'd planned it well, but Lizzie had reservations. Blackmail was one thing. But kidnapping . . .?

"Don't tell me you're getting cold feet. Think of the money," he urged.

Lizzie felt a sudden rush of excitement, the danger, the risk. "OK I'll do it, but for two hundred pounds!" She thought it worth a try.

"Yes-yes, whatever."

274

He had agreed, and from now on there could be no going back.

Early on Wednesday morning Hutchins once again was making a trip to the railway station, this time to drop off Megan.

"It's a pity you couldn't have travelled to Wales a few days earlier, then you would have had the company of your cousin Lizzie," Hutchins said, by way of making conversation. He could tell she was on edge about travelling alone.

"Lizzie's gone home to Wales?" Megan asked.

"Yes, she's gone to visit her mother. Apparently she's not been too well, didn't you know?" They had arrived at the station, and Hutchins politely opened the door for her.

"No, I haven't heard a thing." Megan wondered why her mother hadn't mentioned that Aunt Margaret was poorly in her last letter, but put it down to her mother not wanting to worry her. She herself had a letter, which she intended to post in Cardiff, informing her mother of the recent developments in their fight for an early release date for Jess. Before sending it she would add a postscript sending Aunt Margaret her good wishes for a speedy recovery, and hoping that having Lizzie home would be the tonic she needed. Megan knew how much her aunt loved her only daughter and how glad she would be to think Lizzie had taken the time to visit her. For once Lizzie appeared to be thinking of someone else.

At four-fifteen on Wednesday afternoon Harold pulled the horse to a stop outside Rose Partridge's back garden. With the nights of winter coming in, it was already beginning to get dark as Lizzie slowly stepped out of the carriage, her throat dry, her heart racing. Harold had stressed that she needed to act quickly if she didn't want to be discovered. As she approached the gate she peered into the garden. There, just as Harold had said, she found Mary-Rose happily running along the grass chasing after her ball.

"Hello, Mary-Rose." Lizzie spoke softly.

"I-I —" the child was not sure.

"I'm your Auntie Lizzie, remember? And I've come to take you for a trip up to the downs. Look, I've a horse and carriage waiting outside to take us there, but you'll have to hurry or it will go without us," Lizzie said holding out her hand.

The child looked hesitant.

"Come on, don't be shy. I've cleared it with your granny. She says as long as we're back by five-thirty for tea we can go." The lie worked.

The mention of her granny was all that was needed to ensure the child's complete trust. Mary-Rose excitedly took her hand and together they rushed out of the gate and into the waiting cab, the child still clutching in one hand her brightly coloured ball.

"Well done!" Harold said, then handing her a sodden piece of cloth, "Place this over her mouth for a few minutes."

"What is it?" Lizzie asked. Surely he didn't intend to hurt the child? She hadn't agreed to that.

276

"Don't worry, it's only a little chloroform to send her off to sleep," he whispered, not wanting the child to hear. "I promise, it'll do her no harm. Now just do it!" he snapped.

Sensing the change in mood Mary-Rose started to whimper. "I want my mammy —" She was soon silenced when Lizzie placed the foul smelling cloth over her tiny face. Within seconds the child was sound asleep.

As the carriage slowly made its way through the streets of Bristol heading for the docks, no one would have suspected that a dreadful crime was being committed, a crime against a defenceless child.

Harold felt no shame or guilt. It never once occurred to him that he was hurting his own daughter. Lizzie, while not wishing to hurt the child, only viewed it as a means to an end. All she wanted was to have enough money to leave her old life and become a toff.

Rose Partridge, having fed the baby and settled him into his cot, returned to the garden. To her horror young Mary-Rose was nowhere to be seen . . .

"Mary-Rose! Mary-Rose!" she screamed out, again and again.

There was no reply. Then she noticed the wide open gate. It was always closed. She ran out on to the road.

Robert was driving toward Redcliffe House when he spotted Rose Partridge pushing baby Thomas's pram. She was obviously in a great hurry and looked distressed.

"Cook, whatever's wrong?" he asked, pulling the car to a stop alongside her and winding down the window.

"Oh, Master Robert! I was just coming up to the house for help. I didn't know what else to do. The most dreadful thing has happened. Mary-Rose has vanished off the face of the earth. It be all my fault, I should never have left her unattended . . . I only went to feed the baby . . . she was happily playing with her ball . . . and now she's gone. How will I tell Megan?" She had become hysterical; the baby started to cry.

Robert stepped out of the car, "Try to calm yourself. Look, you're frightening the baby," he said sternly. It worked. Cook quickly composed herself.

"That's better. Now take the baby back to the cottage. I'll follow in the car, and together we shall check every nook and cranny. I'm sure we shall find her playing one of her hide-and-seek games," Robert said, trying to reassure her. He needed to get them safely back to the cottage.

An hour later they had exhausted every possibility.

"You see, Master Robert, she's nowhere to be found," Rose cried into her handkerchief. Luckily the walk in the pram had sent the baby to sleep.

Robert examined the garden gate, "You say you left her playing here in the garden?"

"Yes-yes! I needed to feed the baby and rather than bring her indoors . . . Megan always lets her play alone in the garden around the same time every afternoon — weather permitting, of course. I thought it would be all right if I did the same . . . But I shouldn't have . . . it be my fault . . ."

"Why don't you go and make yourself a nice cup of tea? I'll go and get Hutchins to sit with you while I make some enquiries. Try not to fret. I'm sure there's a perfectly good explanation . . . there has to be." He didn't tell her of his intention to contact the police. As soon as he had examined the gate he knew there was no way a child could have opened it. And if she hadn't — then who the hell had?

CHAPTER
SIXTEEN

As Megan boarded the train she was exhausted. It had been a long day but she felt the visit had been a good one. To have been the bearer of good news for a change had made all the difference. She had left Jess in good spirits after she promised to thank Robert Fothergill on his behalf.

"One day, I hope I shall be able to thank the captain in person," he said. Then, out of the blue, "Megs. Are you sweet on him?"

"Whatever made you ask that?" She felt her colour rise.

"Well, it may have had something to do with the way your eyes light up every time you mention his name."

"Do they? Do they really?" Then seeing him smile, "Jess Williams, you're teasing me. Shame on you —"

They both laughed. It felt good to see Jess laugh, even if it was at her expense. With God's help and Robert's letters, he would soon be released, and could begin to look to the future.

Megan settled into her seat in the otherwise empty compartment. The train moved slowly out of the station, gathering speed as it cleared the platform. After a while the guard came and checked her ticket, he made no attempt at conversation, simply did his job and moved on his way. In a few hours she would be safely back in Bristol with her children, her mother-in-law . . . and Robert.

With this comforting thought she gave way to the motion of the train lulling her into a deep sleep. She dreamt that Jess had been released and there was a big party in the back kitchen of their old house. Everyone was there — Mam, Jess, Olive and John, Phyllis, Bryn, Evan, Granny Williams, Granny Rose, Aunt Margaret and . . . Robert. Robert was sitting in Dad's comfortable big armchair in front of the fireplace. She could plainly see the large tin bath in the centre of the room. Robert smiled at her. But she couldn't see her children . . . where were her children? She awoke with a start as the train jerked to a stop.

"Bristol Temple Meads," the guard called out.

After adjusting her clothing, she proceeded to leave the train. Rose had practically ordered Hutchins to be sure to pick her up. She couldn't wait to get back to the cottage and see her children; she had missed not having them with her. Once on the platform she looked for Hutchins, and she smiled when she saw Robert, not Hutchins, walking briskly towards her. Her smile was not returned. He looked pale, worried . . . frightened even.

"Robert, what is it? What's wrong?"

"Megan. It's Mary-Rose . . . I'm afraid she's gone missing."

As much as he had been dreading telling her, he insisted on being the one to meet her off the train. He'd left Hutchins in the cottage comforting Rose.

"Don't be silly, Robert. She's with her Granny Partridge. Robert, you're frightening me. Please tell me she's safe . . . please!"

"Megan, she went missing from the garden this afternoon. Cook was in the kitchen feeding the baby, when she'd finished there was no sign of her." He felt drained. "The police have been called . . . just to be on the safe side, you understand? I'm sure she'll show up soon." He dared not tell her of his secret fears that she might have been abducted, a fear he knew was also held by the police.

"It doesn't make sense, Mary-Rose would never go from the garden . . . how could she have opened the gate? Someone must have taken her —" She swayed and would have fallen if he had not put an arm around her waist and supported her across the platform to his waiting car.

"Take me home, Robert. I want to be there for her when she returns."

The journey back to the cottage seemed to take forever. Her day had begun with so much promise. Maybe this was God telling her that by answering her prayer to help Jess, she must pay a price. She would have willingly paid with her life, "But, please God, don't let anyone hurt my daughter."

"*Echo. Eve'nin Echo!*" the hawker shouted.

Arthur stopped to buy the local rag and placed it inside his coat. He would read it later. Right now he was eager to get to the purser's office and book his passage to America. It had all happened so quickly, once the initial decision to go had been made. The necessary application only meant filling in a simple form. It seemed that as long as you could prove you didn't have a criminal record — which in Arthur's case was more by luck than judgement, having spent most of his adult life skirting the law — acceptance was virtually guaranteed. Now all he had to do was pay the fifty pounds for a one-way ticket, and in just seven days' time he would be on his way to a new life.

Leaving the booking-office Arthur felt into his pocket, making sure his newly purchased first-class, upper-deck ticket was safe. It would have been a lot cheaper to travel steerage, but, from past experience, he believed opportunities only presented themselves when mixing with the "right people". The voyage across the Atlantic Ocean would give him both the time and opportunity to glean information and make new and, he hoped, influential acquaintances, to help ease his transition into a new country.

As he walked out of the dock gates, his eyes were drawn to a familiar figure on the opposite side of the road. At first he didn't believe his eyes. Surely, it couldn't be Lizzie? She was supposed to be in Wales visiting her mother. Even though she had her back to him there was no mistaking the walk, the hair and the petite figure. She seemed in a hurry. He watched as she turned into a side alley. Arthur ran across the road hoping to catch up with her, but by the time he'd reach the other side she was nowhere in sight. Puzzled, he slowly walked down the narrow cobbled alley. Mystified by her sudden disappearance he decided to check in each of the quaint little shops along the way, a shipwright's, a bookshop and finally a tobacconist, but still no luck. At the end of the alley stood the Queen's Head public house. Although he doubted he would find her in there during the day, he suddenly felt the need of a beer.

Once inside he was hit by a strong stench of stale beer and cigarette smoke. The bar room was dark and much busier than he had expected. Most of the tables positioned around the large open fireplace were taken by fishermen and sailors. One or two gave him a cursory glance but most ignored him. As he made his way to the serving hatch he was surprised to hear a familiar voice call out to him.

"Arthur, my good man. Come, join me." Harold's smile was false, his speech far too gushing.

"Harold, whatever brings you to this area?"

"A bit of business," he answered tapping the side of his nose, and throwing him a look of defiance, daring Arthur to question him further. He immediately turned the table on him. "I was about to ask you the same question, old man."

Arthur hesitated for a moment. He didn't want Harold to know of his plan to leave the country — he would find out soon enough.

"I like you, had a bit of business. You know how it is," he said, and tapped the side of his nose copying Harold's unspoken signal.

Both men sensed the other to be hiding something, but neither pursued the issue. Instead they shared a jug of beer and settled down at a vacant table in a small alcove. Arthur politely inquired about Harold's new wife. Harold joked that marriage was an institution to be encouraged and suggested Arthur should think about finding a suitable wife.

For about an hour they talked — mostly small talk, both awaiting a suitable moment to end their meeting and be on their separate way. Arthur needed to find Lizzie's true whereabouts. Harold wanted to visit the rooms above the bookshop to check on Lizzie and the child.

In the end it was left to Arthur to make the first move.

"Well, old chap, as much as I would like to sit with you all day, I really must be on my way. Some of us have to earn a living, you know?"

"Quite, maybe we could get together later at the club?"

Both men stood up from the table.

"Yes, that would be nice. Until later then . . ." Arthur said, politely shaking Harold's hand. Which seemed unusually hot and clammy.

Once out of the pub, Arthur automatically looked up and down the alleyway, although he was sure that by now Lizzie was well gone — but where? Leaving the alley, Arthur hailed a cab. He would return to his apartment and try to figure out why Lizzie had lied about going to Wales?

A black cab pulled up along side him.

"Take me to 25 Docks Road," Arthur instructed the driver, as he positioned himself on the spacious back seat.

"Certainly, sir, 25 Docks Road it is."

As the car sped along, Arthur reached into his coat and pulled out the local evening paper.

The headlines screamed out at him!

MYSTERY OF CHILD'S DISAPPEARANCE

Arthur quickly read on . . .

. . . the mystery as to the whereabouts of Mary-Rose Partridge, aged three years. She disappeared from the Clifton area yesterday at around four o'clock. Anyone who may have seen the child either while she was in the care of her grandmother Mrs Rose Partridge, or at anytime afterwards, is asked to call at the police station. There is a substantial reward offered for any information leading to the child being found.

Arthur was stunned. Then suddenly everything made sense . . . Lizzie, being on the docks when she should have been in Wales . . . bumping into Harold at almost the same place where Lizzie had vanished into thin air . . . Lizzie, making Harold believe Megan to be the blackmailer . . . Harold's veiled threat to "teach the Welsh bitch a lesson" — It all added up.

"Cabby, take me to Victoria Road, Clifton."

"Victoria Road, it is, sir." Unquestioningly, the cabby turned the car at the next junction and headed towards Clifton.

286

Robert Fothergill had not long returned home from spending a harrowing morning visiting Megan. He could tell she was close to breaking point and felt powerless at not being able to help her. She was suffering so much, he could feel her pain himself. After all, her pain was his — he had long ago realised he was in love with her. She didn't know of course, and he had no intention of telling her. It had taken a long time for her to regard him as a friend — a Fothergill male she could trust — and he didn't want to do anything that might endanger their friendship.

Today, he had tried to assure her that everything would be all right and Mary-Rose would soon be found. But, in truth, he had his doubts. After all the child was only three and she had been missing all night. He omitted to tell Megan that police divers had been scouring the river bed at the bottom of Clifton gorge.

"We have to eliminate all possibilities, sir," the police sergeant informed him earlier.

Suddenly a terrible image came into his head. He could plainly see his fellow soldiers as they lay in the foul-smelling mud, their bodies twisted and mangled almost beyond recognition, and Mary-Rose's small-framed torso amongst them. He shook his head repeatedly in an effort to rid himself of such a terrible vision, praying it was not in some way a premonition. Surely this could not be the fate of such a sweet young child? In the distance he heard a loud knocking. Someone was at the door, distracting him. He blinked, making sure the horrific image had gone.

Hutchins entered, "Sorry to disturb you, Captain. But a Mister Arthur Walters has called to the house. He asked to see you. He says it's urgent." Hutchins thought how tired the captain looked. He hoped that this terrible business concerning Megan's daughter wouldn't affect his recovery. He'd seemed so in control of late.

"That's all right. It may be good news. Please show him in."

The name Arthur Walters seemed vaguely familiar to him and he tried, in vain, to put a face to the name.

"Captain Fothergill, it's good of you to see me," Arthur said, shaking the captain's hand.

"Mr Walters, please take a seat. Can I get you a drink?" Robert knew he'd met his visitor before, but could not for the life of him remember where or when.

"Thank you. I think a stiff Scotch would be in order for both of us. What I'm about to say may come as a shock. But I had to come and tell you of my suspicion."

"I'm intrigued," Robert said, handing him a drink.

"I'll not beat about the bush. I believe you have some connection with the family of the girl who recently went missing from the Clifton area."

"Yes, that is correct. I like to think I am a friend. Have you any news of the child?"

"Well, I have reason to believe the child has been abducted. I also believe I know where the blame lies."

"If you really have such important information, why have you not gone to the police, or are you the abductor? Is it your intention to hold me to ransom?"

"No, no! Although you may wish I was. You see I have come to name your brother as the kidnapper."

"Harold? Surely not! Why would he —?" Although Robert was shocked, in truth, he knew his brother was more than capable of such a thing. "What evidence do you have to support such a claim?"

"I believe Harold to be the missing child's true father. I know for a fact that he had wrongly been led to believe that Megan — Mrs Partridge, the child's mother — had been blackmailing him. Of course it was a lie."

"How do you know all this?"

"Because I believe I know who the real blackmailer is."

"You do? Then you must tell me."

"No. But I'm sure there's a way we can thwart your brother." Arthur handed Robert his empty glass, indicating the need for another.

"And what reason do you have for helping if not monetary?" Robert asked, as he refilled both their glasses.

"All in good time. I'll tell you everything if you agree to join forces with me — together I'm sure we can get the child back safely."

"Megan, do you trust me?" Robert asked, not looking forward to the task ahead.

"Yes, of course I do. Why do you have to ask?"

"You see, I need to know the true identity of Mary-Rose's father?"

The shocked look on Megan's face told him he needed to tread very carefully.

"Megan, I need to know. Believe me, if I didn't think it would help us find Mary-Rose, I would never ask."

"I don't understand. How could it possibly be of any help?"

"Earlier today I had an unexpected visitor, who shall at this stage remain nameless. Suffice to say accusations were made against my brother which, if true, would explain the child's disappearance, although even I, knowing what my brother is capable of, find it hard to believe he would stoop to this."

"Harold. What has he to do with it?"

"Megan, I have to know — is Harold Mary-Rose's father?"

"Yes — yes — yes! I never wanted anyone to know the truth. She's mine, mine and Sidney's. Please, promise me you'll tell no one," she sobbed, her hands covering her face, attempting to hide her shame.

"The evil bastard! I blame myself. I should have known after he attacked you that night in the parlour that he was sure to try again . . . and the bastard did! Oh Megan! I'm so very sorry. How can you bear to even speak to me? I'm ashamed to be his brother. Can you forgive me."

She had stopped crying. She looked up into his sad eyes.

"Robert, I don't blame you — you have nothing to feel guilty about. It all happened a long time ago. Of course Sidney knew the truth and was happy to accept the child as his own. As far as everyone else was

290

concerned, Mary-Rose was mine and Sidney's, and that's how I want it to stay. You must promise to tell no one."

"Of course I promise, although my visitor today has somehow guessed the truth and believes Harold to be holding the child. Perhaps now you will understand why I felt the need to press you for the truth."

Megan was shaking her head in disbelief, "You're telling me that Harold has taken Mary-Rose? I don't understand. For what purpose? Surely he doesn't want to recognize her as his daughter?"

"No, I wouldn't have thought so. If my informer is right then Harold has taken her as an act of revenge." He did not add that he feared for the child's safety.

"But what possible cause could he have?"

Robert felt there was nothing to be gained by revealing her cousin Lizzie's part in it. For the time being she had enough to cope with, without the added burden of family betrayal.

"Who knows the workings of his sick mind? All I ask is that you trust me to deal with him. I don't want to raise your hopes too high but I have agreed to join forces with the informer, and together we hope to find Mary-Rose and bring her safely to you before the night is out."

"Robert, I swear, if he harms one hair on her head, I'll do for him. He may have been able to hurt me but —"

He put his finger to her mouth stopping her short, then, putting his arms around her he pulled her to him. "Please, Megan, my love. Trust me." His face brushed hers and before he knew he was kissing her lips . . . a gentle, friendly kiss . . . for a while he just held her close to him, wishing he could stay with her forever.

Megan felt as if she was floating on air, she was in Robert's arms and he had actually kissed her and had called her "my love", although deep down she knew he was only being kind. She trusted him completely and believed that he would do everything in his power to bring her daughter back safely. He was a true friend.

CHAPTER
SEVENTEEN

Lizzie sat alone in the rooms above the book shop. She was bored — the child had done nothing but grizzle since she awoke early this morning. She had wet the bed during the night, which meant Lizzie had to swill out her undergarments. With none spare — Harold hadn't thought of purchasing clean clothes for the child — she had made a napkin out of a towel in the water closet, much to the child's disgust.

"I'm a big girl now. I don't wear nappies like baby Thomas," she cried.

Harold had ordered her to keep the child quiet. "We don't want to arouse suspicion from the shop below, do we?" he'd warned. It was easier said than done. The child was not happy, she grizzled about the napkin, the food, and cried out constantly, "I — w-w-ant M-a — mmy."

All of this finally proved too much for Lizzie. She knew Harold had left the bottle containing chloroform on a shelf in the water closet. A few drops on a cloth, he had said. "Use it, as a last resort, to send her to sleep if she becomes too noisy." Well, she was getting on Lizzie's nerves. What better reason to silence her?

Lizzie checked the child's breathing. She had only used a few drops of chloroform as instructed, but the child appeared out for the count. Once assured the child was indeed OK, Lizzie returned to sit in the bay window looking out into the street below. It was growing dark. Below her men and women rushed to and fro, some heading for the bright lights of the Queen's Head pub a few doors away. In her mind she reasoned that the child would probably sleep for ages, so why stay in these gloomy rooms alone when she could be sitting in the pub with a small sherry and some lively company? Within minutes the decision was made and her coat was on. Quietly, she crept out of the room, down the stairs and into the night.

A few doors away from the Gentlemen's Club Robert Fothergill lay in wait. The November wind felt cold and damp. He slid his hands deep into the pockets of his warm Crombie overcoat wondering how much longer his brother was going to be. When Harold eventually emerged from the club Robert intended to follow him. Somehow, Arthur Walters seemed convinced he would lead him to the area of the docks.

Meanwhile, Arthur sat in the Queen's Head public house, hoping that Lizzie would show her face. He knew all of her weaknesses too well, and would have laid odds that if she were anywhere near such a lively public house, the temptation would prove too great, child or no child. It was not long before his hunch paid off. He watched her enter the pub, her face flushed with excitement as she made her way to the serving hatch. How she loved having a good time.

"Sorry, Lizzie, I'm about to spoil your fun," he mumbled under his breath as he sneaked up behind her.

"Hello, Lizzie. Fancy seeing you here."

Immediately recognizing his voice she span around.

"Arthur! What are you doing here?"

"I was about to ask you the same question. By the way, how is your dear mother?"

"I-I —"

He grabbed her arm, pulling her into a dark corner under the stairs.

"OK, Lizzie, it's time for the truth. Where is the child?"

"I don't know what you're talking about."

"All right, try this. How about blackmail? Maybe the sum of five hundred pounds will refresh your memory. The same five hundred pounds you boasted you had in the bank and exactly the amount Harold has paid to — Megan? I don't think so. Harold may have believed it but we know better, don't we?"

"Why don't you mind your own bloody business?" she hissed.

"I wonder what Harold would say if he were to find out the real truth? One thing for sure, I wouldn't want to be in your shoes," he goaded.

Seeing her face twitch, he knew he'd touched a nerve, yet she continued to brazen it out.

"I've no regrets. He could afford it. I've earned every penny. Call it payment for services rendered," she said icily.

"I suppose I should think myself lucky. After all, I've had your services for free . . . or was I the next in line to be squeezed?"

She raised her hand to slap his face, but Arthur was too quick for her and caught her wrist. "Now, now. You don't want to add assault to your list of prosecutions. The police are already going to have a field day — prostitution, blackmail, kidnap . . . shall I go on?"

At that precise moment a drunken customer pushed passed him forcing Arthur to move to the side and let go of Lizzie's wrist. Within seconds she had fled from the bar. Gathering himself, Arthur followed close on her heels. Outside the pub he strained his eyes to find Lizzie through the fine mist which had crept in off the sea and settled around the flickering gas lamps. It was then he spotted her weaving her way through the many dark figures rushing about the quay. A strong pungent smell soon reached his nostrils, a sure sign that the tide was high, which explained so much activity, with ships taking on cargo and provisions in readiness to sail on the outgoing tide.

He cursed himself. "Damn it, I've gone and lost her again."

At that moment, not six feet away from him, a black cab pulled to a stop. Out stepped a large man smoking a huge cigar — it was Harold. Arthur stepped back into the doorway realizing all would be lost if Harold were to catch sight of him. He watched as Harold paid the cabby and slowly headed for the alley. He seemed nervous, constantly looking over his shoulder.

Arthur wondered where the hell Captain Robert had got to. He was supposed to stick close to his brother. But just then he saw another car pull up at the end of the docks. Two men stepped out. Arthur gave a sigh of relief when, as they moved closer, he recognized Captain Robert Fothergill and his chauffeur, Hutchins. While mindful to keep a safe distance, he watched the two men gingerly follow Harold down the alleyway and towards the book shop. Then he disappeared through a small doorway. Arthur decided it was time for him to join the party.

"So glad you could make it," Arthur whispered, as he caught up with Robert and Hutchins.

"Mr Walters. As you can see you were right about Harold heading for the docks. He just slipped between these premises and up those iron steps," Robert said. "Do you think this could be where he's holding the child."

"I hope so. And by the way forget the he — it's they. Harold has an accomplice, none other than Megan's cousin, Lizzie."

"But she's in Wales visiting her — Well, I must say, she certainly had me fooled. I even took her to the station," Hutchins guiltily admitted.

"Don't feel bad. She could lie for Wales. And you're not the only one to have been taken in by her. Take your place in the queue behind me!"

"I think it's time we made our move, don't you? If I take the lead will you cover my back, Mr Walters?"

"It will be my pleasure, Captain, and please call me, Arthur."

"Good man, Arthur. Hutchins, you stay here and wait for the police to show. I took the liberty of leaving a message with the duty sergeant."

Minutes later, Robert made a run up the steps closely followed by Arthur. As they burst into the room they saw Harold and Lizzie standing near the window.

"Wh-what th-the . . .?-" Harold stuttered nervously.

"The game's up, Harold. We've come for the child."

"Lizzie, quick, go grab the child." Harold shouted.

Arthur moved swiftly to block her way. "I wouldn't do that, if I were you."

"What the hell are you doing here?" Harold shouted, as he sized up to his brother.

Robert stood his ground. "You can't intimidate me. It might work on vulnerable women and small children. But not with me." Robert made a grab for his brother's shoulders, roughly pushing him aside. In his temper he seemed to have found extra strength. "If you have harmed Megan's child in any way, I swear I'll not be responsible for my actions."

"She's in the bedroom, she's all right, honest, she's sound asleep . . . it's the chloroform. He made me do it —" Lizzie pleaded, realising it was time to change sides.

Robert turned on Harold. "You bloody animal! Did you really believe you could get away with kidnapping a child? You're sick and evil and from this moment on I refuse to recognize you as my brother. The police can deal with you. My only regret is what it will do to our mother."

298

At the mention of the police Harold panicked and made a run for the door. Neither Arthur nor Robert bothered to give chase . . . their concern was for the safety of the child. Robert quietly entered the bedroom where Mary-Rose lay pale and limp. Gently he bent down to pick her up. Almost immediately he could smell the chloroform, and once again he cursed his brother. As he raised the child to his face he felt her soft warm breath on his cheek. Thank God . . . she was still alive.

As Robert and Hutchins stepped from the car outside the cottage, the front door opened and Megan came rushing out, closely followed by her mother-in-law.

"I heard the car. Robert, where's Mary-Rose?" she cried, her voice bordering on hysterical.

Almost without thinking, Robert rushed over to her, taking her in his arms. He felt no awkwardness; it just seemed the right thing to do.

"Megan, the child is safe. I've come to take you to her."

As she looked up into his eyes, she looked but a child herself . . . so small, so fragile, and so vulnerable, "Robert, where is she? If she was hurt in any way, you would tell me, wouldn't you?"

"Of course. But Megan, I promise Mary-Rose is fine, although as you can imagine, she's been through a bit of an ordeal. And just to be on the safe side they want her to spend the night at Bristol Royal Infirmary. You have to believe me when I tell you the child is well."

At which point Megan laid her head on his chest and gave way to tears of relief.

"Thank God!" Rose Partridge exclaimed as they all went indoors.

Once Megan had calmed herself, then came the questions, "And was your informant right? Was it Harold?" she asked, still puzzled.

"Yes. I'm afraid so. The police have taken him and his accomplice into custody."

"Accomplice, what — who?"

"I'll explain on the way to the hospital," Robert answered, playing for time. He dreaded having to tell her about Lizzie's involvement.

"Mam Partridge, while I go with Robert to visit Mary-Rose, will it be all right for me to leave Thomas with you?"

"Of course — if you're sure you still trust me? I feel so guilty 'bout what happened with —"

Megan stopped her in her tracks, "Don't be silly. I never blamed you. I know you would lay your life down for my two babas."

For a while the two women hugged each other. Then, after loudly blowing her nose into her handkerchief, Rose said, "Go on, off with you. Victor and I will be more than pleased to watch over the baby."

Megan felt suddenly ashamed of herself. With all that had been going on she had forgotten to thank Mr Hutchins or, for that matter, Robert.

"Oh Mr Hutchins, Robert . . . please forgive me. I should have thanked you both —"

"Please don't give it another thought . . . after all, I'm practically family," Mr Hutchins said, as he caught hold of Rose's hand, which made her blush like a young schoolgirl.

"And *I* certainly don't need to be thanked. It felt good to see Harold finally getting what he truly deserves."

As Robert and Megan left the house, Rose called out, "Don't forget to give the young 'un a big hug from me."

On the way to the hospital Robert decided it was time to tell Megan the truth — before she heard it from the police.

"Megan? Remember back at the cottage when you asked me about the accomplice? Well the reason I held back was that I did not want to be the one to tell you that it was your own cousin Lizzie."

"I don't understand."

"Apparently, it was Lizzie who enticed Mary-Rose from the garden."

"Oh God, no! My own cousin? Does she really hate me that much?"

"I believe she was driven more by greed than hate. If it hadn't been for Arthur —"

Shocked by the mention of his name, she interrupted, "Arthur! Arthur Walters? What part did he play — don't tell me he had a hand in this?"

"No. Far from it. It was he who came to me in the first place. Megan, Arthur Walters was the informant I told you about. He's the one who worked out that

Lizzie and Harold were up to something when he spotted them by the docks."

"I thank God for his sharp eyes, and I will personally thank him for his help. But" — Megan shook her head in dismay — "how could Lizzie do such a thing to me?"

But if Megan believed her troubles were over, she was mistaken. The week that followed proved to be a difficult one, with the police pushing her to make a statement, eager to secure prosecution. It would have been so easy to have given the police what they wanted — but what would it achieve? Mary-Rose was safe and well and back to her normal mischievous self. All Megan wanted now was an end to the whole sordid business. She had no wish to have all her personal details dragged through the court. She wasn't just thinking of herself . . . there were her children, Mary-Rose especially — having to have it on record how her own father had used her for revenge. Then there was her family in Wales — how could she subject them to another court case, another scandal? And what about Mistress Fothergill? The poor woman — wasn't it bad enough to have found out what her own son was capable of, without being held up for ridicule? Megan even thought of Jane Arkwright, who might have married unwisely, but she had never done anything to harm Megan. No, it was best to have an end to it all.

The only person whom Megan felt deserved the whole truth was Rose Partridge. She took it well. "I always knew in my heart that my Sidney were not the true father. Believe me, Megan, I don't blame you in any way. My Sidney loved you and that little one so much. It didn't matter to him, and it doesn't matter to me. He may not have been her true parent but he was most certainly her *Dad*. Just as I may not be her paternal grandmother, but it doesn't stop me loving her like a granny."

Megan felt as if a huge weight had been lifted from her shoulders.

She decided that, as long as Harold and Lizzie agreed to certain conditions, she would not press charges. The police made their objections loudly, but in the end, swayed by the weight of both the Fothergills' and Arkwrights' standing in the community, they decided not to proceed with their investigation. The next day Harold and Lizzie were set free. Harold agreed to relinquish all rights to the Fothergill Tobacco Company and to leave the country — his wife, always mindful of her marriage vows, chose to leave with him, and promised all concerned that she would endeavour to change his ways.

As for Lizzie, and her blackmail: well she was made to donate all of her ill-gotten gains to the tune of five hundred pounds to a children's charity. Needless to say, she was asked to leave the Fothergills' employ. With no money, no reference and nowhere to live, she was forced to return to Wales in shame.

With everything more or less settled there was only one thing left to do. As Megan walked with purpose across the downs, having left the children with their Granny Rose, there was something she had to do. In the distance she could see Clifton Suspension Bridge. Not long now, she thought. During the bleak period when she hadn't known whether her daughter was alive or dead, she had made a promise to God, that if He kept her child safe from harm, she would stop dwelling on the past; she promised to move on and start a new life. Before she could fulfil this promise she must make her peace with Sidney. She needed him to know she would never forget him, and how she would never have missed the short time they had together. He would always have a special place in her heart. He had taught her the meaning of true love. Where better to tell him all this than at "their bench"?

Megan returned to the cottage, her heart much lighter, her spirit high, especially when she saw the Fothergills' car parked outside. As she rushed indoors she expected to find Robert sitting in the parlour, but instead she found Mistress Fothergill taking tea with Mam Partridge while Mary-Rose and Thomas played with their toys on the rug in front of the fireplace.

"Megan, I'm so glad you're back. The mistress has called to see you," Rose proudly said.

Megan didn't say a word. She just stared at her visitor — partly in disbelief that Mrs Fothergill should take the time to visit her. She hadn't changed much, only her hair a little greyer. She was still a striking-looking woman.

"Look, I shall leave you two alone. I've chores to get on with in the kitchen," Rose said, giving Megan a reassuring smile before leaving the room.

"Mrs Partridge — Megan. I apologize for calling on you unannounced, only I need your help. I know how highly my son Robert regards you, and I thought you might be able to enlighten me as to the way his mind is working. He has seemed so much better in recent months, you see, my dear, so much more in control and enjoying life again. But suddenly he has become — hot-headed."

Megan suppressed a smile. "In what way?"

"This morning he announced that while he is prepared to accept my offer for him to take over at the helm of our tobacco company, he insists on moving out of Redcliffe House, he says there are too many bad memories and assures me he'll not be persuaded otherwise. Apparently a house has become vacant overlooking Clifton Suspension Bridge and he says that he intends to purchase it. I find his behaviour so out of character, I do so worry that he may have to return to the military hospital . . . I have lost one son, I cannot lose another — my dear, are you all right?"

Megan didn't answer, instead she ran out of the room down the hallway.

"Megan? Where are you going? What about the mistress?" Rose called.

"I'm going up to Redcliffe House! Please go and comfort Mrs Fothergill. Tell her everything is wonderful. Especially Robert!"

Megan stood on the doorstep of Redcliffe House. She was out of breath from running all the way from Rose Partridge's cottage. As she stared at the imposing black, high glossed door with its ornate brass adornments, Megan remembered the day she first arrived at the "Big House". How nervous she had been. If it hadn't been for Sidney — she sighed. So much had happened since then. As she raised her arm to tug on the handle of the brass doorbell her hand was visibly shaking, this time not with nerves but excitement.

Mr Hutchins answered the door, obviously surprised to see her.

"Megan? What's wrong? Is something wrong with *my* Rose? Are the children all right?"

"Mr Hutchins — Victor — everything's fine, honest. I'm here to see Mister Robert, is he in?"

His face showed his relief. "Why, yes, Miss. Mister Robert is in the drawing room," he said as he stood aside to let her in. "Shall I announce you, Miss?"

"No thanks, Victor, I know the way. Anyway, I want to surprise him."

Mr Hutchins smiled and with a nod of his head gave her a knowing look.

For a few moments Megan stood in the hallway. How different it looked when entered from the front doorway instead of the service stairway she'd always previously used. Or was it her new-found confidence that changed the once-imposing surroundings to an atmosphere of opulence. Whatever it was, she liked the warm feeling just standing there gave her.

A few moments later she stood outside the drawing room and, taking a deep breath, she pushed open the doors. This was it — there could be no turning back.

As she entered the room, Robert looked up from the newspaper he was reading. "Megan?" Discarding the newspaper he stood up and crossed the room towards her.

She, in turn, rushed to meet him. "Oh, Robert. I just had to come. I need to tell you how I feel, I need you to know —"

Before she could say another word she was in his arms and he was kissing her, tenderly at first, then with so much passion it took her breath away. Megan responded by throwing her arms around his neck and she eagerly returned his kisses.

When they eventually drew breath they stayed wrapped in each others arms.

"Megan —"

"No, me first. I love you, Robert Fothergill."

He squeezed her to him. "Oh, Megan, my sweet, lovely, Megan. We've wasted so much time. I blame myself. I didn't want to frighten you off. I thought that if I told you how I truly felt about you, you'd run a mile. I kidded myself that I could be happy with just our friendship."

"I'm as much to blame. I wouldn't let myself believe, after all that God has thrown at me over the years, it was as if, to acknowledge I loved you, it would be tempting fate."

"What an absurd pair we've been — but no more. From now on I want everyone to know how much I truly love you and how I want to spend the rest of my life with you. Megan, will you marry me?"

Her heart was pounding, "Yes! Yes! But Robert, can we wait until Jess's release from prison? I want him there to give me away."

"Of course, my love." He smothered her with kisses. Then, taking her hand he led her from the room.

"Where are we going?"

"I meant what I said: I want to tell everyone our good news, starting with my mother. She's probably in the garden."

Megan stopped him in his tracks. "Your mother's not in the garden."

"How do you know?"

"Because it was your mother who prompted me to come rushing over here."

"I'm intrigued."

"Your mother called to see me at the cottage earlier. She was concerned about your state of health — your mental health to be exact. And after hearing about your wild scheme to sell Redcliffe House and buy some place near Clifton Suspension Bridge — I too thought you totally mad."

He looked hurt. "I'll have you know my mental health has never been better. I wanted to sell up for you. I thought if I ever plucked up the courage to tell you how I truly felt and ask for your hand in marriage — and if by some miracle you said yes — I was sure you'd never want to live here with all the bad memories. I knew how often you visited the downs and I thought —"

"I know what you thought. When your mother told me, I guessed you were doing it for me. It was then I

308

decided to take the bull by the horns and tell you that I loved you. Even as I ran from the cottage I wasn't really sure you felt the same. But it was worth the risk."

"Well, you know now."

She smiled. "Yes, and I'm so happy. Robert, I really don't want you selling this house. I feel everything that has happened in my life, even the bad memories, was the path fate laid down for me. The path that has finally led to you. It made me into the woman you see before you today."

"And I, for one, wouldn't change you for the world."

Jess walked through the prison gates and breathed in the cold fresh air. Thanks to Robert Fothergill's intervention on his behalf, Jess's prison sentence had been reduced from five to three years. At last he was a free man.

"Jess! Jess! Over here!" Megan called from the other side of Adam Street, furiously waving her arms as she stepped out of Robert's car.

She watched as her brother, before crossing over to her, beamed a smile and waved back.

Also available in ISIS Large Print:

Perdita

Joan Smith

Governess Moira Greenwood's beautiful young charge, Perdita Brodie, is a high-spirited chit. Indeed, she rebels against her stepmama's choice of mate and manages to get Moira and herself positions in a not-quite-shabby travelling acting troupe.

While Moira cooks, her lovely cousin sings, attracting the very insistent attentions of the cold, handsome rakehell Lord Stornaway — who takes the pair for lightskirts!

Although Moira explains the truth, the self-satisfied lord believes not a word; he's positive the two are ladies of ill repute. Moira finds him the most rude, uncivil of men and tells him so. Still, there is something about him she can't quite define that is not completely loathsome . . .

ISBN 978-0-7531-8294-9 (hb)
ISBN 978-0-7531-8295-6 (pb)

Muddy Boots and Silk Stockings

Julia Stoneham

It's 1943 and the country is at war. Yet on one remote Devonshire farm the days are not so dark. An unlikely group of land girls are finding out about life, love and loss, forming surprising friendships along the way.

When Alice Todd's husband runs off with another woman, she is forced to find a means to provide for herself and her young son. Accepting a position as a hostel warden at an old Devonshire farmhouse, Alice finds herself looking after a group of ten volunteer land girls.

The job is not as easy as it first seems. Not only does Alice have to deal with the uncompromising farm owner and her resentful and unhelpful assistant Rose, but as her young charges arrive at the farm, she discovers every girl has a story — and some have rather dark secrets.

ISBN 978-0-7531-8186-7 (hb)
ISBN 978-0-7531-8187-4 (pb)